Y0-BVR-457

# The Empty Chair

# The Empty Chair

*by Bess Kaplan*

HARPER & ROW, PUBLISHERS

*New York   Hagerstown   San Francisco   London*

THE EMPTY CHAIR

Published in Canada under the title Corner Store

First American Edition, 1978

---

Library of Congress Cataloging in Publication Data
Kaplan, Bess.
    The empty chair.

    SUMMARY: A young girl struggles to acknowledge her
mother's death and accept her new stepmother.
    [1. Death—Fiction.    2. Stepmothers—Fiction]
I. Title.
PZ7.K12897Em 1978      [Fic]      77-11852
ISBN 0-06-023092-4
ISBN 0-06-023093-2 lib. bdg.

---

To Phil, who put up with much
during the writing of this book,

and to Penhandlers, whose advice
and criticism were invaluable.

*All characters in this book are fictional. Any similarity to actual persons is purely coincidental.*

*The foreign words in this book are Yiddish words; they are defined in the Glossary at the back of the book.*

**1** Sometimes something can happen that changes everything in your whole life. It's what makes you start to grow up. You never know when to expect it or what it'll be, and it can be triggered by the *tiniest* thing. I remember it began one evening for me. It seems so long ago — I was only a baby then, just nine. I was standing with my little brother Simply Simon (I called him that because we both hated his real name, Saul) and I looked up and saw the first pale stars gleaming overhead, and I crossed my fingers and whispered:
"Star light, star bright,
First star I see tonight . . .
Wish I may, wish I might
Have the wish I wish tonight . . ."

"What are you wishing for?" Simply Simon asked me, even though I had told him a million, billion times that it wouldn't come true if I told.

I shut my eyes tightly and wished very hard. I wish . . . I wish . . . something wonderful would happen. Something so great it would knock me over with its marvelousness.

I uncrossed my fingers and opened my eyes. What could possibly happen that would be so wonderful? I didn't know. I left it up to the stars to decide that for me. Wishing for something tangible never worked. I knew that from experience. For instance, when I wished the old Italian couple next door would move out so a family with girls my age could move in, they planted shrubs, proving that they intended staying forever.

"I'll bet I know what you wished for." He tossed a small pebble into the air and caught it with the same hand.

"What?" I challenged. "But I won't tell you even if you guess right."

"I'll bet you wished for a million dollars! Boy, if I had a million dollars, I'd get rid of this old house, and the old store, and we'd live in a castle full of servants!"

"I didn't wish for that, smarty! I wouldn't wish for
...*money*!" I made it sound dirty.

"Why? What's wrong with money? If we had it, you
could get anything you wanted — lots of new clothes, 'stead of
one that's too big for you, just so it'll last a long time."

I shrugged. If I had a wish coming to me, it better not be
for anything frivolous like that!

"And Mama wouldn't have to work so hard," he
pursued, "and be tired all the time. You know what? She was
even lying down when I came home from school at four."

"Maybe she's sick. . . ." I began to worry. "Who'd look
after us, make meals and stuff like that?"

"I don't know." He opened the gate, swinging it wide.
"Auntie Sadie, maybe."

"Auntie Sadie!" I pushed past him through the gate.
"You bite your tongue!"

He tried, then frowned. "Why should I bite my
tongue?"

"So it wouldn't happen, stupid!"

He bit it, and we clattered up the steps and into the
house. He went through the dark hallway into the middle
room while I ran up the stairs to my bedroom and pulled the
string that hung from the center of the ceiling. My light
clicked on, illuminating the small square of walls that contained all my very own personal things.

I dropped my Hebrew books onto the top of my dresser
which had once belonged to Mama and Papa, catching a
glimpse of myself in the big mirror above it. I stuck my tongue
out and turned away quickly before I could see if She did the
same. I yanked my tunic off over my head and dropped it to
the floor, then opened my closet door and looked for my only
other tunic. It was older than this one, but it couldn't be
helped. I'd have to wear it. I struggled into it, buttoned the
belt around my waist and kicked the discarded one into the
farthest corner of the closet. A flash of gold caught my eye. I
pulled it forward — my new Yontiff dress, the only bright
thing I owned. I gently closed the closet door and looked

around.

Under my window, now shrouded against the night by dark green window blinds, stood the low blanket box Papa had made for me a long time ago. I kept other things inside it besides bedding though. I kept a collection of scribblers, filled with my thoughts and feelings on everything that ever happened to me since I'd started, about six months ago.

I was torn between writing in the scribbler, a Labor of Love; doing my English school homework — Duty; or copying out the Hebrew stories Mr. Lerner had given me — Necessity. I took out my scribbler, pulled the kitchen chair I used as a boudoir seat closer to the dresser, and slid into it. I began to write. I could always do the other things, the homework, the lines, afterwards, but I might forget something important if I left my writing till later.

Both arms resting on the dresser, I wrote in tiny letters, hardly readable except to me. Nobody else would ever see it anyway, and the main thing was getting as much onto each page as possible. Scribblers cost money and every time I asked Papa if I could take one out of stock, he would say: "What? Another one? Didn't I just give you one last week?"

"Yes, Papa. But it's used up already."

"How could it be used up so fast?"

"I don't know, Papa — the teacher gives us lots of work."

I would cross my fingers behind my back. Nobody knew, not even Simply Simon, that I wrote in the scribblers at night. It was my secret and would stay a secret forever.

While I tried to think what to write, I looked up and caught sight of the funny blob in the mirror, the face of the girl who lived there. She stared out at me and stuck her tongue out, the same as I did. I hated her looks yet admired her in a way. How did she always know exactly what I was going to do? Maybe she could read my mind. Very carefully, without thinking about it, I placed my thumbs in my ears and waggled my fingers. She did the same. Then she opened her mouth as wide as it could go so I could see the backs of her teeth.

"You've got a big mouth," I whispered to her and watched her thin lips form the words with me. She looked like she was laughing at me and was probably going to answer me, but then Mama called.

Reluctantly, I closed the scribbler and put it back in its hiding place, pulled the string to turn out the lights and slammed down the stairs, two at a time, landing with a crash at the bottom. Mama gave me Her Look.

"When will you ever learn to walk like a lady?" she asked me for the 573rd time.

Supper always started out formally enough. Everybody sat down at the same time around the kitchen table. Then Mama placed the food out hot, raised her eyes to the ceiling and said under her breath:

"Please God don't let anybody come into the store till after."

God seemed to be busy with other things though, because partway through the meal we'd hear the tinkle of the little bell over the store door and Papa would leave, most of his supper untouched. This explained his slight build, the thin, bone-carved look of his features. By the time he'd return, the food would have been reheated to tastelessness, we'd have finished, and he'd have lost his appetite.

I stopped just inside the kitchen doorway, sniffing the air. Bowls on the table steamed, smelling suspiciously of cooked onions which I wouldn't touch with a baseball bat. Braced for battle, I approached my chair as though it could electrocute me and slid into it gingerly. Simply Simon ate with disgusting enjoyment. I made a face and waited expectantly for Mama's opening shot. It came.

"Why don't you eat, Becky?"

"I'm not hungry for soup."

"Eat it anyway."

I glanced at Mama. Was that the best she could do? It hardly seemed worth answering, and besides, she had her face turned away from the table, looking everywhere but at me.

"*You're* not eating," I reminded her, almost with triumph.

*4*

"What has that got to do?" Mama demanded, giving me a swift, reproving glance. "I made it, you eat."

I looked at the soup. "What else is there?"

"Never mind. First the soup, then . . ." But the words stuck in Mama's throat. She looked towards the sink. I saw Papa's head lift from his dish long enough to look at her.

"You're all right?"

"Yes, I'm all right," Mama said, still not looking in our direction. Papa accepted that and went back to his meal, which struck me as being very hardhearted. Was he so blind? Couldn't he see something was wrong? Even Mama's nagging had lost some of its vigor. I became so worried that I absentmindedly picked up my spoon and began eating the soup, keeping my eyes on Mama, and it wasn't till I felt the spoon scrape bottom that I realized what I was doing and dropped it.

Papa pushed away his empty bowl and looked at Mama. "Nu?" That meant, What's next on the menu, and Mama hurried to her feet. For once she didn't have everything out where Papa could help himself when he was ready. I watched as Mama went to the stove, and I thought . . . Hey! She's getting fat! Not that Mama was ever skinny, but I'd never seen *that* much stomach on her before. I suppose it was all those potatoes she ate. Mama sure liked potatoes and schmaltz — when she was in a mood to eat.

We continued to eat in silence. At least Papa, having loaded his plate with slices of roast beef and browned potatoes, attempted to eat it. But then the tinkle of the store bell jerked him out of his chair. Mama said: Tsk, tsk, but Papa strode past her without comment, slamming the store door shut behind him.

Mama looked stricken, as if she were somehow to blame.

Just to take her mind off it I leaned on my elbows and said: "Why aren't you eating, Mama?" Her bowl of soup sat untouched in front of her. She looked at it for a moment, almost the way I usually did, then rushed away into the bathroom just off the kitchen near the sink.

Simply Simon and I exchanged glances.

"I told you," his voice dropped to a murmur, "that Mama is sick."

We listened to sounds of retching. It was enough to make me want to vomit too.

"Well one thing," I said firmly. "That Auntie Sadie better not come here and boss us around. Or else."

"You can say *that* again," he agreed with me, even though she was a lot nicer to him.

We started to clear things away from the table just to help Mama out, leaving Papa's plate. I hesitated over Mama's soup, then picked up the bowl and carried it, sloshing, to the sink, where I poured it out.

"You spilled some on the floor," Simply Simon informed me as he wiped crumbs off the oilcloth that covered the table. I watched the cold, sluggish soup ooze down the drain.

"So wipe it up."

"Why should I? I didn't spill it."

"Because I said so," I told him, and to prove I meant it I gave him a really menacing look. He sighed and bent over the floor with the table rag. In many ways he was a pain in the neck but he had a few good points, and one of them was that he knew who was the boss.

I wiped my hands on the dish towel and went off to do my homework, the biggest waste of time I could think of but something that had to be done if I didn't want to get killed by Miss Harrison or Old Lerner. First I turned on the radio so I could listen to a program and not have to think what I was doing. I sprawled in the chair by the big desk, spread my books out across its surface and tackled arithmetic determinedly with the half of my mind that wasn't listening to the radio.

Hours later I shut the last book. My eyes watered with tiredness but at least I wouldn't get into trouble with any teacher. I could hear the sounds of Papa closing up the store, the metal bar being shoved clanking through the handles on each side of the door. I knew it must be pretty late.

Mama had joined him sometime during the evening. It

had rather surprised me to see her march past me on her way to the store, acting as if nothing had happened. I rose and stretched, bending way back so my stomach almost popped out of its natural place; then, feeling better, I began to sharpen a pencil for tomorrow with a penknife.

The door between the house and store opened. Glancing up, I was startled to see Papa push Mama through the doorway, both of them smiling. They looked childish and young as Papa came up behind Mama and looked like he was about to give her a playful whack on the rear. In fact, he lifted his hand, then caught sight of me. His face turned white while mine felt hot with embarrassment. I looked down quickly and went on sharpening the pencil, the point breaking off as I worked.

"Why aren't you in bed?" Papa demanded. "Do you know what time it is?"

My eyes slid sideways to the little clock tick-ticking on the desk. It read half past eleven.

"I was doing homework," I muttered to the penknife.

"And Saul?"

I shrugged. "I think he's in the kitchen."

"My *God!*" Papa exploded.

There was the sound of running footsteps and Simply Simon blurred by.

"Good night, Papa. Good night, Mama!"

He disappeared through the door to the hall and I followed him out so I wouldn't have to go up the stairs by myself in the dark. We clattered noisily together, past the small square window near the upper landing, Simply Simon to his room and I to mine. I turned on my light and shut my door.

While I struggled into my pajamas I thought about Mama and Papa. What were they doing now, alone together? Whacking each other, playing like two kids? It disgusted me to think of them behaving in so undignified a way.

Shivering in the chill of my room I buttoned my pajama top quickly and thought about grown-up people and their strangeness. They could go from laughter to anger in a minute; at least, Papa could. And Mama had definitely been sick at supper tonight and other times too. I heard her throw up this very morning in the upstairs toilet, yet afterwards, it was as though nothing had happened.

Papa's face came into my mind. He'd looked young tonight, boyish. I never thought of my parents as being young because they weren't. They were probably close to thirty years old — and they should *act* that way.

I sat on the edge of my bed, floorboards cold under my bare feet. The time had come to turn out the light, and this took a certain amount of cunning on my part. I had to do it with as much of me under the blankets as possible. Reaching up for the end of the light cord, I slithered under the covers, holding the cord lightly so it wouldn't get pulled before I was ready. The important thing was to get my head under the covers at the same time so I wouldn't see the Black Dark when the light went out.

There were people in the Black Dark, unseen watchers who moved around the room while I lay under the blankets, hardly breathing. They were shadows gliding into each other, and passing, arms outstretched as they searched for me, groping blindly but never finding me. If I made the least sound they would get me, so I lay perfectly still in the dark cave of my blankets.

It was no use telling anyone about them. They never believed me. Mama said it was my imagination and to prove it she turned the light on while I hid behind her. As if that proved anything! Naturally the unseen watchers were invisible, and I'd shivered a long time under the covers that night sure they would wreak vengeance on me for telling on them. The only good thing about them was that they went away after a while although I was never sure exactly when it was safe to peek out. Whenever I finally did get the nerve to look though, they would be gone and so would the Black Dark.

In Dim Dark which followed you could see your furniture and anything else in the room including Miss Harrison's glass eye.

I'd never forget the shock the night I'd uncovered my

face in Dim Dark and had seen her glass eye shimmer and wink at me from the wall near the window, right opposite from where I lay. Horrified, I'd covered my face right up, heart hammering inside my ears. After a moment, I exposed one eye to see if it was still there. It was. It pulsed like a living thing, a cold round gleam moving in the wedge of light visible from my window where the blind didn't quite cover at the sides. How had it found me, her terrible eye, and so quickly? And why did it want to watch me all night?

With my head inside the blankets, my stale breath began to choke me, so I wondered which was worse, being frightened to death or suffocating. I made a small tunnel out of my cave with an air hole to allow me to breathe while I kept my eyes closed tightly against any Things that moved out there.

While I waited for sleep, I thought about things, such as my new dress in the closet, and Yontiff next week with its bonus of a two-day holiday from school, and going to Shul. Actually, Shul was boring. All you did was stand at the railing of the balcony where the women had to sit and stare down at the men and boys who could sit downstairs. We weren't allowed down there. If a girl tried to sit on a bench near the men the old long-bearded ones would glare and flap their hands at her and point upstairs. I couldn't figure the reason for that and Mama shook her head at me when I asked her. How I could look forward to anything as uninteresting as looking down at the tops of men's yarmelkes, I didn't know. But I *did* find it appealing somehow.

Of course, I didn't have to stand at the railing. I could sit beside Mama in the third-row seat that she'd had for as far back as I could remember. You couldn't see a thing from the third row except dandruff on the shoulders of the lady who sat in the second row and the gray hairs that dropped onto her collar and the backs of her pearl earrings that squeezed her ear lobes into little pink sausages. Beside her sat the lady with the diamonds. Diamonds dripped from her pierced ears, looped around her thick neck and spangled on her fingers. Whenever she turned and caught me staring at the sparkles, she fluttered her hands around, straightening her funny black hat, moving a hanky or fixing up her hair at the back just to make them sparkle more, I guessed.

Not that Mama allowed me to sit and look very long. She pushed her prayer book into my hand and showed me the place with her finger and made me pray too. I preferred to stand at the railing, careful not to look behind me and catch Mama's eye even though my feet always felt as though I were standing barefoot in a thistle bush. It was very pleasant to think about all the others who had to go to school that day in their ordinary clothes while I wore the new dress.

I peeked out of the blanket not at the wall where Miss Harrison's glass eye stared but at the dresser wall, and was relieved to see Dim Dark, showing my mirror silvery gray, and I thought about the Girl in the Mirror then, the one who thought she was me. It wasn't fair. I wished I could look in the mirror sometimes and see Simply Simon's face on my body instead of that ugly old coot. Why did she have to stay in *my* mirror? A small doubt crept in, as it did whenever I let it. Maybe it really was me and not some horrible stranger. I remembered the time I had asked Mama why I'd been born so ugly and she had been shocked.

"What? Who says you're ugly? Who told you such a lie? Silly girl! Just look what she calls ugly! A beautiful smile, and shining eyes! God forbid you should be ugly!"

Impressed and hopeful, I had run quickly to see the sudden change in me because Mama had put on such a convincing performance. But when I reached the mirror, I was disappointed to see the same face I always saw. Either it had gone back to its original features while I was on my way to the mirror or you couldn't trust your own mother!

I could see my library books on the dresser under the mirror. On Sunday I would take them back and get other books. I wished I could spend all my time just reading. That would be heaven, I thought to read every hour of every day, going through all the books in the library. I had no fear that the library would run out of books either. Quite often I would find a new book by one favorite author or another as though they were working very hard just to keep me supplied. It would be wonderful to be a writer . . . I could imagine myself doing it, bent over a book, writing in it and becoming rich and famous. It gave me goose pimples just to think of it.

People would speak my name. They would say: "Here is a new book by the famous author Rebecca Devine."

"How wonderful," they would tell each other. "A new book! I always look for her books!"

I could see myself as a writer, very tall and beautiful, with long blond hair and a cigarette holder, looking glamorous. Best of all, people would want my autograph and I would give it to the ones I liked. Miss Harrison could forget it, if she thought I'd give *her* one. Not even if she went on her hands and knees, begging me. Or Bella, or Mr. Lerner. I might give one to Betty Greenberg and some of the other kids. I wasn't sure yet. It would all depend on how I felt. I yawned, positive it was very very late.

There were sounds on the stairs and Mama and Papa whispered to each other as they passed my closed door. I strained to hear what they said but it was all mumbles and then their bedroom door closed. I thought of them acting kiddish and felt disgusted all over again. They shouldn't forget even for one minute that they were parents. It looked terrible.

There were so many things I didn't understand about parents — about many things. A long time ago I had asked Mama where babies came from and she hadn't answered me. Instead, she became angry and red-faced and told me my dress was dirty when that had nothing to do with it. It made me wonder even harder. That was before I knew Fat Emma, though.

Fat Emma lived near the park and she'd told me last year that babies were born because mothers and fathers did something in bed. She wouldn't say what but kept laughing behind her hand, her face red as tomatoes. I had grabbed onto her elbows and tried to shake her, demanding to know what it was.

"Never mind," she snickered. "You're too young to know."

"I am not!" I protested, still shaking her but not able to move her a single inch, because she was a year older than I and at least thirty pounds heavier.

"Yes you are!" she'd laughed infuriatingly. "You're almost like a baby yourself!"

This was the supreme insult. Unable to think of anything as devastating as this, I sank my teeth into her fleshy arm in a soul-satisfying bite that nearly jarred my teeth out of my head. Although she'd yelled, I hung on grimly, and it took two passing grown-ups to pry me off her arm. Later, Papa had walloped me and I'd hidden in my closet crying for hours. But it was there in the dark closet while lying on top of blouses that had fallen off their hangers, and wiping my tear-reddened eyes on the sleeves and hems, that I figured out how babies were started. Babies came from kissing.

I turned onto my stomach in bed and tried to visualize Mama and Papa kissing but the image wouldn't come. I pulled the pillow underneath the covers and with my face buried in its softness, I made Mama and Papa kiss in my mind. Mama looked sick and Papa looked angry and the kiss was a fake. But they must have, I thought sleepily. They must have done it, because . . . here I was, and there in the next room was Simply Simon, so they must have done it twice. I really *was* their child, not a Princess, wasn't I? Nobody would leave a Princess on somebody else's veranda, would they? So they must be my real parents, and that meant they had kissed twice, didn't it?

I wished they would do it again. If only I could have a big sister, somebody who would tell me things, who would be my friend forever. A sister would be the most wonderful person in the whole world, especially a big one. But of course it was too late for that. I had been born first so nobody could be older than me. My head began to drift, gently leaving my shoulders. . . . Oh well, I thought, that's all right. If I can't have a big sister, a baby one would do. I really would love to have a baby sister sometime. My head drifted farther. . . . A dear little baby sister . . .

**2** When Mama called us into the kitchen to tell us A Very Big Secret, one day near the end of October, I couldn't imagine what it would be. That whole Sunday had been unusual in a sense. Not that the outdoor concert put on by the Salvation Army on our street corner was an unusual happening, but it was the forerunner of more to come. Actually, the members of that band liked our corner for some reason and we looked forward to their vibrant and loud music. I particularly liked the snappy way they looked in their trim navy blue uniforms.

The tips of my fingers were numb with cold and my nose seemed to have swelled to twice its size, the way it always did when chilled, as we stood in a semicircle with a motley group of other kids and listened to the horn, tambourine and drum produce their stirring religious sounds. Absentmindedly we wiped our noses with the backs of our hands, gazing up into the nostrils of the leader, a red-faced man who led in the tooting, jangling and booming songs of salvation. That part was all right, but then they stopped and he stepped forward and in loud, ringing tones, commanded:

"Come to Jesus, all ye sinners!" And Papa opened the front door to holler:

"Saul! Becky! Get in the house!"

I couldn't see what he was mad about. The man was talking to sinners, not to us, but when Papa yelled, we didn't waste time arguing. At least, not too much time, except when Johnny Felange, the biggest pest on two legs crossed his eyes at us and three of his copycat sisters did the same. So I put my thumb on my nose back at them and would have done a lot more.

"Becky!" Papa yelled, "I told you to come in!"

Later, I went to the public library and brought home more books, which was what I usually did on Sunday, but while I sat reading, all curled up on the chesterfield in the front room, we heard the most exciting sound of all — the wail of the fire siren. In no time both Simply Simon and I had pulled on our jackets and joined the running crowds into the middle of our block where bright red fire engines vibrated and roared.

We could see bits of flame shoot out of an upstairs window and smell the acrid odor of burnt wood. We didn't know many people on this side of Boyd, so we could view it all objectively, as entertainment put on for our benefit. But the smell hurt our throats and made our eyes water, and black smoke hung tangibly in the air. There was the buzz and mumble of people asking each other for details even though nobody knew any more than the next one.

"Is somebody trapped up there?" a lady asked no one in particular, and several others hastened to assure her that, yes, there was an old lady in that bedroom, and no, of course not; nobody was at home.

Firemen pushed us back; others rushed around bringing equipment closer to the house while we watched breathlessly. It was thrilling to have this drama happen so close and yet not close enough that we should feel sorry for the occupants when we didn't even know them.

Simply Simon stood tensely beside me, his eyes alight as he watched the firemen scale their ladder towards the window that belched black smoke.

"Boy, just look at them," he breathed. "Boy, that's what I want to be when I grow up. I'll be a fireman and save people's lives!"

Johnny Felange loped up behind us. "Ho, ho. I'll bet," he laughed and dropped to his knees in a pantomime as though he'd been shot. "You go ahead and be a fireman, big hero. I'd like to see that. Probably drop into the fire yourself and burn to ashes." He looked pleased, as though he hoped it would happen that way.

Simply Simon stared at him. "I will not."

"Bet you will."

"I bet he won't *either!*" I leaned menacingly over him, my fist poised above his head. "Nobody says that about *my brother!*"

Quick as a cockroach, Johnny rolled out of my reach and stood up, skinny body braced. Bits of grass stuck to his wiry hair and on his thick beige sweater.

"Try and stop me!"

"You're asking for it," I said in my most threatening voice, confident I could beat him up although we'd never gone past the face-making stage.

"Yah!" He stuck his tongue out at me. "I don't fight with girls!"

"Ha! You're scared!" I wanted once and for all to let him have it so he would know who was superior.

His foot shot out and hooked my ankle. I fell but now a great fury shook me. My brain screamed: "Kill him!" and in a flash my fist connected with his face. The fire that raged in front of us paled in importance with teaching him a lesson. We rolled on the ground, panting, as I grasped for his hair which was infuriatingly short. I hit him with all my might and an instant later he hit me back.

Dimly, I could hear sounds connected with the fire, men racing around, another siren, hoses gushing, crackling flames and muted excited voices, but mashing Johnny into the ground held more excitement for me. Breathing hard I got to my feet and aimed a hefty kick in his direction, missing by a scant inch because he rolled quickly away, got up and made another face at me.

"Bloody Jew!" he yelled, backing away and darting into the crowd that stood enthralled, gazing at the fire.

"You're bloody yourself!" I shouted at him. "And next time, I'll *really* let you have it."

I turned to find Simply Simon, feeling satisfied with myself for having avenged him, but he had disappeared. I searched all over, becoming more indignant by the second, then found him, his head wedged between Mrs. Samowitz, with her flapping brown sweater, and Mrs. Wurster, who lived across the street from us. All I could see of him was one shoulder and his green jacket and pants.

Isn't that lovely, I thought. I fight Johnny Felange on account of him, and he's busy watching the fire. Incensed, I grabbed Simply Simon's jacket and yanked him back so his head popped into view. He turned, surprised, and stared at my face, then slowly down to my torn stockings and up again.

*15*

"What happened to you?" he asked. "You look like you were in a fight."

"I've got some brother." I glared at him. "Some brother, boy! That's the last time I stick up for *you*, Saul Devine!"

"They took a lady out of that bedroom" he said, trying to change the subject and get back in my good graces. If I called him by his real name, he knew I was furious. "She was still alive, I think," he added, looking hopefully at me for signs of interest. "An ambulance took her away."

I glared coolly past him, above his head to the top of the house, with its blackened roof, smoke still billowing out.

"So?"

"So, and then they went in with the hose and axes and they were chopping away! You should've seen!"

"I know I should've seen!" I flared at him — "I missed the best fire we ever had on account of you!"

"Well, gee whiz! I didn't *tell* you to!"

"Next time, fight your own battles!" That was all the thanks I got, and my stockings were torn. Mama would take one look at me and I'd be dead.

The fire was over. There were signs of equipment being pulled back as the smoke lessened considerably. In a few minutes, the ladders were lowered and people drifted home. We stayed till the trucks rumbled away. The taste of smoke in my mouth began to nauseate me.

"Let's go," I said, turning towards home. Obediently, he followed me.

At the door, Mama gasped and held her heart.

"How many times did I tell you not to fight?"

"I couldn't help it," I said, and then inspiration hit me — "He called me a bloody Jew." That part of it was, technically, true, and the effect on Mama satisfying.

"I hope you fixed him so he wouldn't be able to walk!"

"I made his nose bleed."

"He tore your stockings. And look at your coat — it's dirty!"

"He didn't do that. Fighting did it. Anyway, I let him have it good." She didn't even ask me who "he" was, as if it made no difference.

"Take off the coat and brush off the dirt," Mama sighed. "Those stockings look finished to me. And go wash your face so Papa doesn't see how you look. Sometimes . . ." She shook her head. "I don't know . . ."

I became quickly aggrieved. "It wasn't *my* fault, Mama! I *had* to!"

"I'm not talking about that." Mama absently patted her round belly that seemed suddenly to have grown larger. "I mean, in the world the way it is, to bring more children in . . ." Her eyes looked far away into what vistas I didn't know.

I shrugged, then took off my coat to examine it. Grass and dirt, nothing very permanent.

"Take it in the cellar," Mama said, "and shake it good." She put her hand on my arm as I turned to go and gave me a surprising squeeze. "Then, when you're finished, hang up the coat and you and Saul come into the kitchen."

"What for?" he asked.

"Because," Mama said softly, "I have A Very Big Secret to tell you."

We stared up at Mama. She smiled her almost-smile, one hand resting on her round belly. "Fast!" she said then, so I jumped. Questions raced through my mind too quickly for me to sort them out into words, as I ran down the rickety cellar steps. I hesitated near the bottom where the permanent Black Dark skulked. There was a light bulb which I had to grope for, and pull the tiny chain that dangled against it so my way would be faintly illuminated.

I shook my coat. What could Mama possibly have to tell us? My eyes darted around the shadows, avoiding the thing on a ledge farther back of the cellar. It looked like a coffin. . . . I shook my coat again. A Very Big Secret . . . What could it be? I shook my coat two more quick shakes and shivered in the cold.

I knew it wasn't really a coffin, but that's what it looked like. It drew my eyes like a magnet, so I had to fight my curiosity and just before my eyes reached the spot, I turned and rushed up the steps, my heart beating very fast. The coat brushed past cobwebs in the corners so it came up dirtier than when it went down. Something had been about to open that coffin . . . I was sure of it! At the top of the steps I stopped and looked at my coat. Oh well, it would clean itself sooner or later. I hung it on a hook, hoping that Mama hadn't started telling Simply Simon first.

"What's the secret, Mama?" I ran into the kitchen where my brother sat, a look of expectation on his face. She pointed to the chair next to his and as I perched on it she pulled a third one over to the table.

"We're ready," I said impatiently.

Mama held up her hand, her expression serious, yet in her eyes something softly glowed. She seemed to be holding her breath. Just as I thought I would explode if Mama didn't tell us, she said:

"Kinderlach . . . we're going to have a baby."

Several emotions seemed to come over her at once: pride, fear, happiness. Almost as though she wasn't sure how she felt about it herself. But I knew how I felt. Instant and overpowering joy. A baby! My wish had come true! I was going to have a baby sister. I leaped out of my chair and ran to Mama in an ecstasy of excitement, almost knocking her out of her chair in my breathless assault. I barely noticed that Simply Simon hadn't moved or uttered a word. It was all just too unbelievably wonderful!

"When, Mama? When will the baby get here?" I couldn't wait to see her.

Mama smiled, leaning away from me so she could look into my face. I knew which of her emotions had won — happiness.

"In about four months."

Four months! She might as well have said four years! What was I going to do for four whole months while I waited for my sister to get here? It would be the middle of winter then!

"Why does it have to take so long, Mama?" You couldn't take a baby for a walk in February!

"We have to have patience, Becky. It takes time till the baby is ready to be born."

"Does Papa know?" I suddenly asked, and wondered how he would feel about having a baby around.

Mama laughed. "Yes, he knows. Now sit down and don't get so excited. There's plenty time yet for that."

I scarcely heard her. In my imagination, I pushed the baby carriage with my little sister inside it, and I could visualize how beautiful she would be, like a Shirley Temple doll, with pink skin and golden curls and big blue eyes. The baby waved her adorable little arms and smiled at me. Oh how she loved me, and I loved her ten times back. No, a thousand times more.

Simply Simon suddenly climbed into Mama's lap, as much of it as he could and leaned on her. I stared at him in astonishment. What was the matter with *him*? I wondered.

"I'm tired, Mama," he said, half-closing his eyes, and stuck his thumb in his mouth, a habit he had given up a long time ago.

Mama smiled and rocked him for a moment while I watched in disbelief, then she pushed him off.

"Do you want to feel the baby?"

How could we? I looked around quickly to see if she had been fooling us. Maybe it was here already. But no. There was no sign of a baby anywhere around, and besides, she was holding Simply Simon's hand against her stomach. He didn't really want to, but Mama held his hand firmly so he couldn't pull it away, and then he had a funny look on his face.

"Hey! It kicked me. I felt it!"

"What did?" I hated to be left out of anything.

"I felt it." He turned to look at me. "Like a foot or something."

I stared at Mama. "Is the baby in *there*?"

"You didn't know?" Mama appeared surprised. "But where did you think . . .?"

"It's there . . ." Simply Simon assured me. "Something is, anyway."

"Let *me* feel." I adjusted to this new knowledge in an

instant. If babies had to be someplace, that was as good a place as any and I could see the logic in it. Mothers grew them in their stomachs and that was why they were mothers. Fathers couldn't possibly do it. Their stomachs were too small. Mama took my hand in her other one and placed it against the other side of her stomach. I didn't feel anything except the roughness of the material of her skirt.

"I *still* feel it," Simply Simon said. I was ready to protest that I hadn't felt anything and it wasn't fair, when suddenly, I did. A faint but deliberate pushing against my palm by something that slid, came back, and pushed again. There really was a baby inside Mama. So it was true then, and my sister was in there, just one inch away from my hand, wanting to come out!

It all made sense. . . .

"You and Papa kissed in bed, didn't you?"

I wanted Mama to see that I was old enough now to know everything. It must have happened that night a month ago when I'd heard them whispering and Mama had giggled. To think that while I lay in my bed, trying to hear their whispers, they had started this baby that tried so hard to get out now!

"What do you mean?" Mama looked bewildered.

"I mean," I said on a deep breath, "that I know where babies come from."

Mama looked alarmed. "Who told you?" Her voice came out sharp as a penknife.

"Nobody. I figured it out myself." I felt proud about that. . . . "Fat Emma thinks she's the only one that knows things, but I know too. She wouldn't tell me it was kissing, but I guessed anyway."

"Kissing?" Mama looked relieved. "You think it's from kissing? Well, it isn't, and when you're old enough, I'll explain it to you. Right now you're too young. Believe me."

I sighed very loudly, exasperated.

"I'm old enough now, Mama. Fat Emma knew when *she* was nine years old and I'll be ten in January."

It was no use arguing with her once she made up her

mind. Mama was even more stubborn than I.

"I have to get myself a smock," she said, almost to herself. "I'm getting too big for my clothes. Nothing fits."

The bump that grew inside Mama had made her fat. I looked at it in awe. How had it gotten in there in the first place and how would it get out again? And if kissing didn't start babies, what did? There wasn't anything else that could. Mama must have said that because Simply Simon was listening and he was a boy. He really *was* too young to know about things; he was only eight. I smiled at Mama, a knowing kind of smile. She thought she'd thrown me off the track by pretending I'd guessed wrong but I was too smart for that. Kissing did *so* start babies.

What I couldn't understand though, was how a kiss got into Mama's stomach and turned into a baby? Unless . . . I felt myself grow hot just to think of it . . . unless Papa had kissed Mama right on the . . . belly button. It sounded disgusting. I couldn't believe Papa would do a thing like that or that Mama would let him. But, even though I hated to admit it, it did sound logical. Maybe that was what they were for. I had often wondered what good they were. Now I knew and the knowledge made me feel kind of . . . old, as though I'd discovered the secret of the ages.

"Go upstairs and take off your stockings. Maybe I can fix those holes," Mama said.

I'd forgotten all about those stockings, Johnny Felange, the fire and the lady trapped in her bedroom! I'd forgotten everything that had been exciting, because they were nothing, compared to the wonderful news of the baby!

Mama's hand suddenly pulled my head down so our eyes were level. She patted my head for a moment.

"I wish you would try to act more like a lady, Becky. You are getting to be a big girl, you know."

I would have promised her anything. I gave her the biggest hug ever, almost knocking the breath out of her. "I'll try, Mama!" My voice choked up on me. "I'll really try to act like a lady. Even if it *kills* me!"

I ran upstairs, taking them two at a time as though I

were being chased by monsters. Mama's hand seemed still to be touching my head. I stared at myself in the mirror, and saw the same old face with the same old nose and the same old hair. But the eyes were different. They were wide open, and seeing, really seeing. I could look outwards now instead of always inside my own head and I knew I was happy. Mama loved me. Her touch on my head said so. And in four months, just one, two, three, four months, I was going to have a brand-new, gorgeous, darling sweet and adorable baby sister. What could be more marvelous than that?

**3** "Did you go and see the doctor yet like I told you?" Auntie Sadie's voice, like sour wine, puckered in my ears as I walked through the door after four o'clock. I stopped, surprised. What was she doing here this time of day?

The teakettle humming loudly on the stove almost drowned out Mama's answer: "Not yet."

I imagined her leaning against the sink while Auntie Sadie stood, straight and thin as an accusing finger. I couldn't see either of them from the desk in the middle room where I slowly began gathering Hebrew books together. That stupid Simply Simon. He hadn't waited for me and now I had to walk by myself to Cheder, Hebrew school.

"What are you waiting for?" Auntie Sadie's voice snapped and for an instant I thought she was talking to me. "I'm telling you, Minnie, I don't like the way it looks. Your legs are so swollen."

"So what do you want me to do? Lie on my back all day?"

"I'm saying for your own good, Minnie. Don't blow up at me. Look at you . . . anybody would think you're in your eighth when you're what . . . going into the sixth? If I were you I'd make an appointment and not wait till it's too late."

I stood, my books cradled in my arms, reluctant to leave yet not wanting to be late either.

"So come, sit down and drink your tea," Mama's voice

said placidly. The humming of the kettle stopped abruptly, followed by the sound of water trickling into a cup. A chair scraped loudly.

"Did I come for tea or to try to talk some sense into your stubborn head?"

Mama sighed. "Suit yourself. I need tea."

Water trickled again. "Don't worry so much, Sadie, I'll be all right. What could happen?"

"What could happen! God forbid what could happen! The doctor would take fits if he saw you. That's one thing could happen."

"Oh, the doctor!" Mama's voice dismissed him airily. Spoons clinked into cups stirring stirring stirring. I stood half in, half out of the hallway that led to the outside door and took one step backward then another.

"Anyway," Mama's voice suddenly pursued the subject. "I haven't anything to wear. How could I go to the doctor in this kimono even if I had the strength to walk that far?"

"All the more reason! And you'll take a taxi, never mind walking."

Mama gave a short laugh, "A taxi!"

Auntie Sadie's voice went on, unperturbed. "Maybe I got something at home will fit. I'll have a look."

"Sure, tomorrow they'll fit me. They wouldn't even fit my hanger. Take a piece of chocolate cake."

"No. I shouldn't. I have to go home and make supper for my Morris."

"One piece"

"All right."

By now I'd back-stepped all the way to the outside front door when I heard Papa's footsteps sounding hollowly on the linoleum coming out of the store. I stopped dead.

"You're here?" His voice spoke in tones of resignation.

"Fool!" Auntie Sadie hissed. "Look what you did already!"

In a flash I was back inside the entrance to the house, so I could hear better while still being out of sight. Papa laughed. "It's your business? Besides, it was her idea, not mine."

"You should know better. Don't you remember what the doctor said after Saul? No more, remember?"

"Doctors," Mama said. "What do they know? Are they God? It's only lately, this pain bothers me and all this extra heaviness."

"Take my advice, Minnie," Auntie Sadie said urgently. "Put yourself in the hands of the doctor. Don't let it get worse. Maybe he can give you something. If I were you . . ."

I didn't wait to hear more. Clutching my books to my chest I turned and ran down the hall to the outside door, out of the house and across the street. My stomach churned with a lot of undigested emotions so I hardly felt the nip of November cold or the ache in my throat from inhaling chill air.

I didn't stop running till I could see the brick building that was Cheder, and as I slowed to a walk I realized that the feeling I had tried to outrace, my chilling fear, was inside me all along. I hadn't been able to leave it behind.

I shivered, pulling my coat more tightly around me and tried to understand what Auntie Sadie had said. But all that came through was one fact: The doctor had told Mama not to have any more babies after Simply Simon. I crossed my fingers, closed my eyes and counted backwards from ten three times for luck. Now it would be all right. Nothing bad would happen to Mama and the baby. Especially the baby!

I wasn't altogether relieved though, and Mr. Lerner's giving me twenty pages of lines to do for coming late didn't help much either. But I was one hundred percent sure of one thing. God would take good care of Mama and the baby. He wouldn't let anything happen to them, doctor or no doctor! Just to be on the safe side I counted from ten backwards another three times but this time I forgot to cross my fingers.

**4** Betty Greenberg and Marjorie Adams weren't really snobs! This came as a great shock to me during recess one day when I finally, in a lull in conversation, blurted out my secret.

Marjorie Adams, pushing her glasses up — they were always sliding down her nose — stared at me.

"Oh are you ever lucky!" she screamed and Betty Greenberg edged closer.

"What are you hoping for, a boy or a girl?" she asked.

"Well, it's going to be a girl," I said, happy that they were so interested.

"How do you know?" Marjorie pushed her glasses up again.

"Well, because," I said. I couldn't really explain how I knew. "It just will, that's all."

"Even *doctors* don't know, so how do you?" Betty persisted.

"I guess," I had to admit, "I don't *really* know. I just have this positive feeling. I want a sister anyway."

The bell rang then but I didn't mind because I was afraid we would start to argue about it and one thing I didn't want was an argument just when things were going so well. We went inside, one of them on each side of me, and it was the most marvelous feeling.

"You lucky fish," Marjorie whispered in my ear. "All I've got is a brother!" She pushed her glasses up again. I felt sorry for her suddenly, not only because she had a brother and no prospects for a baby sister but because she had to wear glasses and they were such a bother. I had never felt sorry for any of the girls before. It felt strange.

Later Betty Greenberg told me she was an only child. I began to see the flaws in the perfection of her life. In spite of expensive tunics and the beautiful big old house on Machray Avenue, where the really lovely old homes were, she was an only child and that would be pretty awful. I'd walked her partway home going two blocks out of my way just to have her to talk to for a change.

"Do you want to come into my house?" she asked.

"I'm going to be late getting home," I said regretfully.

"How many rooms do you have?"

"Six," she said casually, "Of course they're pretty big

ones."

"They *must* be," I breathed and wondered why a family of only three people needed six rooms. We parted company then and I galloped all the way home. I'd be late for Cheder again.

Simply Simon had changed. He didn't wait for me anymore so I had to walk to Cheder by myself and I had to walk home alone too. Now that it was winter it grew dark earlier and I didn't like walking home by myself. Snow crunched under my overshoes, making sounds like somebody chasing me, and the bare trees looked like hunched-over old men with their arms stretched out to grab me. I could hardly wait to get home from Cheder. Besides, when I was away from Mama I worried about her.

She sat, her face puffy and tired, and for once her hands lay idle in her lap.

"Did you go to see the doctor yet, Mama?" I asked anxiously.

She raised her eyes and looked at me.

"Why should I?"

"Because you don't feel good, do you Mama?" I asked. "I don't see why you don't make an appointment with the doctor. Was it this bad when you were having us?"

"I was younger then, faigele," Mama assured me. "Now I'm older, it's a little bit different."

I hung up my coat, not entirely convinced, and started on my homework. I could see that supper hadn't even been started. There weren't any pots on the stove. That meant I would have to peel potatoes as soon as I got finished and maybe fry some slices of meat for the family. I didn't blame Mama but I made up my mind that when I grew up, I'd have all my babies at once: one, two, three, six, maybe even twelve. And then I'd stop and never have another one. Then I wouldn't be having them when I was older like Mama. I didn't want to turn out to be big and fat like she was.

I finally figured out how babies got out of their mother's stomachs—the same way they got in: through the belly button. It opened up somehow and the doctor put his hand in and took the baby out. I hated to think of old Dr. Goozer touching Mama's belly button or even seeing it. It made me sick to the stomach to think about it but that's the way it had to be. Doctors probably got used to seeing them and they didn't think anything about it. I was sure I'd never get used to a doctor touching *my* belly button though. I decided to face that event when the time came and firmly pushed it out of my mind. I still had thirteen pages of lines to do.


**5** Snow fell in great lazy flakes. I stood on the sidewalk, my head tipped back and mouth open. I could feel the snow, tasting like sparks of fire as it landed on my tongue. No wind stirred, not even a breath. It was a good thing because winter had really arrived.

Wednesday, December 2nd, and the whole winter still ahead of us. Snow clung to my high three-buckled overshoes. I hugged my coat tighter around me. It was getting too short but when I asked Papa if I could have a new one he barely glanced in my direction.

"You can wear it another year. We have expenses to worry about now. Anyway, what's *wrong* with this coat, eh?"

"Nothing, Papa," I said because that was what I knew he wanted to hear.

"All I got to worry about is a new coat," he grumbled under his breath. "A baby coming, doctor's expenses, the hospital, and all she can think about is a coat."

"It's okay Papa," I said quickly, wishing I hadn't spoken. "I can wear it another year."

"And business," he went on, still talking in the same undertone to himself, "toig oyf kapores. People stopped eating."

I tiptoed away not wanting to hear any more. I knew people hadn't stopped eating. It was just that there was too much competition and Papa hadn't adjusted to that fact. He kept sending his customers away so they'd get on their high horse and gallop off across the street to nurse their hurt

*27*

feelings, Papa's shouts ringing in their ears.

"How much you tomatoes?" Mrs. Deburni would ask. Papa would tell her.

Inevitably (she never learned), she would say "So *much*? I can go across street, get it maybe fi', ten cents cheaper!"

"So *go*!" Papa would holler. "Who dragged you in? Me?"

I'd hear Mama go tsk, tsk, and later she would try to calm him.

"Jake, why do you do it? You know we need their business more than they need us. Why do you have to get mad and start yelling?"

Papa maintained an icy silence.

"Why," Mama persisted, "do you keep sending them across the street? Does Corkman keep sending you *his* customers?"

"Don't mention his name in my house!" Papa roared. "That nothing, that Shabbas goy! A man doesn't believe in God, he'd sell his Bobba for a nickel."

"Shah. Don't yell. I told you not to yell so much. You'll get a high blood pressure."

"Who's yelling!" Papa shouted. "Why do you keep saying I'm yelling? You know that always makes me mad!"

Mama sighed and closed her mouth and Papa stalked away. I kept my head bent over a book so I wouldn't meet anybody's eye. If it was Papa's eye I'd get a lecture for wasting time reading instead of sweeping the floor. If it was Mama's eye I'd be criticized for sitting bent over like a hunchback instead of straight like a lady. No matter how arguments started, they usually ended with me.

I wished things were different. I wished Papa was different, because if he smiled a lot we'd have more customers and then Papa would make a lot of money and I wouldn't have to feel like a poor freak wearing a coat two inches too small with frayed sleeves and a plain collar. I couldn't help comparing mine with Betty Greenberg's, which had a fur collar that felt soft as a kitten. I almost expected it to purr when she let me stroke it.

But one thing I had that they all envied me, and that was my coming baby sister. Next to that nothing was of any great importance, not the cold, not my appearance, not Miss Harrison's meanness or Mr. Lerner's brutishness. I closed my eyes and whirled joyfully on one foot. In two months or so, I would actually look at her, touch her, hold her, hug her!

Mama said she was as "big as a house" and I heard her wonder if it could be twins. Such an idea had never occurred to me, but the thought of it sent me into happy hysteria. Two baby sisters! Or maybe a baby brother for Simply Simon and a sister for me. I could afford to be generous. After all, he already *had* a sister, and it could be that the thought of another one didn't thrill him half as much as it did me. Strange, how I didn't doubt for a moment that it would be a girl. . . .

Mama seemed better too. Happier. I wondered if she'd finally gone to see the doctor and he'd given her some pills but she said no, she didn't have the time, and anyway, there was no need.

"Women had babies," she reminded me, "since Eve, and they didn't always run to see a doctor. If they could do it, so can I."

"But Mama," I protested, "they didn't have doctors then, that's why they didn't go to see them. I bet even *Eve* would've gone if she could!"

Mama merely smiled and dropped another hamburger patty into the hot oil in the frying pan, sending wild and angry hisses up from its black bottom. The aroma was delicious. My appetite had improved wonderfully lately. I was hungry all the time and this made Mama happy. Papa always said: "Eat with bread." But Mama didn't care whether we did or not, and loaded my plate with potatoes and hamburgers or chunks of fried liver with onions, which I loved. Of course if Papa sat and watched we did cram ourselves with bread too, which was cheap and filling, but even so, in an hour or two I'd be looking for something to eat in the ice box.

"Eat . . . eat," Mama said. So I ate . . . and ate.

There was a craving inside me for something, a hunger deep, not easily satisfied. I didn't know what I hungered for and thinking it was a physical kind of thing I concentrated on food. It was the nearest thing to satisfaction I could find, although once, when Papa had been in a particularly benign mood and played a game of cards with me, my happiness had bubbled like a pot of boiling sugar and I hadn't thought of food that whole evening. Times like those were rare though. Mostly Papa paid no attention to me. Luckily, I didn't get any fatter than a shoe lace no matter how much I ate, otherwise my coat would have been impossible to wear whether we could afford to replace it or not.

I stepped into Simply Simon's footprints all the way to school, walking half a block behind him. When he crossed to the zigzag lane, I didn't but kept on till the end of the street and crossed at the corner.

I didn't mind school these days. Miss Harrison, the approaching season no doubt in mind, became slightly mellow, even smiling occasionally when she looked at us. The sight of a smiling Miss Harrison brought me up short, especially when she looked in my direction, but her stinging sarcasm was as potent as ever, season or no season.

"Did you notice how sweet Miss Harrison has been acting lately?" Debbie Hanson said at recess. We huddled together in our usual corner of the school out of snowball range of the bratty boys.

"I'll bet Becky doesn't think so!" Betty laughed.

"Oh yes I do!" I nodded my head vigorously. "She even said something nice about my English composition!"

"I'll bet I know why." Marjorie grinned. "She's making sure we all get her presents for Christmas. That's why she's acting like that. And in January..." She made a slicing motion across her throat with one finger.

"What if someone doesn't get her a present?" I asked apprehensively, thinking of the money situation at home, not to mention Papa's reaction to a "Christmas" present for the teacher. Marjorie laughed gaily and repeated her throat-slicing gesture casually. Since it was my throat that would be slit, I didn't laugh quite as heartily as the others.

"Boy," I said with feeling, "am I in trouble!"

"Why, Beck? It doesn't have to be expensive, you know. You could get her something cheap, like a nice lace hanky or a bottle of toilet water."

"What are you getting her?" I asked.

"A book of poetry," Betty said. "Mummy's already got it wrapped in red and green paper with a big red bow!"

I could imagine Mama rushing out in her kimono and going downtown to get Miss Harrison a book of poetry.

"Boy," I said again, "am I in trouble!"

"Well," Marjorie said cheerfully, "there's still plenty of time to worry about it. It isn't for almost three weeks, you know. And then . . . the *holidays!*" She did a happy dance in the snow.

Because I had plenty of time to worry about it, I worried all the rest of that day and the next day too. By Friday evening I had worried myself into a chronic stomachache and decided it was time I did something about it. After the table had been cleared away and the kitchen straightened up I stood beside the Shabbas candles and looked into the flickering flames.

"Mama," I said, watching the deep blue and orange in the heart of the fire, "all the kids are getting the teacher a Christmas present."

"So?"

"So I was wondering . . ." My heart pounded like a hammer. "Do you think we could . . . afford . . . to get her something, too?"

I stole a glance at her over my shoulder. She looked at me. "Since when do Jewish people give Christmas presents?"

"Betty Greenberg's Jewish and her mother bought a book of poetry for Miss Harrison and wrapped it with red and green paper and bows and Mama . . . *they're* Jewish."

"They're Jewish," Mama said. "They put up colored lights on their house and you call them Jewish?"

"Well they are anyway even if they use colored lights and anyway, what's wrong with colored lights? I think they're pretty."

"Only Goyim put up colored lights. That's what's wrong. What's the matter, are you ashamed of being Jewish?"

"Of course not, Mama. All I said was all the kids are getting Miss Harrison presents and if I don't, I'll be the only one and you know what she'll do to me?" I made Marjorie's gesture across my throat.

"You mean," Mama's eyebrows shot up, "if you don't bring the teacher a present she'll kill you?"

"Well, not really but she'll sure pick on me more than she already does."

"The teacher picks on you?"

I bit my lip. Why did I have to say that? I didn't want Mama to know and till now she hadn't known. Mama had enough to worry about without me adding to it, and besides there was nothing she could do about it anyway.

"Why does the teacher pick on you? What do you do?"

"Did I say she picks on me? Well she doesn't. I don't know why I said that. It just slipped out. Forget it, Mama. Okay?"

Mama sat back and looked at me.

"Does she, or she doesn't? Which is it?" Mama looked exasperated. "You better tell me, because I'll find out. I'll go to the school and they'll tell me."

I could just imagine it: Mama plodding into school, the ends of her kimono flapping like big maroon-colored wings and all the kids staring at her with owl's eyes and maybe snickering. Then the principal would call me into his office and Miss Harrison too and she would act shocked and say of *course* she didn't pick on me, why I was her favorite pupil, and afterwards when Mama went home she really would kill me.

"Mama! You wouldn't go to the school!"

Mama folded her arms across her chest.

"You're telling your mother what she shouldn't do?"

"Honest, Mama! The teacher doesn't pick on me. She's very nice really. In fact that's why I want to get her a present.

*32*

To show my appreciation. A sort of . . . Chanukah present?"

"A Chanukah present. You have to give the teacher a present for being nice? She doesn't get paid for teaching? Isn't this her job? By us we never gave presents."

"I know Mama," I said, getting desperate. "But this is Canada and here they give presents when a teacher is nice."

I hoped I'd be forgiven for the outrageous lie but I was playing for high stakes—Miss Harrison's good will. Mama looked at me and sighed and then I realized I was leaning forward so intensely my body arched. Mama saw this too. She put a hand out and twisted the hair beside my face into a sausage. I knew I had won even before she spoke.

"I'll talk to Papa," she said.

The next day, Saturday, while Papa and Simply Simon were at Shul, Mama stirred cold cocoa while I ate my corn flakes with milk.

"Today we get your teacher a present," she said.

Relief washed over me in tidal waves. Then a thought hit me.

"What are you going to wear?"

I couldn't visualize Mama going downtown in her kimono.

"Don't worry," Mama said. "I've been saving."

"Money?" I wrinkled my nose. You couldn't wear money.

"No. A dress. What I was saving to wear to the hospital when the time comes. I'll wear it just this one time if it's so important to you. How about Saul? Do you think he needs too?"

I nodded. Anybody coming to school without a present for the teacher would look pretty cheap. It was even a kind of insurance. If you give the teacher a present, she has to be nice to you after that.

Downtown was a madhouse, Mama kept saying as I clung to her so we wouldn't get separated in the shoving crowds. People pulled things out of each other's hands and glared at each other, just as though there weren't a hundred other items exactly the same. I hated it when we had to shop in the Basement because that was where nobody had to be polite to anybody else, but the prices were lower there along with the standards of human behavior.

Mama kept picking things up from counters and asking: "Would she like stockings? Would she like an address book?"

I didn't know what Miss Harrison would like. The only things that sounded safe to me were the things Betty mentioned: a book of poetry, a lace hanky or a bottle of toilet water. The book of poetry was out. Betty would get mad and call me a copycat if I got something like that too even if we could afford it. That left only a hanky or toilet water.

In the end we got toilet water with pretty purple pansies painted on the side of the bottle and the small box it came in, one for me and one for Simply Simon. Thanks to me now he wouldn't have to get into trouble with his teacher. Not that he deserved my help.

We stopped at the notions counter for wrapping paper and some bright red ribbons.

"Don't show the paper to Papa," Mama advised me in a low voice. "When you wrap it, do it in your room."

I carried the parcels in Mama's big shopping bag. The world was a marvelous place and I loved everybody in it. But most especially, I loved Mama who really and truly understood everything.

**6** It turned suddenly cold on the last day of school. All bundled in our scarves and mitts with two pairs of stockings on over our long winter combinations, carrying our gaily wrapped gifts, Simply Simon and I stepped out into swirling snow. My scarf tasted woolly and faintly of moth balls. I pulled it up higher over my nose. It kept sliding down. In a few minutes, Simply Simon became a blur up ahead but it didn't matter. This way, I could pretend I was lost in the Great Northland and hadn't seen a living person for days.

She struggles on, I told myself, bravely fighting the blasts of icy wind. The Girl squints into the vast whiteness, her eyes almost freezing up solid. If she blinks, they'll crack and she'll be blind for life. She has walked for days and days without food and water, and wild animals howl in the distance. . . .

I was glad to see Machray School loom solid and comforting up ahead. We'd get our report cards today and for the first time I could look forward to it. Everything had seemed so easy during the exams, even arithmetic. And it was all because of the baby. She brought me luck. Every time I thought about her, happiness surged through me. I thought about her constantly.

We didn't have to wait for the bell on really cold days like this one. I figured it to be about sixty below zero, at least. The big school doors were so heavy. . . . After the glare of snow the hall seemed dark. I pulled my scarf off my face so nobody would see me looking like a little kid and went inside.

Against the wall in the center of the corridor stood the biggest tree I had ever seen, and as I stared at it brightly colored lights flickered on, tiny ball-shaped lights. Tinsel, silver ornaments and colored strawlike ropes were strung from branch to branch and I gazed at it with the fascination found in any forbidden thing. It was a sin to think a Christmas tree looked pretty so I kept from thinking anything at all by counting all the lights I could see. Who paid for them, I wondered . . . Mr. Fudge, the janitor, or the principal?

A trickle of children spilled past, running up to the tree, oh-ing and ah-ing, shadows between me and the tree. I could see the colors reflected on upturned faces and I envied them. They could admire it all they wanted without feeling guilty or wondering what Papa would say if he knew.

Why couldn't *we* have something pretty like that? On Chanukah, all we did was light the menorah with the eight little candles, starting with one on the first night, and adding another till, by the eighth night, all of them were lit, but they were so small they burned down to nothing very fast and all we had was a smear of hard wax when it was over. That wasn't my idea of celebrating.

I moved my feet slightly and felt the soles of my overshoes stick to the floor in a slushy mess. Mr. Fudge hated anybody walking in with rubbers on. I slogged over to the wall to lean while I took them off and still keep my eyes on the tree. Then I carried my overshoes, scarf and present into the classroom.

Miss Harrison's desk held a mountain of gaily colored packages. I had never seen so many all in one pile before, although I supposed every teacher got them, even Miss Smith last year. I placed mine on top. I'm the King of the Castle, I said to myself.

"What did you get?" Betty came up behind me.

"Toilet water." I made a face because whenever I thought about it, it sounded like water from the toilet. Then, just in case she felt the same way about it, I added:

"It smells real nice. I hope she likes it."

Betty pointed to one, longer and flatter: "That one is mine," she said.

Miss Harrison made a grand entrance so we scurried to our seats. She stopped just inside the doorway, made a small gasping sound and pretended surprise. As if she hadn't expected to see all those presents on her desk.

"Merry Christmas, children," she said.

"Merry Christmas, Miss Harrison," we parroted back at her. My lips moved but the words didn't come out. I could never actually say them.

Miss Harrison fussed with the gifts and said: "My, my!" and I wanted to see if she would open them but she didn't. I felt vaguely disappointed. I had wanted her to know right away that I brought her one too. Now she would have to wait until the holidays to find out!

"Class stand!"

We snapped to our feet.

"Class by rows, forward march!"

She opened the door and we filed out into the dimly lit hall. Other classes were filing out too in a congestion of sweaty bodies, damp stockings, muffled giggles and whispers, and shuffling feet. The tree stood omnipotent, the central point of our assembly, glowing wickedly, beckoning, winking, tempting me to admire its grandeur.

I stared at it, the symbol of so many terrible things that happened to Jewish people at Christmas . . . things Papa had told us about. In Russia, where he and Mama had married, the priests told the peasants to kill the Jews and they did. That was how Papa's mother had died, my grandmother whom I was named after. Papa would have been next if he hadn't escaped through a small kitchen window. I always felt my stomach tie into knots when Papa started talking about it. I didn't want to hear the terrible stories even though they were true. I didn't want to hear that we were hated because of our religion. I wanted people to love us, and hearing the truth made me sick. I wanted to vomit.

"Everybody, squat!" Miss Courtenay, the grade six teacher with the trombone voice yelled. We squatted. The floor felt dirty but I sat on my knees anxious to get the whole thing over with. The singing of Christmas carols began.

I could see Betty ahead of me, silhouetted against the tree lights. She had her head lifted, her eyes fixed on the tree, lights reflecting on her white hair ribbon. To my amazement she was singing the words to the carols. I sat with my lips closed not even pretending to sing, yet there was Betty, Jewish like me, singing *Christmas* carols! I stared in horror, then moved my eyes to see if anybody else had noticed. After all, it wasn't *her* holiday. But nobody paid the slightest attention to her. All had eyes fixed on the tree, heads lifted, lips moving at the same time.

I must be the only one who noticed and no one else even cared. I was the one who was different, not Betty. She was more like them than like me. She was really Canadian, with both her parents born here (she had told me that) and all her grandparents living close by. Betty's father was young with black wavy hair and a small moustache. And he smiled a lot. Once he had kissed Betty good-bye right in front of me. Embarrassed, I had looked away, feeling alien, an outsider. He laughed as if he knew how I felt and when I looked at him again he had winked at me.

After the carols, we were sent back to our classrooms where we endured the little speech Miss Harrison felt she had to make, the have-a-happy-holiday-and-I-hope-Santa-brings-you-everything-you-desire one. The peppermint candy canes in cute red and green striped packages were handed out to each of us, a sort of tradition at Machray School and we were almost ready to be dismissed. There was just one more thing, one I looked forward to this year as I never had in the past: report cards.

On the way out, all bundled in our heavy coats and scarves and mittens, Miss Harrison handed each of us our report cards. Pleasepleaseplease, I prayed to myself. . . . Out in the hall I took a quick look to reassure myself, straining to see in the dim hall light. There were my marks, not one encircled by red pencil. No failures! Wow! Thank you God, thank you, Baby Sister! I slid the report card back into its beige envelope and gave a quick skip on my way to the door. Funny how light I felt even weighted down with all those clothes.

"Hi!" Betty's voice came breathlessly behind me. "How did you make out?" I turned and saw her lift the fur collar around her face.

"Pretty good," I said modestly. "At least I won't mind showing *this* report card to my father!"

Together we pushed the front doors open. Swirling snow hit us in the face. A regular blizzard!

"I wish my daddy was waiting for me with the car!" Betty wailed, ducking her chin into the collar. I pulled my scarf over my mouth.

"I wish I was home already!"

"Well, good-bye!" she called to me, waving her candy cane. "Have a nice . . . holiday!"

"You too!" I laughed, because I was sure she'd been about to say Christmas.

At the corner we went our separate ways. Home seemed like someplace on the other side of the world. With my head bent into the wind, I watched my feet disappear into the soft snow, hunched my shoulders against the cold and squinted.

There were bright spangles everywhere I looked through my squinty eyes. I held tightly to my candy cane and report card. Papa would be so happy when he saw it. I almost skipped with the anticipation of it.

I became the Lost Brave Girl again, outwitting wild wolves and death in the form of freezing. I knew I would get to civilization just in time. When I could see the grocery store, rising specterlike through the snow, I ran panting and gasping, chased by wolves and wild men with spears. They were going to capture me and make me their Great White Goddess like in the movie I had seen last Saturday at the Palace Theatre. If they caught me, I'd never see my parents again. I made it up the front steps, stamping snow off my overshoes, safe at last.

Mama looked surprised.

"Is it time for dinner already?" We always called lunch dinner.

"No, Mama. It's the beginning of the holidays. We get out early. Remember? My report card!" I placed it in front of her with a flourish.

"You look so happy it must be a good one." Mama pulled it out of its envelope, quickly scanning the figures. "Well! You came in fourteenth in class, Becky! Better than last time!"

I glowed.

"Very very nice," Mama said, reaching up to pull my face down to hers so she could kiss me. "Wait till Papa sees!"

I unbundled myself from my coat and cap, the warmth that coursed through me only partly from the heat of the stove. Then I remembered to ask.

"How are you feeling?"

"Fine. Did your teacher like her present?"

"She didn't open it. She had about a million presents on her desk, Mama. You should've seen! I bet it'll take her a month to open them all up. The lucky fish!"

"What's so lucky about fish? We eat them, don't we?"

"Well, she's a lucky fish anyway. When I grow up, I'm going to be a teacher, so I'll get all those presents!"

"If getting presents is the only reason you want to be a teacher, never mind."

I turned to look out of the window.

"It sure is a gyp that when the holidays start, the weather has to be rotten. Is Simply Simon home yet?"

"Simple-Shmimple," Mama said. "If it's Saul you mean, he isn't home. I wonder what's taking him?"

She seemed to notice the weather for the first time. "Oy vay, look at that storm! Did you see Saul on your way?"

"Saul-Shmaul." I grinned at her. "If you mean Simply Simon, no I didn't. Don't worry, Mama. All the classes didn't get out at the same time."

But I stood at the window and watched for him, even though you could hardly see anything through the flying white flags hurled against the panes by blasts of wind. Then I caught sight of a small shape bent forward, struggling into the wind.

"He's home!" I shouted, and ran to open the door for him. He looked like a snowboy.

Papa came in from the store at that moment.

"What are you doing home so early?"

"It's the holidays, Papa," I reminded him. "We get home early on the holidays."

A nerve twitched ominously beside Papa's mouth. He held out his hand.

"Let's see the report card."

This was the part I had always dreaded. Papa would look at it while I tried to make myself disappear, keeping my eyes on the floor. If I didn't see his expression, it wouldn't be so bad, and meanwhile I'd try to think of reasons why I was almost last in class. I would try to remember if I'd been sick during the past two months, if maybe that was why I'd done so poorly.

But now I handed it to Papa, keeping my eyes on his face as he scanned it so I could savor his pleased surprise. Just once I'd have the joy of watching him look happy about my marks. His expression didn't change.

"Marks are higher," Papa commented. My heart

pounded suffocatingly. He looked at me, his blue eyes piercing my complacency. "Fourteenth in class," he said without inflection. "Better than before." I prepared to glow. "Why couldn't you be tenth?"

The glow faded.

"Fourteenth is good," Mama said from the kitchen. "Don't forget she's in high grade four, where the smart kids are."

Papa grunted and held out his hand for Simply Simon's report card. I didn't stay to hear how great *his* marks were. I ran up the stairs to my room, taking my candy cane with me. A bitter taste welled up from my throat.

I threw myself onto my bed, hating Papa. Anger and disappointment rolled together inside me, choking me. Hell, damn it, goddam it, I whispered, letting the bad words repeat themselves over and over in my brain. I hate him, I hate him. He's . . . I couldn't think any further. I could hate him, but he was still my father. Maybe. Probably not. I dug my shoulders deeply into my pillow. And that Simp . . . *Saul*. Goody-goody Saul. I hated him too. For being so smart, so cute, so adorable, *Saul*, Saul, Saul, Saul. That's who you are. You're *Saul*.

I glared at the ceiling, staring at its yellowing crusty surface with the spidery network of cracks beginning in one corner and fanning out towards the center. Then I peeled the cardboard container off the candy cane and popped the peppermint candy into my mouth. I hoped it would spoil my dinner. But that would make Mama unhappy, and I certainly wasn't mad at *her*. Still, I didn't let that stop me. I twisted it around in my mouth, making a sharp point at the end, sharp as a dagger.

When I grow up, I thought, I will never be mean like Papa and make my children hate me. I would be more like Mama, who was kind and good. But one thing I would make sure about was that I would only marry somebody as good as I was. I tried to imagine the man I would marry. For some reason, his face resembled the face of Betty Greenberg's father. I was sure *he* never said things like: "Why can't you be tenth in class?"

Of course Betty was always among the first ten students anyway. I sighed very deeply. I would be just as smart as her, I told myself, if I had a young Canadian father and mother, was rich, was the only child in the family, and had all my grandparents living where I could see them, and wore expensive tunics. Suppose *she* had to live here, and have a brother like Simp . . . *Saul*, and wear the same tunic for three years and have a father who never smiled at you, no matter what? Would she be so smart then?

My candy cane grew smaller. I sat up suddenly, swung my feet over the side of the bed and got out my latest scribbler. As I bent over it, a stub of pencil gripped tightly in my hand, I began to feel better. Later I went down for dinner, just as if I'd never been angry.

# PART TWO

**1**  The day I became ten years old was like any other. I went to school because it was Friday, January 15, my nose buried in the damp folds of smelly scarf, thinking what a gyp it was. I didn't feel any older. For all it mattered I could still be nine or even eight. When would it happen, that miracle which would proclaim me old enough to know everything? How would I know?

The cold bit my fingers through the woollen mittens, so I tried to keep one hand in my pocket all the time, changing hands frequently. The other hand would be holding my books. I'd be glad when winter was over . . . glad? I'd be delirious!

I didn't tell the girls it was my birthday. First thing they always did was grab the poor victim's arms and legs and give her the royal bumps. There was nothing very royal about them, and what really hurt was that the boys would get in on it, which wasn't fair because they didn't let us return the favor when it was a boy's birthday.

Then they would ask me what I'd received from Mama and Papa and as far as I knew the answer would be "nothing." Mama hadn't even been awake when I'd left for school in the morning and I had a hunch she'd forgotten all about my birthday in spite of the fact that I'd dropped massive hints all week.

I wasn't surprised, because Mama hardly did anything anymore. For instance it was only weeks away instead of months and Mama hadn't bought a single thing for the baby. When I'd realized how close it was, I said:

"Mama! When are you going to start getting some things for the baby? We haven't got a crib or anything!"

Mama had said casually: "There's lots of time."

"But it's only a month now, and it'll be time and we won't be ready!"

"When the time comes," Mama had assured me, "we'll be ready. It's bad luck, God forbid, to have anything in the house before the baby comes. Something could happen."

"What? What could happen?" I hadn't thought of anything as dire as that since the time I'd overheard Auntie Sadie in the kitchen. "Why is it bad luck?"

Mama stood solid as a tree, a wisp of hair escaping from the braid around her head, stirring something on the stove.

"*What* could happen?" I repeated, but Mama shook her head at me and made me set the table for supper. So it didn't surprise me very much that she had let my birthday pass by without even saying the words: Happy Birthday!

Of course, we didn't exactly make birthday celebrations last from morning till night, so I didn't give up hope altogether, and when I walked through the front door at dinnertime and kicked off my overshoes, Mama stood there.

"So, look who's ten years old already!" she cried, holding her arms out to me. I ran to her, pleased. That was more like it, I thought.

She pecked my cheek. "Happy birthday."

I looked over her shoulder just in case there were some packages lying around for me to open.

"I smell something baking." I sniffed the air and made a beeline for the oven door.

Mama grabbed my arm. "Don't touch. You'll let the heat out and good-bye birthday cake."

On the way back to school for the afternoon session Simply Simon walked with me. Lately he'd begun to mellow so sometimes we were friends.

"Did you notice," I asked him, "that Mama kept holding her stomach? I'll bet the baby will soon be ready to come out."

"Well, it better wait and not come out till after *my* birthday cause I want Mama to make *me* a cake too."

"It will come out long before your birthday, Dopey," I informed him. "Your birthday isn't till March and the baby is *supposed* to be born in February."

"Well then, what makes you think it's ready now?"

"Just a feeling I have," I said smugly. "Just something a *girl* can tell, but boys can't."

"Oh you think you're so smart!"

"Well, I am. After all, I'm ten years old now and it makes a big difference."

The afternoon dragged but finally we were on our way home again. I wanted to run all the way. I felt a new power within me. I felt bigger, older, stronger, smarter. It was my birthday; it was Friday so there would be no Cheder tonight and soon the winter would be over. But the very best thing of all, soon I'd be able to actually see and touch and kiss my baby sister.

Eagerly I went through the front door, being careful to hang my coat, cap and scarf in the closet, place my wet overshoes against the wall so nobody would trip on them, and see the cake Mama had baked . . . the aroma of it having met me in the hall.

A white tablecloth covered the kitchen table, and Mama, moving slowly, brought out our best plates. I counted eight settings and wondered . . . who could be coming over for Shabbas supper? I inhaled deeply, identifying roast, potatoes and kugle, among other things. Mama had been busy today!

I walked behind her as she set out the cutlery. Her apron strings hung down in back so I retied them into a huge bow.

"Who's coming?"

"Ohhh, Auntie Sadie and Uncle Morris, and Auntie Leah and Uncle Dave. . . . "

"Oh." I stood still, disappointed. "How come?"

"I just wanted everybody to be together," Mama said surprisingly. She lifted out the silver candlesticks, which she'd brought with her from Russia, the only things that had survived the journey, and placed candles in them. It was still too early to light them though.

I walked over to the kitchen cupboard where my birthday cake sat resplendent in pink icing, decorated with tiny red rosettes which Mama made with her special gadget, bought one day at a sale. On top of the cake, Mama had scrawled my

*45*

name in red icing. She had become quite expert at decorating cakes and cookies with it.

"It's beautiful," I said, scraping up some loose icing along the edge of the plate and licking it off. "Will you teach me how to do that some day, Mama?"

She smiled her almost-smile.

"Maybe," she said, "if God spares me."

"Mama, why do we have to have the aunties and uncles on my birthday? We never had them before, and they'll spoil everything. They always do. They'll talk and talk and tell me to behave and I'm a big girl now and everything like that. I can't see why they have to come *today*!"

"Because I asked them. I want you to be nice when they get here. Be a helper to me, you understand?"

I understood all right. My birthday was going to be ruined, that's what I understood.

Papa washed his hands and went up the stairs to his room, and when he came down in a little while he wore a white shirt and tie and his Shabbas suit. Papa, who was very religious, shrugged into his coat and hat and without a word to anybody went out. I knew he was going to Shul and when he returned we would have supper.

I played piano at the edge of the tablecloth, letting my fingers run in wild crescendo from one end of the table to the other. The music sounded in my head, loud, grand, absolutely tremendous, and I stopped to tumultuous applause, all very gratifying. Inside my head, I rose to acknowledge the applause, bowing, and noticed that I wore a white shimmering gown.

Mama said: "Go upstairs and change into your Yontiff dress. On your birthday you shouldn't wear a tunic."

I moved dreamily towards the stairs, applause still rising in waves of approval. It was beautiful to be appreciated. I threw kisses to the audience with both hands. I had seen it done in a movie once and had been terribly impressed with the gracious gesture.

I took my time getting changed, savoring the specialness of the occasion. While I had my clothes off, I took the opportunity of looking at my belly button very closely. It didn't look to me like any baby could ever get out of there but I supposed that when I grew up it would get a lot bigger, like a cave. Not only that, but I expected it would have changed quite a bit. I'd never seen Mama's so I had nothing to go by, but I was sure that women's belly buttons looked nothing at all like a little girl's. I pulled on my underwear and slipped the Yontiff dress on over my head.

The sounds of people arriving with a big noise and clatter informed me that the relatives were here. Laughter, mostly from Auntie Leah, who was Uncle Dave's wife, spurred me to dress a little faster. Uncle Dave was Papa's brother, of course. If I had to have favorite relatives it would be them, mostly because Auntie Leah was fat and jolly and not sour like Auntie Sadie, who had been an old maid most of her life. She and Uncle Morris were just married about five years and had no children. I figured that any couple without children couldn't help but be miserable for the rest of their lives.

I pulled the belt tightly around my waist, buckling it on. In the mirror I spread out my skirt and curtsied and a sudden thought hit me. Maybe they'd brought me presents! I ran out of the room, down the steps and into the hall as though I were being chased by Things.

Auntie Sadie frowned, her thin lips turning in on themselves. "She's growing into a wild Indian!" she greeted me. "If she was mine I'd know what to do!"

That was just the kind of thing Auntie Sadie would say, birthday or no birthday, but Auntie Leah beamed, enfolding me in layers of flesh. She bestowed a wet kiss on my cheek.

"A happy birthday, Becky! You look already like a big girl. When did I see you last?"

"On Yontiff," I reminded her, wiping the kiss off my cheek. Although I liked her, I didn't care for her spit on my face—or anybody else's either.

"Yes, Yontiff." She smiled.

Mama beckoned to me with one finger and drew me into the kitchen. Both uncles were in there and so was Simply

Simon. I wondered what she wanted till I saw her draw a small black comb out of her apron pocket. While I held myself rigid Mama proceeded to pull at my hair in the usual agonizing way. I said: "Ouch! Mama, you're hurting me!"

"Stand still," she said without sympathy.

"Nu, Becky?" Uncle Dave stood in front of me. "How does it go?" He was older than Papa and had been in Canada longer. Where Papa's face went in Uncle Dave's came out so his expression was one of permanent contentment. Religion wasn't as important to him or he would have been at Shul too. I smiled back at him.

"Okay, I guess." Impatiently, I turned my head from side to side. "That hurts!" I said to Mama.

"I'm finished." Mama sighed, stepping back to view her work, like an artist. "Now if you don't run, your hair will stay nice."

"So now you're ten years old," Uncle Dave went on, as though Mama hadn't spoken. I nodded, feeling the sausages beside my face bounce up and down like springs. He put his hand in his pocket. "For a girl on her birthday," he said with a twinkle, "maybe I can find something in here."

I stood in front of him, my hands behind my back, and waited to see what would magically emerge from his hand. It gleamed dully at me ... a quarter! Twenty-five cents! I grabbed at it but he pulled his hand away teasingly, out of my reach.

"What do I get for it?"

I stood on my tiptoes and kissed his cheek. It felt like Papa's sandpaper that he used on rough wood after he got through fixing chairs and things that came apart. I reached for the quarter and felt it hard but warm from his fingers. You weren't supposed to handle money on Shabbas and since Mama had lit the candles when I was upstairs it was already Shabbas but if Uncle Dave could hold it, so could I, and it wasn't a worse sin for me.

"Thank you!" You could buy a lot with a quarter but I was going to save this.

Uncle Morris, feeling outclassed, fumbled in his pockets.

I blinked hopefully in his direction, waiting to see what would happen, but he yawned, took his hand out of his pocket empty and scratched the back of his neck with it. It didn't surprise me at all but I couldn't help glaring at him. He ignored me and stood staring out of the window into the darkness.

"What's taking Jake so long?" he wanted to know. "Does he have to be the last one out?"

Mama frowned warningly at me as though she could read my mind. He and Auntie Sadie were perfect for each other, I thought, both of them equally nasty.

The candles still flickered, about halfway through their burning. I watched the soft warm drippings as they slid off the top in liquid form and solidified at the base of the holders. The flames licked and waned, hypnotically, twin spears pointing to the ceiling.

The aunties walked into the kitchen.

"What's this, a meeting?" Auntie Sadie demanded. "I'm waiting in there to give Becky her birthday present!"

She held a thin narrow package out to me, disappointingly small. Her eyes gleamed like bright blue nuggets and were just as hard.

"Thank you." I took it out of her hand.

"You're welcome. Open it."

I did, untying the string that held it together. I lifted the cover of the slim box which could only contain underwear. It did. I held the cotton undershirt with a small blue bow at the neck, looking at it.

"Wear it well." Auntie Sadie made it sound like an order. "I hope it fits."

"Thank you," I said again, my eyes sliding to Mama's. She smiled at me and nodded her head once.

"Just what she needs," Mama said with enthusiasm. "There's plenty of winter left yet. Give Auntie Sadie a kiss, Becky."

Dutifully, I pecked the dry cheek and stepped back. Then Auntie Leah, who had been keeping one hand behind her, brought it forward with a solid-looking parcel gripped tightly, as though it were heavy.

"Does she need this too?" she asked me, smiling.

I took it, determined that no matter what it was I would make a big fuss over it even if it was *panties*! Breathlessly, because it couldn't possibly be this heavy and contain clothing, I unwrapped the brown paper. It felt like...it was...a book!

"*Tabitha's Promise,*" I read the title out loud. The first book I had ever owned, my very own book which I would never have to give back to the library, and could read over and over any time I wanted!

Auntie Sadie sniffed.

"What foolishness," she said, "wasting money on a book."

"You like it?" Auntie Leah asked anxiously. "In the store they told me it's the latest girl's book...."

I threw my arms around her neck.

"Thank you, thank you, thank you! How did you know I love to read?"

"Mama told me." They smiled at each other. I held the book against my chest, keeping it as close to me as possible. I felt the weight of it, the anticipation of reading it when everybody had gone.

"Money thrown away for nothing," Auntie Sadie grumbled. "What she needs is a heavy pair of stockings."

Papa came in then. "Good Shabbas," he said and hung up his coat. We all answered him except for Uncle Morris, who said loud enough for me to hear:

"It's about time."

I showed Papa my presents while he washed his hands.

"Very nice," he said. "Who got you the book?"

"Auntie Leah!"

He looked at Mama. "Now we can eat," he said.

Later, after we had eaten and cleared away the dishes, we had tea and birthday cake in the front room, carrying the kitchen chairs in there so everybody could sit down and hold the plates on their laps.

"I'd rather sit at the table," Uncle Morris complained, but Auntie Sadie gave him a sharp elbow in the side. I liked her a little bit better after that.

When Mama sat down with the rest of us and lifted her cup of tea, though, Auntie Sadie ruined everything.

"You didn't by any chance go to see the doctor." She made it a statement of fact. I could see Mama tense for a moment; then she smiled and shrugged. Auntie Sadie opened her mouth and took a sharp breath, her usual preparation for a verbal attack. Mama headed her off neatly.

"And now," she said dramatically, "it's time for the present from us."

Auntie's mouth snapped shut, but I hardly paid much attention to her after an announcement like that. Papa went into the kitchen while my heart started to pound with excitement. What could it be? We'd never made such a production of birthdays before, and this meant something out of the ordinary, as far as I was concerned.

Papa returned carrying a large box. Where had they hidden something that size where I wouldn't find it? I knew every good hiding place in the house! Papa wore the most peculiar expression on his face and as I stared at him, I suddenly realized what it was: excitement. Papa never got excited about anything. Angry, yes, but not happy-excited! I slid to my knees in front of the box and began to unwrap it. Everybody leaned close, breathing on me, as I pulled the paper away. I didn't want to guess to myself what it could be . . . I wanted to be surprised.

My hands trembled as I lifted the lid of the box and looked inside. A coat! A new brand new bright red coat with a *real . . . fur . . . collar*! I took it reverently out of the box and stood up, holding it in front of me. It had the softest gray kitten fur of a collar, exactly like Betty Greenberg's! I made little screaming noises, unable to help myself, and slipped it on, running to the mirror above the sink in the kitchen, but it was a small mirror that let you see to your chin and I had to content myself with looking down and patting the collar.

I ran to Mama and flung myself on top of her, my face in her shoulder. Her hands touched my head and my back, and the baby moved tantalizing inches below. Till this moment nobody had spoken a word but now Auntie Sadie broke the silence.

"You came into a fortune maybe?"

"Hinda got it." Auntie Leah's voice sounded complacent. "In the factory where she works as a bookkeeper. They let her have it half price. It's a second, but you can hardly see it. You wouldn't find it in a million years. Jake asked her to pick one out, and then me and Dave brought it with us."

"Hinda got a real metsieh," Auntie Sadie sniffed. "There's the second, right in back."

I felt myself being grabbed and everyone bent over the flaw. I didn't care. It was a beautiful coat, and Hinda was the nicest cousin a girl could have even if I hardly ever saw her. I craned my neck to see the second but it was barely noticeable. That was Auntie Sadie for you. Just because she hadn't had anything to do with picking it out. She always tried to spoil things.

I took the coat off reluctantly, and hung it in the closet, and went back to finish my piece of birthday cake. The others were carrying their empty dishes to the kitchen.

"You help Mama with the cleaning up," Auntie Sadie ordered, just as if I didn't always. She stood at the door, Uncle Morris right behind her buttoning his coat up to his chin. I didn't mind them going but I wished Uncle Dave and Auntie Leah would stay longer. I hated my birthday party to end, except that soon I'd be able to read my new book!

Auntie Leah, tying her kerchief firmly around her hair, looked anxiously at Mama, who leaned against a chair.

"Minnie, I told you we shouldn't come. I knew it would be too much for you. . . ."

Mama smiled. "It's all right. I'm glad. It isn't too much for me."

"Don't argue with her," Auntie Sadie broke in. "She doesn't listen to anybody. She thinks she knows what she's doing. She's just like Jake. Stubborn."

Auntie Leah intervened for Mama. "Shah. If this is what she wanted to do then I'm glad she did it. The supper was delicious. Anyway the family should be together more.

Who else is there?"

"At a time like this? She should've been in the hospital for a month already, instead of making parties and suppers!"

"I enjoyed myself," Mama protested.

"Some enjoyment. Well, it's too late to worry about it. I talked till I turned blue and what good did it do me? I wash my hands of the whole thing. Just remember one thing: don't come and complain to me if anything happens!"

"I won't," Mama promised, smiling.

This was definitely the wrong answer because Auntie Sadie snorted as she left but Auntie Leah hugged Mama and kissed her, and this left a better feeling inside me. The door closed on our company and I breathed a sigh of relief. We finished cleaning up, bringing dishes out of the living room for washing, while Simply Simon carried all the chairs back into the kitchen. As he plunked the last one down at the table where I placed the cups and saucers I had finished drying, he bumped me in the leg.

"Don't forget," he said ominously, "on *my* birthday, I don't want any *clothes!*"

Boys certainly were queer.

**2** People moaned in a swirling dark; there were tendrils of black that floated in air. Hands were outstretched claws; faces were grinning skulls. They were chasing somebody. Me. I ran, my face white, eyes staring, just inches ahead of them. Over hills, through valleys I ran, my mouth open, my face a skull. . . . The moans grew louder, urgent, insistent.

"Becky!" they cried. "Becky! Becky!"

A hand gripped my shoulder, a hard bony clutch.

"Becky!" the voice cried in my ear. "Wake up!"

I gasped, heart pounding, and suddenly opened my eyes. In the dark, Papa's face leaned over me.

I blinked, trying to unblur my eyes. From somewhere I heard a moan, muffled, starting low then rising, a weird animal-like sound. Was I still dreaming? My skin prickled, sending shivers through me. "Papa," I whispered. . . . "what's wrong?"

The moan reached a peak and died away to silence.

"What was that? Did you hear it?"

Papa sat heavily on the edge of my bed. I could see him dimly. He was fully dressed. I wondered what time it was.

"Are you big enough," Papa said in a low voice, "to be by yourself with Saul?"

I sat up, leaning on my pillow, feeling my elbow gouging through the thin feathers to *Tabitha's Promise* underneath. I always slept with it there since my birthday last week.

"I guess so . . . but why? What's happening, and what was that noise?" It hadn't sounded like anything human. It belonged to my nightmare.

"You have to be a big girl now, Becky," Papa said, his thin fingers clasping and unclasping in his lap. "I have to take Mama to the hospital and I have nobody to leave here with you."

My mind sluggishly grappled with Papa's statement, then gave up.

"Why do you have to take Mama to the hospital? Is she sick?" Suddenly, even as I asked, it came to me in a brilliant flash. "Is it time for the baby? But it isn't supposed to come till next month!"

"The baby decided to come tonight," Papa said drily. He rose to his feet, swaying slightly, as though he were drunk. But I knew better than that. Papa never drank, except wine on Shabbas.

"I'm waiting now for a taxi. Mama is downstairs. If you want you can get dressed and sleep on the chesterfield downstairs with Saul. But hurry up. It's cold in here."

Quickly I threw the covers off and without turning on the light, I groped for my clothes. Papa went out and opened Simply Simon's door while I shivered out of my pajamas and into my shuddery-cold clothes.

I tried not to think; I wanted to stay desperately ignorant. I buttoned my blouse with trembling hands, not caring whether the buttons and buttonholes matched. The moan began again, very low. My blood became ice. I couldn't move or draw a breath. Time hung suspended on the thread of sound growing higher, jagging, curving over my head then fading to nothingness. My fingers shook as I pulled on my tunic, fastening the belt around my waist. I shoved my feet into my shoes, bent over to tie the laces. I couldn't believe those terrible sounds had been made by Mama. . . . I just couldn't!

Papa loomed, a shadow in the doorway, with Simply Simon a smudge beside him.

"You're dressed? Good. You stay here now till we go. Mama doesn't want you to come downstairs."

"Why not? I want to! I want to say good-bye!"

"Say it from the top of the stairs then. Mama knows what she's talking. You can't help her and it won't do you any good to see her the way she is."

Papa's shadow disappeared down the stairs. I could hear Simply Simon's shallow breathing behind me. We were alone upstairs. In the dark. Neither one of us thought of turning on the hall light. His hand gripped mine.

"What's going on?" he whispered, and in the dark I could make out the iridescent shine of his eyes. "Did you hear it too?"

I swallowed, unable to speak for a moment. Fear rose into my throat in a tangible, tasteable lump.

"The baby is coming," I whispered when I had safely pushed back the thing that stuck in my throat.

"Is the baby making that noise?"

"No, dummy! It's Mama! It must hurt an awful lot!" I felt like crying, and stood swallowing over and over again. We stood in the small upstairs hall, unaware that we gripped each other's hands, staring at the wall where the steep stairs curved downward. I could see the tarnished roses on the wallpaper—mostly because I knew they were there, dark or daylight—with curving vines and thorns making a geometric pattern in between. Simply Simon jerked my hand slightly.

"What's going to happen next?"

"They're waiting for a taxi. Papa must've gone next door to the Gallianis' to use their phone."

I visualized him banging on the door and the old Italian couple standing in their nightclothes peering out at him. It was a good thing they had a telephone.

The silence stretched out, pounding in my ears with the rhythm of a heartbeat. We strained, standing at the top of the stairs, unable to see down to the bottom, but forbidden by Papa to come any closer. When the moan began again our fingers tightened together. We listened, not wanting to hear, not wanting *not* to hear, trembling. Papa's voice said something. Was he praying?

It stopped. Almost immediately, there was the sound of a car pulling up in front of our house, the motor coughing loudly, sounding as though it had caught a cold. Papa must have been watching for it because the downstairs door opened and we heard the sound of footsteps going through the hallway towards the front door.

"Mama!" I cried, staring at the roses climbing the wall. "Mama!"

The footsteps stopped. "Be a good girl," Mama's voice replied. She sounded weak and tired. "Take care, and keep the doors locked. Don't let anybody come in."

"Are you all right, Mama?"

"I'll be all right. When I come back..." Her voice seemed to break here. "I'll tell you all about it."

"I want to kiss you good-bye!" I screamed, and letting go of Simply Simon's hand, I flew down the stairs. I could hear him clatter right behind me. They stood at the front door.

"Make it quick," Papa said. "We can't waste time."

Mama looked the same. Somehow I'd expected, feared some awful change in her but except for the hollowness under her eyes she still looked like Mama.

We clung like vines twining around the trunk of a tree. She kissed us both and tried to push us away. I didn't want to let go of the solidness of her flesh; I wanted to keep her with us as long as possible. Papa pulled us off as though he were peeling a banana. Mama gave her almost-smile.

"Be very good. I'll come back as soon as they let me."

Then they were gone, a blast of cold air from the front door all that remained. We ran into the front room to look out of the big window and watched Papa help Mama through the snow and into the back seat of the taxi. Neither of us spoke as the taxi moved away in a cloud of exhaust fumes. The fumes hung motionless in the air for long moments, and when they too were gone the street looked empty and aloof. We turned away from the window and looked at the house, lit up as though it were early evening. I decided to be cheerful.

"Next time we see Mama, " I said, "she'll have the baby with her. I wonder what we're going to call her. . ."

"Who cares?" Simply Simon stared at me morosely. "I wish she never started to have that stupid baby! We were okay without it and now look . . . we're all by ourselves!"

I became suddenly maternal, feeling protective towards him.

"There's nothing to be afraid of, Simply Simon. I'm here and I'm ten years old now. I can take care of you. Anyway, let's go and lock the front door like Papa said."

He shrugged, frowning fiercely, but came with me as I locked the front door then inspected the house, going through all the rooms to make sure no burglars had gotten in. Satisfied that all was as it should be, we brought our pillows and bedding downstairs from our rooms just in case we felt like sleeping. We'd fix up the chesterfield with our blankets and whoever felt sleepy could lie down on it. I knew that I wouldn't be able to sleep at all, but Simply Simon might.

"D'you think Mama is going to be all right?" he asked. Because I'd been wondering the same thing myself and didn't want to admit it, I spoke louder than necessary.

"Of *course*, Mama didn't look any different, did she? I mean, there's nothing really *wrong* with her. She's not sick, you know."

"But did you *hear* her? Did you know it was her at first?"

I shuddered. We sat side by side on our blankets. "At

first," I admitted, "I thought it was in my nightmare. . . ." I looked around the front room which was shrouded in shadows cast by the light fixture in the middle room. It seemed unreal, all of it. I felt as if I still hovered between sleeping and waking. . . . The old overstuffed chair in the corner hulked in the half-dark, its greenish plush covering almost bald. I stared at it for a moment then glanced at Simply Simon, whose eyelids drooped. He leaned back against the chesterfield.

"It sure didn't sound like her," he murmured.

I didn't want him to fall asleep and leave me wide awake by myself. I wanted him to talk to me so I wouldn't have to think about what was happening to Mama right at that moment.

"I didn't know having a baby hurt so much," I said slowly, watching him to see if he'd heard me.

"D'you think it hurt her to have us?"

"I don't know. Mama would never tell me. I always asked her things and she always said I was too young to know. Well, now that I know, I'm not ever going to have a baby. *Never.*"

He didn't answer. I looked at him. His eyes were closed. I shook him.

"Hey! Wake up! I'm still talking to you. Don't you hear me? I said I'm never going to have a baby! Not even one! Did you hear me?"

He murmured in his sleep and turned away into the back of the chesterfield, his face pressed into the material, curling his body up to his chin, knees bent. He lay without moving. I stared at his back. The lucky fish . . . How could he sleep at a time like this? I leaned against my pillow, my lids heavy but I knew I wasn't going to be able to sleep, not even for a minute all night long.

Twelve adorable sweet babies smiled and waved their dimpled little hands, all looking amazingly like the newest baby on the street, Stella Hodnik. Her mother shopped at our store and let me look after Stella in the baby carriage. I always imagined myself growing up and having twelve babies, all beautiful. I'm going to have twelve, I used to say in my ignorance. And Mama would laugh and say: "Tell me again when you grow up and have the first one!" And Mrs. Hodnik, who had five all together, Stella being the latest one of the bunch, would pat my head and say: "You have lots of babies, be strong like horse first."

The twelve babies began to dissolve, one by one, as I sank deeper and deeper into a dark mist and for a long time there was only darkness. Then I woke with a start and for a moment I didn't know where I was or remember why I lay, half on the chesterfield, half on the floor, with all the lights in the house blazing.

Turning my head slightly, I could see Simply Simon sprawled on top of the blankets, eyes shut, mouth open, breath wheezing in and out. I let myself slide all the way to the floor, landing with a gentle thump, and blinked at the wall opposite where the door to the grocery store stood securely locked.

The mist began to clear. Mama — Mama was at the hospital having the baby! I rose painfully to my feet, neck and seat stiff, and stood at the window looking out. Maybe I'd be lucky and see Papa coming home. Maybe the baby was born already! Maybe I had a little sister and didn't even know it yet . . . or twins!

Boyd Avenue looked serene in the half-light. The store across the street with dark windows stared blankly at me, and the string of houses, as though they were joined together, were all dark and still. Our house was the only one in the whole city where the lights still glowed. I leaned my face against the cold windowpane, my breath creating a circle of frost, and watched down the street for a sign of a human being, Papa. Would he come striding up Powers Street? Or would the taxi pull up again and Papa step out of it? As far as I knew, nobody in our family till now had ever ridden in a taxi. It would have to be a very special occasion. But of course it was, wasn't it?

I stood a long time feeling the chill that came from the window glass, the dark wine-colored drapes enfolding me, hiding me from the rest of the house. My eyes began to water, to blur so the street lost its sharp outlines. It became a white-carpeted landscape with nearby hills, the rooftops forming the hills and the chimneys the jagged peaks. I blinked several times to clear my vision and the street came back to normal. I yawned and turned away from the window, going back into the room. I needed a place to lie down. Grabbing my pillow from under Simply Simon's limp arm, I placed it at the opposite end of the chesterfield. He mumbled something but I moved his feet together, clearing a space for myself. My head sank into the pillow and a brown cloud drifted over me as I sank lower and lower, falling slowly into a pit. . . .

. . . Stella, Papa and a nameless baby played ring-around-a-rosy, while Mama muttered words to Mrs. Hodnik. They were struggling over the baby carriage, their voices growing louder. The Mrs. Hodnik turned suprisingly into Auntie Sadie who said: "I told her and I told her, but would she listen? No." Papa stopped playing with the babies and glared at Auntie Sadie.

"Enough already," he said, in a gruff voice unlike his, "I don't want you to talk."

Mama looked up and smiled her almost-smile and faded. So did the carriage, but Auntie Sadie stayed and sat heavily down in a chair that creaked and hit her forehead with her fist. She began to wail in a high voice.

"The children . . ."

My eyes opened slowly. It wasn't a dream . . . Auntie Sadie was really here. I rubbed at my eyes and sat up on one elbow, listening to the thin wail. It hadn't disappeared with my dream. If I moved my head outward, I could see straight through the middle room and into the kitchen, all the rooms opening into each other as they did. My heart began to beat with dull thuds that echoed inside my head.

Papa sat at the table, and all I could see of him was that his head was in his hands. Behind him stood Uncle Dave, silent, his hands on Papa's shoulders. The kitchen seemed to contain the entire family, and over their figures, frozen as statues, the ribbon of Auntie Sadie's tightly drawn wail wound round and round, tying them closer together into a compact bundle.

My hands and feet were paralyzed. A ball rose up in my chest gathering momentum as it neared my throat. My mind stayed blank pushing the edges of knowledge away. I didn't move. I would stay in this spot forever, and they would stay in the kitchen, and I wouldn't have to know what had happened, ever.

A new sound ran counterpoint to Auntie Sadie's wail. Muffled sobs, loud sniffles. I cringed from feeling, consciously fought it. It overtook me. I knew. Dreadful knowledge overwhelmed me and I could no longer refuse to admit my thoughts. I sat up, my feet accidentally kicking Simply Simon, who raised his head and turned, a look of puzzled concentration on his face. The ball in my throat began to dissolve, leaving a bitter taste.

"What's going on?" Simply Simon said.

I couldn't hold back any longer; the tears gathered, gushed as though they would never stop. My cries drowned out every other sound for me. I felt myself being touched. Arms, hands petted me. A soft something, familiar, smothered my face while hands pressed the back of my head forward. I resisted. My cries were being stifled and I wanted to make a big noise. I wanted Mama!

"Shah, shah, faigele," a voice above my head murmured. "It doesn't help."

I stared through my tears at Auntie Leah's comforting bosom, her hands thrusting me back between the solid mounds covered by a flowered crepe. A cloying smell of perspiration and stale cologne swept up from the vee of her neckline. Wildly gasping, I fought her hands. I caught a glimpse of Simply Simon still where I'd last seen him just staring at me.

"Where's Mama?" I cried. "Where's Mama and the baby? I want them . . . I want them *now!*"

Papa stood a moment and looked at me, his face tightly controlled. He seemed to have shrunk within himself, his face clinging to the bones underneath for support. His eyes were somber, deep pits of darkness which made me draw back from him, afraid. The tears dried on my face, tightening my skin as I watched Papa, knowing that when he spoke, that would be the end of it, not wanting him to speak but helpless to stop him. Papa said nothing.

Simply Simon sprang at Papa then, crying, his legs digging into Papa's back, his arms like a noose around Papa's neck. It was as if he suddenly realized something had happened and tried to make up for his lateness. Watching him, I dried my face with the back of my hand, and then I had to know, to hear the words with my own ears.

"Which one?" I looked straight into Papa's terrible eyes.

"Both," he answered.

**3** A grayish light seeped around the edges of drawn window blinds, bathing everybody in a green pallor. Friends and relatives stood or sat, expressions frozen, speaking in murmurs over Papa's head. Restlessly I roamed from the front room to the kitchen looking at things: dishes, or a pot, or the back of a chair. Everywhere I looked I saw Mama. This was her house; there was her apron on the back of the bathroom door near the sink. Here was her mixing spoon. This was the chair she sat in. . . . Uncle Morris, even as I watched in horror, began to lower himself into the chair.

"No!" I screamed, rushing at him, trying to push him up out of it. He rubbed his bald spot and stared at me, his expression none too friendly.

Auntie Sadie hurried in. "What? What? What's the matter?"

I pointed a finger at her husband. "Make him get up! He's sitting on Mama's chair!"

"So?"

I stared at her. "Make him get off!"

"What's the difference where he sits? Don't make so much noise, you'll upset Papa!"

"He can't sit on Mama's chair! Nobody can!"

Papa appeared in the kitchen doorway suddenly, a

pained expression on his face. Behind him I could see Uncle Dave. I knew Papa would understand.

"He's sitting on Mama's chair! Make him get off!" I stared up at Papa, seeing the thin lips, the pinched nose, the distant eyes gazing at Uncle Morris.

"It's just a chair," he said finally. "That's all it is. Just a chair."

"It's Mama's!" I tried to shake Papa so he would understand.

"Mama won't sit there anymore."

"He has to get off!"

Papa sighed and turned away from me and Uncle Dave placed a hand on his shoulder, leading him back to the front room. I stood rooted, shocked. Papa didn't care. Nobody did. I glared at Uncle Morris. To show me how little it mattered to him, he lifted his right leg and crossed it over the left one, sitting sideways on Mama's chair, hooking his elbow over the back of it. He yawned without covering his mouth so I could see into the black cavern with the rotting teeth. Then he looked at me very deliberately, a little smile rising out of his rock face, the green eyes triumphant. I loathed him with burning hatred, wanting him to die on the spot.

I turned and walked quickly to the bathroom door before anybody else could think of it and snatched Mama's apron off the doorknob. Then I balled it in my hand and grabbed the big mixing spoon off the countertop and ran with them out of the kitchen, dodging around Auntie Sadie, past Cousin Hinda who stood talking somberly to some elderly cousins of Papa's, and through the hall. In my bedroom I shut the door, my heart pounding. From now on, nobody was going to have anything of Mama's but me. Only me.

Carefully I spread Mama's apron on the bed, smoothing out the wrinkles. Touching the material, tracing the pattern of small pink flowers with one finger, I could feel Mama's stomach underneath and hear her breathing, and feel a warmth of love. I knew she must be somewhere close even if I couldn't see her.

Time passed but I wasn't aware of it, and then I heard a

strange thumping sound out in the hall. Simply Simon opened my door and looked at me, his face small and round as a baby's.

"Uncle Morris says you're crazy," he announced.

"Did he send you here to tell me that?"

"No. He said not to talk to you because you're crazy."

"Look who's talking! He picks his nose in company, sits on Mama's chair when it isn't even *his* house, and then *he* calls *me* crazy!"

"I don't like him either." Simply Simon grinned suddenly. "So guess what I did?"

I couldn't guess.

"I waited till he got off Mama's chair, and I grabbed it and look. . . . " He opened my door wider. Mama's chair stood beside him. He'd lugged it up the stairs all by himself.

I went to him. "You're the only person in this whole house that I still like."

I felt a terrible compulsion to cry.

"Even Papa, he . . . I don't blame him really but . . ."

"D'you want the chair in your room?"

"Yes! Oh yes, Simply Simon. If Mama ever comes back she'll find all her things here . . . look, see? Her apron, and . . ."

"Mama won't come back." Tears swam in his eyes, darkening them even more. "Don't you know that? She's dead. She can't, can she?"

"Simply Simon . . . can you keep a secret?" He nodded, looking solemnly at me.

"Swear that you'll never tell."

"I swear. Hurry up and tell me!"

"It's about Mama. . . ." Maybe he'd think I was crazy too. Maybe he'd agree with Uncle Morris.

"What about Mama?"

"Give me your hand." I took it and place it on top of Mama's apron, looking eagerly at his face, "Well?"

"Well what? I thought you were going to tell me a secret."

"Don't you feel anything?"

"Sure. An apron. I feel the material."

I placed my own hand on it, beside his. Material. Simply Simon was right. There was nothing else.

"That's funny. I felt it before. . . ."

"What? What did you feel?"

"I felt Mama. I felt as if she was here. It was wonderful."

Dubiously he moved his hand over the apron, running it over the folds of cloth, but I could see by his face that nothing had changed.

"She's gone," I whispered. "She's really gone. I felt her in this room but now she's gone."

"Maybe she went into her own bedroom," Simply Simon suggested.

I picked up Mama's chair and placed it inside my room. Then together we stood outside the closed door of Mama and Papa's bedroom. I hadn't been in there since before . . .

We looked at the closed door fearfully yet expectantly. It was scary in a way. I put my hand on the doorknob, half expecting it to turn by itself. My heart pounded and by Simply Simon's expression I could see he felt the same apprehension.

We pushed the door open together, huddling against each other, cringing at the loud drawn-out squeak. We held our breaths, staring at the bed, rumpled as if someone had been sleeping in it. No one was there now, though. We pushed the door wider, peering in all the corners without moving from the spot. The room was empty. Together we let out our breaths, then looked at each other.

"Did you really feel Mama?"

Now I began to doubt. "I . . . I think so. At least, I suddenly had a good feeling again."

He shrugged. "We better close the door. Papa said we should stay out of his bedroom, remember?"

He closed the door with a gentle click and we went back into my room. I placed Mama's chair against the wall next to the dresser and then I folded Mama's apron, placed the mixing spoon inside it, rolled them up together and slipped them into one of my dresser drawers. It was as if Mama really died for me then. She wouldn't use her things ever again.

"Do you believe in Heaven?"

He thought about it. "I think so, I mean, everybody says there's a Heaven so I guess I believe in it."

"Me too. Especially if we have to die someday. Did you know that everybody is going to die some day?"

It had taken me a long time to come to terms with this thought. Even now I couldn't really believe that I wouldn't live forever. The idea of my death made my eyes sting with tears. I would be the chief mourner at my own funeral.

"Well, maybe," he said slowly, "but not for a long time. Not till we're very very old and maybe not even then."

"Maybe by the time we're that old, they'll know how to make people live forever." I began to feel hopeful.

"It didn't do Mama or the baby any good."

I stared at Mama's empty chair. "Why did it have to happen?" It was a question I'd been asking myself over and over ever since yesterday morning.

"Why did God make them *both* die? It could've been just the baby. Then we'd still have Mama."

"I don't know." I tried to imagine it. "I bet Mama would've felt awful if the baby died. Maybe she'd have been very very sad and never got over it."

"But we'd still have her," he insisted.

"And then, maybe she'd have gotten sick over it and *then* died anyway."

"And maybe not." Simply Simon was stubborn.

I leaned back on my pillow and stared at the ceiling. Dusk was gathering in all the corners of my room.

"I wonder what Heaven is like," I mused. . . . "*If* there's such a place as Heaven. I wonder if Mama and the baby are there already."

"No," he said authoritatively. "They can't go there till after the funeral tomorrow. They're still at the hospital, I think."

"Yes, but even so, I think a part of them went already

and didn't have to wait for the funeral."

"I wonder what's going to happen to us." He gazed at me soulfully. "I wonder who's going to take care of us. . . ."

"Well bite your tongue so it isn't you-know-who. I'd rather starve to death than have *them* living here. Oh if you only knew how much I hate him!"

Someone knocked at my door, a gentle hesitant tapping. I sat up as Simply Simon opened the door. Cousin Hinda stood there, her expression half afraid, half eager-to-please. That was Cousin Hinda, tall, gawky, her red hair pulled back into a bun so she looked like an old woman of thirty. She was only twenty and Mama had sometimes said that Hinda would have the boys chasing her if she didn't act and dress already like an old maid.

"Hello kids," she said in her breathless little-girl voice. "Can I come in?"

I shrugged, tears welling into my eyes again. She'd come to try to cheer us up, her manner so sympathetic that it reminded us forcefully of our loss. Not that there was the slightest chance of our forgetting it.

She looked quickly around for something to sit on and saw Mama's chair against the wall. I tensed as she looked at it and then at me but relaxed again when she headed for the kitchen chair beside my dresser. Hinda sat as awkwardly as she did everything else, her thin knees spread apart and yards of black skirt material dipping between them.

Now she sat and looked at me, a helpless sort of smile playing around her lips.

"How come you aren't working today?" Simply Simon asked her. She seemed grateful that he brought a change of subject.

"I took the afternoon off," she explained. "I mean, my boss didn't like it but it doesn't make any difference to him anyway. I mean if I'm not there I don't get paid."

"Oh."

"Well, when I found out what happened I decided not to go to work this afternoon. I'll take tomorrow afternoon off too, for the funeral. If he wants to fire me, let him." Her eyes filled with tears. "Auntie Minnie was my favorite person. I'd give up ten jobs if it would bring her back."

We stared at the unaccustomed sight of a grown-up girl crying. I gave Simply Simon a sideways look, a signal that he should think of something to say that would cheer her up. It was a cinch I couldn't think of anything.

Simply Simon wiggled onto my bed.

"We were just wondering," he said looking earnestly at her as she tried to wipe her nose without benefit of handkerchief, "who was going to take care of us."

She finally settled on the back of her hand.

"Don't worry about that," she said between sniffs. "One thing you're lucky, is that Uncle Jake is a storekeeper and stays home all the time. If he had a job somewhere, then you'd have a problem."

"Yes I know," he continued. "But who's going to do our cooking and cleaning? Papa can't and we can't either."

"Well"—she gave a final sniff and lifted her head, exposing her swollen red nose and puffy eyes—"we'll all pitch in and help. My mother and Auntie Sadie, and oh—everybody. As a matter of fact there's some supper waiting for you right now. I was asked to bring you both down to eat."

"I couldn't swallow anything if you put a gun to my head," I said flatly.

"Me either." Simply Simon stuck up for me. "If you put a knife in my back *and* a gun."

"Not even if it's a good hot kroit borscht with lots of beets and meat in it?"

"Well . . ." I looked at Simply Simon. "I suppose if we don't eat, Papa'll get all mad and upset and everything. . . ."

He nodded. "Yeah, and we don't want to make him any more upset than he already is. . . ."

With a great show of reluctance, we went down with Hinda, walking so subdued and quietly that no one even knew we were down until they saw us there. Two bowls of borscht sat steaming side by side on the kitchen table. I looked at the faces of the assembled female relatives and announced loudly:

"I'm not even going to sit down if anybody is going to watch me eat!"

They took the hint and left.

Voices in the other rooms filled the house. I stared through the doorway as I ate, listening to words without meanings. Nothing made any sense, not even eating. My eyes roamed over the kitchen walls, so familiar that I hadn't really seen them in years. It made no sense at all. A few days ago, Mama had been alive, had talked to me and the baby had been my dreams come true. Now they were gone forever and I sat here and ate borscht. It was crazy; it was stupid. I dropped the spoon. It clattered to the table, then bounced off and landed with a dull clunk on the floor. Simply Simon gave me a sideways look but kept on eating. His bowl was nearly empty.

I jumped up and ran out of the kitchen and up the stairs to my room glimpsing startled faces in my wake. I shut my door hard. I wished I had a key and could lock it. I didn't want to see them or hear their voices ever again. I looked wildly around for something heavy, then in a frenzy of crying I yanked and pushed my bed till it rolled against the door.

I threw myself onto the bed, pressing my face into the pillow, hugging it, holding it hard against me, and very soon, the place around my pillow was soaked with tears. I let them come, sliding out of my eyes, and in a deep place within me I felt the roaring of the waterfall. It made no sound but roiled up the water inside me and made it stream upwards through a canal in my head. I knew I could lie here forever and cry, and I would be very old and frail, like Meema Lyuba, with nothing but a tiny curled-up body and delicate bones covered with tissue-paper skin, and deep holes in my head for eyes.

In the darkening room where the Unseen Watchers danced along the walls, and Miss Harrison's glass eye winked and flickered, I had no reason to be afraid anymore. I was a skeleton and my bones rose out of my prone body to join them in their dance.

Someone banged on my door and tried to open it but it held fast. Voices called my name but the tears rolled on. In the sound of a rushing river, the doorknob rattled and my skeleton bones rattled and some very strange music came out of nowhere to drown out the voices. I didn't move. The river dried up and the music stopped and my pillow dried and my room was dim dark and I lay on my bed in my clothes and turned and saw that everything was at a tilt.

Things seemed out of place although I couldn't remember why and wasn't sure if this was a dream or not.

Inside me lay a vast emptiness. The pit which had been filled with water had dried up and my heart which had floated in it, bobbed in it sometimes with happiness, sometimes with anger, had dried up too. I felt my heart the size of a peanut and hard as a peanut and it would never again be big and full and float free.

My room swam in a strange green light as I looked up between half-shut eyes, my eyelashes filtering out the solid mass of space above me. I drifted, my head touching nothing, my body made of air. I felt at peace. My head lolled, my fingertips disappeared, or at least I couldn't feel them still attached to me. I sighed and slept, my eyelids shutting down on the room.

"Be very good," she said.... "No fighting. I'll come back as soon as they let me."

I stared. Mama . . . Mama come back! I had seen her. I knew I had seen her! She wore a white robe with long sleeves, very wide so they hung down to the ground, and her huge white wings rose behind her. She'd hovered between the ceiling and my bed near the window, in the corner of my room. I hadn't dreamed it. She was real, and the echo of her voice saying the ordinary things still lingered in my ears. But she wasn't there. There was nothing in the corner where I'd seen her. I sat leaning on one elbow, squinting around the room, but there was no sign of Mama, even though I stared at the spot for a very long time. But in the back of my eyes I could still see an afterimage, a spot of white, and I knew she had really come back.

I finally lay back on my pillow and closed my eyes. I would tell Papa tomorrow, and he would be happy. Very very happy.

**4** I couldn't believe that the sun could still shine. Today they were going to bury Mama and the baby, yet it was an ordinary cold morning near the end of January. The brilliant gold of sunlight illuminated the world as though nothing had happened.

I lay in bed, not moving, and realized my perspective was all wrong. Staring straight ahead of me, I saw the corner of my room instead of the window wall. My lightbulb string dangled from the wrong place too, over the center of the bed instead of at its edge. Till that moment I'd forgotten I'd pulled my bed over to block the door. I was still dressed, I noticed, exactly the way I'd lain down last night. I got up and pushed my bed back till it stood against the wall again, then I crawled under the covers, clothes and all, wrapping them around me.

Looking up, I wondered if I'd really seen Mama there or just dreamed it. It had been too realistic to be a dream, her voice too ordinary. I closed my eyes, trying to bring back her image, and in the silence of the house I wanted to hear her voice again. But in the diamond-hard light of day it seemed foolish. I covered my face and lay like that for a long time. Till I heard Papa open his door. I tensed.

My doorknob rattled, then Papa stood beside my bed. I uncovered my face and looked up at him. He was fully dressed, his eyes encased in ridges of skin so they looked as if they were imbedded in old wood.

"Today," he said in a voice that cracked like dry straw, "I want you to stay close to Saul all day. I want you to take care of him like a big sister, and not run away into your room. Do you understand?"

I nodded, my eyes sliding away from his. Papa was displeased with me and it hurt.

"He was afraid to be by himself, and he slept in bed with me."

I didn't move, letting the realization take form in my

mind. Simply Simon had slept with Papa in the big bed, had huddled close to him so they gave each other comfort, while I had lain here alone, locked in my room in the dark. It wasn't fair!

"Get dressed, and listen Becky. You make some breakfast for you and Saul. Then clean up the dishes before anybody gets here."

"Who's coming?"

"Everybody. The house will be full, before the funeral and after. And remember, you are going to sit where everybody can see you and take care of Saul. I don't want to hear a peep out of you all day. No crying, no running away, no nothing."

It was on the tip of my tongue to tell Papa what I had seen last night, to point out the very spot, but somehow, from his expression and his attitude, the time didn't seem right. I wondered if the time would ever be right.

The day passed as in a dream, and I sleepwalked through it. I took care of Simply Simon as I'd never taken care of him before until he complained to Papa that he couldn't even go to the bathroom without me trying to follow him. We stayed close as twins and kept to ourselves as much as possible to avoid the kindness and pity in the eyes of people we hardly knew.

"Poor little orphans," a plumpish young woman said, stinging me out of my dreamlike state long enough for me to glare at her.

"We're not orphans! We have Papa!"

Papa gave me a warning look from his place on the chesterfield where he'd sat since after the funeral. We hadn't been allowed to go. A coterie of women had moved rustlingly through the kitchen preparing eggs and other food for the return of Papa and the other mourners, so we hadn't been left alone.

When, after the day had dragged to its end and people had finally gone home, Papa touched my shoulder, I knew he was pleased with me again. But we all slept in our own beds, although for the first time we kept our doors open.

In bed I reviewed the day. People walked softly, bringing pots and pots of food. Some things had to go into the ice box to keep cold until we could get around to using them, and Auntie Sadie had brought the most. Carrot tsimmis, prakkiss, roast beef and roast chicken. It was as if in grief we had to stuff ourselves to death. If anybody else had brought the food I would have appreciated it but I couldn't forgive Auntie Sadie for too many things. Whenever I looked at her I could see her wagging her bony finger at Mama and hear her voice say: "Now remember—don't come and complain to me if anything happens." I could never forgive her for that. Somehow she was responsible for even thinking something bad could happen. I was sure it was her fault.

In the dim glow of light from the bulb in the hall, I could believe again that Mama had come to me the night before, and if she could do it once, she could do it again. I hoped and waited expectantly for a return visit and after awhile I began to worry. Would it be impossible for her ever to come back because now they had buried her? Maybe she could come before because she was still free. And what about the baby? Had they buried her with Mama, or separately, and wouldn't I ever see her . . . at all? What about those big white wings Mama had worn? What good were they if she was buried in the ground forever? I didn't solve the puzzle that night or any of the nights of the seven days of mourning, or Shiva as Papa called it.

It was a strange time, an alternating quiet and noisy time with people coming and going and an emptiness when they left and we climbed the steps to our bedrooms.

Then people stopped coming altogether and the emptiness of the future stretched ahead into infinity as I stood in the middle of the kitchen and looked at the wood-burning stove, the sink and the kitchen table with the extra dining-room chairs around it. I looked at the floor and it needed washing and there were crumbs on the oilcloth of the table. It would stay that way unless somebody did something about it. Then I realized the enormity of our loss. We not only had lost Mama, who had been the center of everything in our family, we had lost also the order and smoothness of our lives. Auntie Sadie or Auntie Leah or somebody might clean the oilcloth, but they wouldn't wash our floors or do our laundry.

Papa opened the grocery store again, and shook me awake. It was early in February and I tried to remember why February had been the month I'd looked forward to for so long. Something wonderful was supposed to happen in February.

"Get up," Papa said. "It's time to go to school."

"Do I have to? I don't want to go to school anymore."

"Yes you have to." Papa had a no-nonsense air about him. "Get up and get dressed. You don't want to be late the first time."

I didn't want to think yet about school. I moved sluggishly, dressing slowly, unconsciously. I heard Simply Simon clattering around his room in a very disorganized way, and I supposed he felt the same as I did.

Papa made breakfast, hot cocoa and toast. We gulped it down, pretending not to notice that his hands shook when he held the kettle to pour water for our cocoa. I felt sorry for him then, because after we left he'd be all alone in the house and the store. It would be the very first time for Papa and I didn't see how he'd stand it.

My coat snuggled warmly around me, the collar pressed against my cheeks, but all I could think about as we walked slowly to school, shuffling through the snow, was how it would be talking to the girls again. I dreaded it.

Betty Greenberg detached herself from the clot of girls. Her face, which had been smiling, turned grave. I sensed that she knew and felt instantly relieved. She stopped a few feet away from me and took a deep breath.

"Hi," she said then, keeping her eyes on my collar. "Are you . . . I mean, is everything all right?"

"Who told you?"

One of her curls had escaped from her knitted cap. She bit on the end of it, a habit she indulged in whenever she was nervous.

"Miss Harrison," she said finally. "Larry told her. . . .

He's . . . one of your . . . father's customers, so he knew. Becky, we feel . . . well, you know."

I nodded, afraid to speak, and watched Marjorie approach. She walked carefully as though she stepped on eggs, concentrating on each step. I blinked back my tears and used the back of my woollen mittens. After a minute. I said:

"I . . . can't talk about it."

Betty put an arm around my shoulder as if we were best friends and Marjorie fell into step on the other side of me. We walked to the school yard together.

"You sure missed a lot of work," Betty informed me.

I shrugged. "I guess I'm going to fail now for sure." I didn't even care. What did it matter?

"No you won't," Marjorie said. "We'll help you if you want us to."

I shrugged. "Thanks." It really was nice of them. "Did . . . did Miss Harrison say anything?"

"Well, she said a few things about it. I don't really remember. We were all so . . . shocked."

We stood in our usual corner of the school near the entrance, humped up against the cold weather. I remembered the times we'd stood in this same spot while I told them the wonderful things I was going to do with my baby sister. . . . I only hoped Miss Harrison wouldn't feel she had to say something. I hoped she would let me go to my seat quietly. It was a vain hope.

She stopped me in the doorway.

"Well, it's Rebecca." Her expression became human. This so unnerved me I stood rigidly against the wall, looking down at the floor.

"Rebecca. We were very very sorry to hear about your mother" she said. I held my breath, trying to block out the sound of her voice, not to hear her words. Please don't talk, I said to myself, but she went on and on, and when I glanced quickly at her face, she continued to look human and her words broke through the mist in my mind. " . . . and if you try to look at it that way, you will see that everything will turn out fine. I want you to stay after four so I can give you extra homework. We mustn't let you fall behind, must we?"

She released me then, and I stumbled almost blindly to the back of the room where the coats were hung and found an empty hook. A few of the students stared at me curiously but I refused to meet their eyes and went to my seat, glad that I sat right at the back.

Papa had dinner ready when we came home at noon. It was warmed-over leftovers from the ice box. I wondered what would happen when we'd used it all up. Would I have to learn how to cook? Maybe I could quit school and stay home and take care of the house and Papa.

Papa looked depressed, so to cheer him up, I said: "How was it in the store?" It was the wrong question, because he became even more depressed.

"Not even a meshuggener hindt came in."

I didn't know why Papa would want a crazy dog to come into the store, but his expression didn't invite further conversation. Simply Simon and I finished our meal in silence and left Papa brooding at the table. I was glad that at least we had someplace to go and didn't have to stay around and watch Papa moodily break a crust of bread into millions of crumbs.

Later, when Miss Harrison had kept her promise and loaded me down with extra homework, Marjorie stopped me in the school hall.

"D'you want to come over to my house so we can do our homework together, Beck? And I'll let you look at my scribbler for last week's work . . . ."

I hesitated. "I'd better not, Marj. My father won't know what happened to me and he'll worry."

"Well, you can phone him from my place."

"We don't have a telephone." I hated to admit it.

Her eyes widened. "No phone?" It sounded almost as bad as if I'd said we had no bathroom.

I shrugged. "You can live without a *tele*phone!"

"Oh sure," she agreed quickly. "They're not *that* important. I hardly ever use ours that much either."

"Yeah. Well, I'd better be going. I've got to get started on that homework. If I get stuck, though, I'll let you know tomorrow. Okay?" I didn't want her mad at me.

"Oh sure. Don't forget though, eh? Well, so long."

"So long." I hurried home to Papa.

He stood in the doorway as though he'd been waiting for me so I braced myself for what would follow. One thing I'd made up my mind about was that I would never go back to Cheder again. School was compulsory. It was against the law to play hookey, but Cheder was something else.

"Get your books ready," Papa said, "so when Saul gets home you can go to Cheder together."

I took a deep breath.

"Papa . . . even if you kill me, I'm never going back there, ever."

He was astonished. Halfway into the store he stopped and turned around. I wavered, seeing the anger clouds in his eyes, but the thought of Mr. Lerner and his punishments stiffened my nerve.

"What?"

"Even if you beat me black and blue I won't go, Papa. I won't ever go back to Mr. Lerner's room." My voice trembled noticeably.

Papa came back and stared at me.

"What are you talking? Who's going to beat you black and blue? Where did you hear such foolishness?"

"I just want you to know how I feel about Cheder, Papa. I hate it so much, and I *always* hated it!"

He sat down. "Why didn't you tell me before?"

"I did, once. You yelled at me and said I was going to be late."

Papa refused to believe that he had ever yelled at me. "When? When was this? I yelled at you? I don't remember."

"It doesn't matter, Papa. Honest it doesn't. I just don't want to ever have to go back there again."

"You have to learn Hebrew. You have to learn how to Daven."

"Then you can teach me, Papa. I don't mind the Hebrew. It's just the teacher that I hate, and the Cheder, and all the lines I always have to write for punishment. . . ."

A sense of victory came to me.

"I can't teach you," Papa said flatly. "I'm not a teacher. I'll see what I can do. Maybe a tutor. I'll ask at the Shul. . . ." He turned and began to walk towards the store door. He didn't get two steps because I leaped at him, yelling, my arms snaking around his neck, almost pulling him to the ground in my joy. Papa disentagled himself, not sure how to cope with this new situation. "All right," he said brusquely. "Don't get so excited. You have some homework to do, no?" And that was how I rid myself once and for all of the daily horror of my life. I knew I could handle any tutor with my eyes shut and both hands tied behind my back.

I couldn't do the same with Auntie Sadie though. Before I'd settled down at the big desk to do homework, she sailed in carrying a pot of borscht ahead of her, Uncle Morris shuffling in behind her. My heart sank. Did they *have* to eat with us? Couldn't they stay home and let us eat sandwiches instead?

She plunked the pot down in the kitchen, picked up a piece of kindling wood from the box behind the stove, and started talking while she poked at the flames in the stove.

"Wash your hands and set the table." She could only be talking to me, I knew, because the only other one in the house was Uncle Morris. "Make sure your hands are good and clean. Use soap. And put away your books. Don't leave them lying there. You didn't even hang up your coat. Do you want your Mama's memory to be ashamed how you turned out?"

I stood in the kitchen doorway to glare at her back. Who did she think she was anyway? My boss? She whirled from the stove to look at my feet, ready to bawl me out for not taking off my overshoes except that I had taken them off, and hers were still on. I let my indignation flare.

"I *always* take off my overshoes!" I answered her unspoken thought. "But *you're* still wearing *yours!*" I pointed to the trail of wet footprints she'd left on the linoleum from the front door to the stove.

"So? Wasn't I holding this heavy pot? You watch I don't take this stick to you." She brandished a piece of kindling at me. "Now do what I told you and hurry up about it. Then you can take a rag and wipe up the floor. It wouldn't hurt you to wash the floors once in a while too, you know. They're a dirty mess."

I pressed my lips together and told her off mentally. Then moving slowly, just to show her, I hung up my coat, caressing the fur collar, remembering as though it had happened a thousand years ago what my birthday had been like and Mama's face when I took the coat out of the box. I still hadn't figured out why we couldn't afford the coat before and could now. I wondered if Mama had had something to do with changing Papa's mind. Did she know then that something was going to happen to her, and did she want to make sure in her mind that I would be warm and taken care of?

I wiped up the footprints from the door to the stove, where she'd finally taken off her overshoes, and then washed my hands *with soap*, not because she said so, but because I felt like it. I set the table for five; then, ignoring her as pointedly as I could, I went back to my homework.

Later, after the ordeal of supper and doing dishes was over and I was alone in my room, I wrote in my scribbler for a while, something I had stopped doing. Now I asked all the questions that kept bothering me. The questions that nobody seemed know the answers to—not Papa anyway. If he couldn't tell me why Mama and the baby had to die then nobody could. I had a feeling he kept asking himself the same question too.

I couldn't help wondering whether I had really seen Mama or just imagined or dreamed that I had. If I had, then why didn't she come back, and if I hadn't, did that mean I was crazy like that rotten bum Uncle Morris said I was? I wondered too what it felt like to die. Was it peaceful and quiet like going to sleep or did it hurt like having a baby? One thing was pretty sure, and that was that the baby didn't feel a thing. It had never known it was alive so it couldn't know it was dying. That was the only good thing about it.

I took Mama's apron out, unrolled it and placed it with the big mixing spoon on my pillow. Sometimes I liked to sit on Mama's chair and pretend I could feel her close by but mostly I let it sit beside my dresser, unused, so when she came back it would be waiting for her. I wished she would hurry up though. I missed her terribly.

# PART THREE

**1** The air became milder some days in March, and brave birds twinkled through still-bare branches. Crunching through crackles of thin ice on my way home from school I left water-filled footprints behind me. I looked hopefully for wispy blades of grass, even though I knew it was too soon. Simply Simon came panting behind me. "Hi! Look what I found!"

I turned thinking: the lucky fish, he always finds money! But it wasn't money that he held out to show me, it was a dead bird. I screamed and hit his hands so it flew into the air and landed in a snowbank where it sank out of sight. "Don't you know it's full of germs?" I yelled. "Don't you know you should never touch anything that's *dead?*"

"It's only a bird I found frozen. There's nothing on it."

"You can't see germs, stupid! You'd better wash your hands real good when you get home! And use lots of soap!"

I turned and stomped off so he had to run to keep up with me.

"If you can't see germs, how d'you know they're there?"

"Because they are! Germs are everywhere, Mis Harrison says and she should know; she's a teacher. Even if you can't see them, they're there, especially in dead things."

"In all dead things? In people too?"

"I don't know. I guess so."

"You mean, Mama too?"

I stared at him, a cold shiver going through me. No. Of *course* not in Mama! Not in *Mama!* We turned and ran, both of us, back to where I'd sunk the bird, scrabbling through the snow till we found it. Miss Harrison was a liar, a dirty filthy liar, and I'd never believe another word she said. Except school stuff.

Simply Simon found it first and picked it up with care. I was glad because I didn't want to be the one to touch it even if it wasn't full of germs. I didn't want to feel the dead stiff body. "See?" He held it out to me. "There's nothing on it, no germs or bugs or anything. It's just a poor frozen bird."

I shrank away a little, staring at the gray feathers, the tiny slits where eyes were closed, the small pitiful beak. We would have to do something to make it up to the poor little bird. "We'll bury it under the tree on the boulevard. I think a bird would like to be buried under a tree."

I left him holding the bird outside while I ran into the house, tossed my books onto the desk and ran down to the cellar where Papa kept his tools. I knew exactly where the spade would be and didn't even have to look deep into the shadows and see the coffinlike box. I grabbed the spade and dashed up the wooden steps to light and safety.

Simply Simon stood where I'd left him. We found a good spot to dig and cleared some of the snow away. It was like digging into cement, but I finally made a dent in the frozen ground. "This'll have to be deep enough," I panted. "We can do it again in the summer if we have to."

He placed the bird tenderly in the hole and covered it up. "Should we say something?" he asked then.

"I don't know. What could we say?"

"Well, like in that movie we saw where those kids buried the cat. Remember?"

I wrinkled my nose. It didn't seem appropriate. They had spoken to Jesus Christ and we were Jewish. It would have to be something else. "How about Boruch Atoh?"

"You mean what Papa says when he blesses the wine on Shabbas?"

"Sure. He says it to God, doesn't he?"

Simply Simon nodded. "Okay." We stood at attention, gazing down at the small mound of snow. He cleared his throat. "Here goes: Boruch Atoh Adoinoi, Aloihanu Melech Ha-Oylum, Boiray Pree Hagoffen." We said "O-Main" together. It was good enough, I figured, seeing as we didn't even know the bird when it was alive.

"When we get into the house," I said, "let's wash our hands extra good. Even if there aren't any such things as germs."

Papa prodded a lump of meat in a pan on the stove when I came up from the cellar again where I put the shovel away. "What did you need the shovel for?" Papa asked.

"We buried a bird." I placed my hands under the tap and let the water run over them. Papa said nothing so I glanced over my shoulder at him. He looked so sad all the time. I knew it was harder on him than on us, so to get his mind off Missing Mama, I said:

"Is there such a thing as germs, Papa?"

"Yes."

Simply Simon and I stared at each other but Papa didn't seem to notice and went out to chop some wood for the stove. I heard the chunk! chunk! chunk! of the axe and the ka-chunk of wood being thrown into the summer kitchen adjoining the back of the house.

The meat sizzled on the stove untended so I stood where Papa had stood and moved the meat around the frying pan with the long fork. It looked horribly unappetizing but this was the full extent of Papa's cooking ability and we would eat it without hurting his feelings. We had no choice really.

"Better go and help Papa," I advised my brother, who leaned against the table, reading a comic book for the seventieth time. He put on his winter jacket and went out, heaving a great sigh. I had sounded almost like Mama just then!

I tried not to think about germs, about Miss Harrison being right after all, but the picture of horrible slimy germs crawling all over the dead bird came back into my mind. In almost the same instant I saw germs all over Mama and the baby. Superimposed over them I saw myself lying dead in a coffin, germs eating away at me. I shuddered violently, squeezing my eyes shut tightly to erase the image from my mind.

After supper when everything had been cleaned up and put away and Papa sat working on the customer accounts in a scribbler, I thought I'd give Papa one more chance. After all, he hadn't been paying too close attention to what I was saying. Maybe he didn't hear me. "Papa, you're sure about those germs?"

"What?" Papa frowned.

"You know . . . what you said. Are you sure there are such things as germs?"

"Yes, yes I'm sure. Why do you keep on talking about germs so much?"

"Because," I said. "How come we can't see them?"

"You can only see them with a microscope. They're very tiny." He bent over the scribbler again.

"Where do they come from?"

Papa shrugged. "Why do you have to know? Is it part of your homework?"

"No. But I have to know. I have to know if it's true or if the teacher's lying."

"She isn't lying. Teachers don't tell lies. Are you taking up about germs already?"

"No. But in Health, we took up about flies and she said they're covered with germs and that germs are in all dead things. Like birds and animals." I looked closely at Papa for a reaction. "She didn't say about people though. Are there germs in dead people?"

Papa didn't answer right away, putting down a few more figures in the scribbler. Then he looked at me.

"Where do you think sickness comes from? Germs. Germs are in the air, that's why people catch colds and other diseases. They're in living people, never mind the dead ones." Papa wet the tip of his pencil with his tongue and went on writing.

Suddenly I felt itchy all over. Invisible things marched up and down my skin, into my nose, mouth and ears, down my back. I shook my head violently to shake them off and rubbed at my face and arms. Simply Simon watched me and grinned.

"What's the matter with you?" Papa finally noticed.

"It's her germs," my brother said matter-of-factly. "She's trying to get rid of them."

Papa threw back his head and laughed. It was the first real laugh we'd heard from him in a long long time. I felt confused. It wasn't funny! But when Papa stopped laughing he had a gentle expression on his face so I didn't mind being laughed at.

"Forget about germs," he said. "Even if they're there, you couldn't get rid of them that way. They don't fall off. Only medicine helps when you need it. Now go finish your homework."

He shook his head for a moment, still smiling. I couldn't help feeling silly, and gave Simply Simon a dirty look just in case he was thinking of making a comment. Which he wisely didn't.

Later on in bed, with my head covered, I fell asleep and then Mama came to me and showed me the baby. See how she's growing, Becky? She's starting to look like you, Mama said. And so smart. Already she knows I'm her mother. Be good and take care of Papa and your brother. Be a good girl.

In silent anguish I watched Mama recede into darkness with the baby in her arms when I hadn't really been able to take a good look at her. Other faces, the faces of strangers, emerged from behind them and grew larger and larger and as I stared I saw that it had arms and legs and waving antennas. It had turned into a giant germ, carrying an awful sickness. I tried to run but I couldn't. I couldn't move at all because suddenly I realized my feet were stuck in the ground like roots and I had turned into the tree on the boulevard, and the germ landed in my branches. I squirmed and bent and twisted every way I could to dislodge it but I couldn't get rid of it. Sickness crawled all over me so my leaves withered and died, dropping off and landing on the ground. I was helpless, doomed; I shook my branches as hard as I could and woke myself up.

I sat up, staring into dim dark. It had seemed so real; I couldn't believe it was just a dream. I looked at my arms to make sure they were really arms and not branches. I moved my fingers, staring at the pale fingernails and thought about Mama. The part about Mama coming back to show me the baby hadn't been a dream. I was sure of that.

I tried to remember what Mama had said. The baby was growing! That meant she was alive somewhere and so was Mama. New hope surged through me. Death didn't mean the end: It just meant something different. I didn't know what it was, but someday I would find out. Oh yes, I knew it was true.

On the wall near the window, reflected light shimmered and danced from the end of the window blind. Miss Harrison's glass eye gleamed wickedly at me but I wasn't afraid. Tonight I had learned something important and I wasn't going to be afraid again. Would I remember about that in the morning?

I could hear Papa's footsteps as he paced back and forth in his bedroom. The floor creaked and squeaked, first at one end of the room, then at the other. I wondered if Mama haunted him the way she haunted me. I wondered if that was why Papa couldn't sleep. I felt like running to tell him about Mama's visit to me with the baby but something held me back. Maybe Papa wouldn't like it.

**2** Another thing Papa wouldn't like, I knew, was getting the house ready for Pesach. It was such a big job that it really needed an army of women . . . or Mama. The cleaning alone took nearly three weeks, not to mention all the cooking for both Seders, which were the feast meals on the first two nights. And Papa was just a man.

When I looked at the calendar and saw that it was a little over a week till Pesach, March 27th to be exact, and Papa was only just starting, I had a sinking feeling that we wouldn't be ready, an unthinkable sin.

I wished we could afford a cleaning lady, like Betty Greenberg's family had. I wished a lot of things, especially after I found myself unwillingly dragged into the cleaning process. Washing the floor behind the dirty wood stove and under the leaky old ice box was not my idea of having fun. If I had my way, I would also not wash dusty shelves in cupboards or go through the clothes in drawers to make sure nothing yicchy crawled around in them. What did all that have to do with Pesach?

I could understand washing the dishes on the top shelves and putting them away because we never used them and they had a film of dust an inch thick on them. And I could understand bringing the Pesach dishes and pots and pans and cutlery from the basement and washing them with cleanser because they'd lain in boxes a whole year, but why did I have to look for little worms in drawers where we kept underwear and stuff like that? Papa insisted though, so I did it.

What really worried me was who would have to wash the walls and ceilings in all the rooms? Mama had always done that, standing on chairs or on the kitchen table spread with old newspapers, her head bent back as she worked, water dripping off her elbow into little pools on the floor, and when she would step off she would move slowly, holding the back of her neck or her back or something else, and make groaning sounds. It didn't seem worth it to me, especially since you couldn't even tell where she'd washed and where she hadn't.

When I grow up, I promised myself as I poured water into a basin, you won't catch *me* killing myself for any holiday. Nosiree. I would enjoy myself and let someone else do the work the way Betty's mother did. I would either marry a rich man so I could afford a maid or I wouldn't get married at all; I'd become rich all by myself. Maybe I'd make a million dollars. I'd be famous as something—a singer, a beautiful glamorous movie star, a tap dancer, or a great author. Whatever it would be, I'd become very rich doing it, I decided.

I wondered if Mama had ever daydreamed about being rich when she was a young girl in Russia. It sure hadn't come true for her. Nothing good had happened to Mama, only hard work and pain. Like last year when she fell off the chair she'd been standing on. We never used it anymore because you couldn't trust it. I could see it still in the corner of the middle room (we never called that the dining room, although that was what it was supposed to be).

By the 26th of March, which was Erev Pesach, the walls

and ceilings still hadn't been washed. I could see now that they wouldn't be. I knew that the whole issue had been set aside for this year and I didn't care. I was pretty sure Papa didn't care either and as for Simply Simon, he not only didn't care, but we hardly ever found him when we needed his help.

Auntie Sadie and Auntie Leah came early in the morning to cook our Seder suppers for us. They divided up the work between them so they wouldn't have to keep bumping into each other at the stove or sink and I managed to stay out of their sight for reasons of safety. If they saw me, they'd both put me to work, and more and more I was beginning to think like Simply Simon. I detested work.

Pesach without Mama wasn't really Pesach. Although everything happened that was supposed to happen—like chicken soup and gefilte fish and matzo balls and farfel—the main ingredient, Mama, was missing. We went through the motions—the reading of the Haggadah, the ritual things—but they were empty gestures, habits we had gotten into over the years. My eyes kept roaming around the room, towards the far wall, the ceiling. If Mama could come back, I thought, she would do it tonight. I watched for her and every once in a while Auntie Sadie would tap me on the shoulder and point into the Haggadah, frowning at me. I wished she didn't have to sit so close to me.

After the first two days, which were Yontiff, we didn't have to go through any rituals. It was still Pesach but we didn't have to be formal about it. We could eat our supper in an ordinary way, but of course there couldn't be any forbidden foods at the table or anywhere in the house for that matter. Pesach was something you had to get over with before you could enjoy the springtime. Once it was past we would be able to relax.

Auntie Sadie hated to see me sitting around. If I even sat studying for exams, it offended her. I had to be busy, cleaning silver, washing the mirror. She picked really ridiculous jobs for me to do. It was unbelievable. What did she care if I failed? She treated me like a slave.

"Hurry up and peel potatoes, Becky, if you want to eat

tonight."

"I'm still full from dinner," I protested. "I won't even be hungry for supper."

"Never mind. Just go get some potatoes from the cellar and start peeling."

"I don't see why I have to do everything! I'm not a servant!"

"AHA!" She croaked. "Now you said something! You think *I'm* a servant? Eh? Is that what you think? Do I have to do everything? It's time you learned to do some work around here!"

I stomped down the cellar steps, too angry to remember to be afraid of the Black Dark, and brought a basket of potatoes up from the bin under the steps. I stomped to the sink and, blinking furiously, I began to peel one, gouging out great chunks of potato till there was little left of it.

"I *am* doing some work around here!" I told her off. "What does it *look* like I'm doing?"

"It looks like," she said grimly, "you're wasting some good potatoes!"

"Huh!" I said to myself. As if she was such a great peeler. As if she was such a great anything. I wished she would go home and leave us alone. And take her stupid old husband with her.

Auntie Sadie stalked out of the kitchen. I heard her go into the store, probably to tell on me. Well, let her, the old tattletale. I braced myself for Papa's entrance and the things he would say to me, and I tried to prepare a defense for myself.

"I'm only ten years old," I could say. "*She* thinks I'm an old lady like her. *She* thinks I should cook and bake and clean everything, like a wife. I didn't even do my homework yet!" That would get Papa on my side. But he didn't come into the house, to my disappointment. I had relished the thought of getting her into trouble with Papa.

"Just wait!" Auntie Sadie, triumph in her voice. I turned around and stared at her. She nodded, her lips pursed together, sharp eyes gleaming. "Just you wait! You'll see.

. . . I don't know why I didn't think about it before!"

"Think of *what* before?" I asked suspiciously.

"Never mind. You'll find out soon enough." And she wouldn't say another word. She left soon after, acting very mysterious. Simply Simon said: "What's wrong with *her?*"

I shrugged. "You know Auntie Sadie. She likes to act important." But a tiny worry nagged at me. That triumph in her voice. I didn't like it at all.

When I tried to question Papa about it, he didn't react. He had his own troubles, he said. I watched with surprise as Mrs. Wurster, the old hag who lived across the street, waddled out of the store. "What's she doing here?" I asked. "She never buys at our store."

Papa sighed, and went on marking prices on cans. "Who knows? The tsedrayteh. She bought one egg."

"One egg?" She really was tsedrayt . . . crazy as a loon, I thought. It almost made me forget to worry about Auntie Sadie.

I sat on an upturned wooden box behind the counter. My head was on a level with the top, and hidden here, I could play with the big spool of string on the shelf, and just be with Papa. While Papa worked I made knots in the string and when the bell tinkled over the door, I was in a perfect position to snoop on whoever the customer was. It was her again!

I peeked over the edge of the counter, then stared. What had she done to herself? This wasn't the same Mrs. Wurster who flapped her sweater sleeves at the little kids on the street, screeching at them in a foreign language, her flaming red hair a frizzled halo, agate gray eyes encased in pouches of skin while her S-shaped body heaved and lunged after them. No, this Mrs. Wurster wore a bright smear of lipstick, a circle of rouge on each cheek; a chalky substance covered the rest of her face, ending abruptly at the chin so her wrinkled neck looked black as it extended into the collar of a purple suit. A heavy aroma of perfume hovered over us, an invisible cloud. What was she up to?

"Mr. Devine!" her voice tinkled as musically as the bells on the door. "I need another egg! One more, please? I want to bake a cake and don't have enough eggs!"

"Why don't you take a dozen?" Papa said, "Then you'll have enough for two cakes!"

She seemed to be thinking it over, then, with a coy twinkle in her eyes, she pursed her lips together. "I'll tell you what I'll do, Mr. Devine! I'll take half a dozen now and half a dozen later. Is it a deal?"

Papa went to the cooler for the eggs and without another word he counted out the six eggs, put them in a bag, and waited for the money. She kept wrinkling up her face in smiles and blinking her eyes rapidly at him. I was repelled by the sight of her and wondered how Papa felt. She paid and wiggled out. "Bye-Bye!" she called as the door closed behind her.

I looked up at Papa. "What was that all about?"

Papa gave me a long level look. "Don't you know?"

I shook my head in wonderment. "No."

"That's good," he said cryptically, and wouldn't say another word, to my mystification.

Auntie Sadie and Uncle Morris were back at suppertime. I had almost forgotten the problem I'd had with her but now it came forcefully back at me and even though I looked very closely at her, I couldn't read her mind and find out what she'd been talking about earlier. I decided then that she was just making it up to scare me and she didn't have any plans at all.

"Well," she said to Papa after we'd eaten. "Did you think over what I was talking to you about?"

I felt cold chills go through me. So she *had* told Papa some stories about me. Apprehensively, I looked at him to see his expression. Papa's mouth closed, a muscle twitched in his cheek and he looked down at the table.

"Don't talk about it," he said fiercely to her. "I don't want to hear anything about it now."

"When then?" She looked very cross. "What I say, the sooner the better. I don't mind coming here and cooking, if I don't have to do it long. I don't want to do it all the rest of my life!"

"So don't!" Papa snapped. "I thank you for what you did already and don't do any more. We'll get along."

Auntie Sadie drew back as if she'd been slapped. "That's the thanks I get," she said in an injured voice. "I'm only thinking of you and the kinder, and that's all you can say!"

Papa made as if to rise and leave the table but she reached out and grabbed his sleeve.

"Sit. And listen. Listen to me, Jake. I'm only saying what's best for you and them. Believe me, for you it may be all right like this. But *they* need a mama!"

I froze. A *Mama*! What was she talking about? I looked around for Simply Simon to see his reaction but he'd left the table already. I stared at Auntie Sadie, convinced she was crazier even than Mrs. Wurster. She looked right back at me and I could tell she had said it so I could hear.

"Yes," she said, as if I'd spoken. "A mama for you and a wife for your Papa. What's wrong with that? We have to think about the future. And I have somebody in mind would make a good wife. You might as well know it, Becky, because when I bring her, I want you and Saul to be on your best manners. Understand?"

Papa sighed, all the fight gone out of him, and leaned his head on his hand. I wanted him to tell her not to bring anybody; I wanted him to make her shut up, to say she should mind her own business, that he wouldn't get another wife, that nobody was ever going to take Mama's place. I wanted him to say all that and more. But Papa sat there breathing in and out heavily, audibly, as if he was concentrating only on breathing.

"Nobody is going to come here and be my mother, so you might as well forget it, Auntie Sadie. I wouldn't let anybody take Mama's place!" I hardly even knew I was going to speak before the words burst out of me.

"Who's talking about taking her place? All I want is somebody should be here to do the housework and the cooking, and learn you some manners so you don't talk back to an auntie like that. And it's about time, I see."

I was highly insulted. Just let her bring somebody here. Let her see what good it would do. Nobody would stay where she wasn't wanted and I would make sure the lady, whoever she was, would know without a doubt that she wasn't wanted.

"And I'm not the only one," Auntie Sadie gloated. "Your Auntie Leah has somebody and so do the cousins. So you're going to see a lot of ladies here soon. Make sure you don't bring shame on all of us, they should think your Mama, she should rest in peace, didn't bring you up right. She would turn in her grave."

"I bet she would turn in her grave if she knew you were trying to make Papa get married again."

"Your Mama *wanted* your Papa to get married again!"

"No, she doesn't!" I'd never believe that. Papa gave me a warning look, then got up and walked away from the table. I bit the inside of my lip. The least Papa could do was help me, forbid her from bringing anybody to the house.

Later, when we were alone, Papa placed a hand on my shoulder. "Becky, I know how you feel but it's no use fighting all the relatives. They mean well and they think it's for our own good they're doing this. Don't talk back, don't argue, be polite and don't worry. Let her say what she wants and do what she wants—and we'll do what *we* want. Understand?"

I nodded. "Then you're not going to get married again?"

"Right now, that's the last thing I want."

"What about the later though?" I didn't like the sound of that "right now."

"Later is later. Who knows about later? In ten years I could change my mind."

"Oh well, ten years . . ." I wasn't going to worry about it before I had to. I threw my arms around his neck. He felt wooden, unyielding, a statue. Then, as if thinking it over, he put his arm around me and kissed the top of my head.

"When is it starting?" I asked. I wanted to get it over with. The sooner they brought their ladies, the sooner we'd be able to relax and forget the whole thing. I hoped they would all bring them at the same time, then we could see them all together, reject them, and everybody would go home. Papa shrugged, uninterested.

I went upstairs to find Simply Simon. He sprawled on top of his bed, reading comic books in the poor light of the bulb that dangled from the end of a cord. He looked so innocent. He didn't know.

I bounced onto his bed. "Guess what. Guess what big surprise everybody has for us."

He turned a page. "Give me a hint."

"Okay. They're planning to give us a new mama."

"Huh?"

I nodded. "They're looking for a wife for Papa!"

"Who is?"

"Everybody. The aunties and the cousins. Everybody that has an old maid friend. Even Mrs. Wurster!"

"She has an old maid friend too?"

"No, dummy. Even Mrs. Wurster wants to marry Papa."

"You're crazy."

"You don't believe me? Go ask Papa."

"You just want to get me into trouble!"

"Why would I do that?"

"Sure. I'll ask Papa, and he'll hit me on the head."

"Simply Simon, I swear it's the truth. I swear on a stack of bibles. Auntie Sadie is bringing a lady for Papa to look at, and that isn't all. Even Auntie Leah, that I always liked, is going to bring over a lady. Everybody is."

"Papa wouldn't marry anybody."

"I sure *hope* not."

He suddenly looked worried. "Do you think Papa would? What for?"

"How should I know. But it happens in the movies, doesn't it?"

"Well, that's only in movies. It doesn't happen in Real Life."

"It does so. Did you ever hear of a stepmother? Huh? Where d'you think that word came from? If Papa got married again, his wife would be our *stepmother!*"

"You mean," Simply Simon said, ". . . a *wicked*

*stepmother?*"

"That's right," I said with relish, glad to see him do a little worrying for a change. I'd worried by myself long enough.

He bit a fingernail, frowning. "Does Papa *want* another wife?"

"Not that I know of."

"So what are we worrying over?"

"We're worrying over: what if one of the ladies that comes happens to be gorgeous, beautiful, glamorous, sweet and kind, and Papa falls in love with her?"

He burst out laughing. "You stupe! We say hurray, that's what!"

I glared at him. "You're the stupe. Would you forget about Mama so fast? Just like that? And besides, she would still be a stepmother. She could order you around and make you work like a horse and then act sweet and innocent when Papa was around and he wouldn't believe you! Is that what you want?"

He looked gloomy again and bit another nail. I left him and went into my own room, satisfied. But as I sat at the edge of my bed, the nagging fear came back. What if the lady Auntie Sadie brought was all those things? What if Papa couldn't resist her? I wished I knew what to do. I wished there was somebody I could ask for advice, someone who would tell me the best thing to do.

I got undressed and into my pajamas, covered my head and reached up for the light cord. In the dark, I visualized a procession of gorgeous women, all of them looking like movie stars, parading in front of Papa who sat, one leg crossed over the other, shaking his head in a bored way. I knew in my heart that Auntie Sadie wouldn't know anybody who looked like a movie star and even if she did, the lady wouldn't have to depend on Auntie Sadie to get her a husband. She could marry anybody she wanted and she certainly wouldn't want to marry someone who wasn't rich. And although I loved Papa dearly, I knew deep down that he wasn't ... uh ... handsome. Well, he wasn't. But he was Papa, and wonderful, and anybody that married him would be very lucky. So there. Except that he wasn't going to marry anybody. Ha ha.

I saw Mama in my dream again. She wore a robe, like one of the prophets in my Hebrew book. She just stood there and looked at me. Filled with overwhelming joy, I rushed to her, but when I got close it turned out to be Mrs. Wurster who laughed like a loony. Suddenly she whirled away and I saw the broomstick she'd hidden in the folds of the robe. I screamed and screamed and felt my head jerking back and forth as though it might break off. I opened my eyes. Papa stood in his underwear, shaking me. "What's the matter?"

"She's a witch! She's a witch!"

Papa shook me again. "Who is?"

"Mrs. Wurster! She's a witch!"

"You had a nightmare," he said. "Go back to sleep. Forget about it." He kissed me on the forehead.

Now I felt wide awake. "Okay, Papa."

He loved me. He would never marry anybody. I knew it deep in my heart. Papa really and truly loved me. I turned over comfortably in bed and went back to sleep.

**7** Miss Blustein was a complete washout. I knew it the minute she stepped carefully through our front door behind Auntie Sadie, flicking nervous quick glances at Papa, at me and Simply Simon and at our furniture.

She jerked her head silently at us without quite meeting anybody's eyes when Auntie Sadie made the introductions, and I knew instinctively that she had come under protest, bullied by Auntie Sadie. I almost felt sorry for her now that I knew we had nothing to fear from her. From the top of her coiled brown hair to the bottom of her prim black shoes, she was blushing maidenhood. Her round plain face, shyly peeping eyes and pale lips gave her an ageless look as though she was born looking like that, and twenty years from now would still look the same. I wondered if she was older than Papa or younger but I didn't wonder very hard. Now that I saw her, the matter was of complete indifference to me.

Auntie Sadie, however, hadn't admitted defeat just yet. She pulled chairs around and like an usher told everybody where they had to sit—Papa and Miss Blustein facing each other, Auntie Sadie next to her, and Simply Simon and me, anyplace. We were ignored but not completely, judging by the fierce frowns she threw in my direction even though I hadn't done a single thing to deserve them—yet.

"Now this house," she said to Miss Blustein, as though continuing a conversation begun earlier, "will be paid for in twenty years. There's a nice little business in the groceries. People got to eat! And the family—a boy and a girl; they go to school most of the day."

I listened in disbelief. Auntie Sadie was actually trying to sell Miss Blustein on the idea of joining our family, as if we wanted her and she had to be convinced! I looked cautiously at Papa to see his reaction and was rewarded by a brief sideways glance out of his eyes, then a very straight, stolid stare that seemed to be aimed at a space between Auntie Sadie's and Miss Blustein's heads. Papa had turned his ears off, and paid little attention to the goings-on.

"Becky," Auntie Sadie's voice snapped. "Go make tea and cut the cake that I brought. Saul. You help her."

I knew we were being banished so that grown-up talk could flow more freely and as far as I was concerned, it was okay with me. The whole thing had become boring. As we walked into the kitchen, I half hoped for a diversion, something that would add a little comic relief, like Mrs. Wurster making one of her periodic attempts to woo Papa. She came bursting through the grocery store at the oddest times and we were beginning to accept her presence as we accepted, for instance, Edgar Bergen and Charlie McCarthy on the radio, or Fibber McGee and Molly, strictly as entertainment.

"You get the cups and saucers and things," I told Simply Simon who had practically been walking on my heels in his eagerness to get out of there, "and I'll fill the kettle."

"Boy," he whispered, "if that's the best Auntie Sadie

can do, she better forget it."

We set up a deliberate clatter getting things ready. I pitied Papa that he had to stay there but at least we could make their conversation a bit less cozy. They'd have to raise their voices to hear each other over our racket.

Over the loud hiss of the kettle boiling on the stove, I heard Auntie Sadie say: "She has a good job in a sewing factory, making overalls. She can make overalls in her sleep."

I giggled, imagining Miss Blustein in bed next to Papa, sitting at a sewing machine and making overalls while Papa was trying to sleep. But I didn't care too much for the idea of her next to Papa in his bed. I stopped giggling and sloshed hot water into the teapot and partly on the floor.

When we carried the trays in, the little tableau looked as though it had run its course and nothing remained but to drink tea, eat the cake, and leave. Auntie Sadie's expression bore grim testimony to what she would have to say to all of us later. Well, was it our fault she had brought a hopeless case into the house? Did we have to accept whatever Auntie Sadie decreed, just to keep her happy? As far as that went, I could see by Miss Blustein's lips that she wished she had never come, that she was safely seated at her sewing machine making another pair of overalls. The sight stirred something in me so I approached her, without realizing in advance that I was going to do it and held the tray out to her.

"Would you like some tea, Miss Blustein?" I inquired politely and found myself looking into panicky gray eyes almost on a level with mine.

"Than—kyou," she said, and reached a hand out to grasp a cup, and at this range, I saw the fine hairs of her moustache and what I hadn't seen before; one long hair grew out of a wart on her chin.

The little bell tinkled in the store. As if jerked by strings, Papa jumped up, barely excusing himself. Auntie Sadie's mouth drew up like the pouch of a purse being closed by the cords and she breathed audibly through her nostrils. In the silence we heard the electric voice of Mrs. Wurster coo:

"Oh Mr. Devine, I was so afraid you'd closed early! I

wonder if you have . . . oil?"

I stood patiently beside Miss Blustein holding the tray under her nose. "Do you want some sugar?" I asked her. "Or cake?" Since we had won, I could afford to be kind to the enemy. After all, I was sure she had feelings, and right at the moment she looked sort of squashed inside.

Simply Simon pushed the plate of cake at her. "Have some cake," he ordered. There were crumbs of cake clinging to his mouth and on his striped jersey. He had cut big hunks which lay on their sides and, as she tried to comply, most of the serving dropped onto the floor. Miss Blustein blushed, looking appealingly helpless, and I wished for her sake that the farce could end. One look at Auntie Sadie though, and I knew she would sit there till the bitter end.

Papa returned, an air of irritation in his step, and in the way he jerked his chair around and dropped into it, I understood his feelings exactly but I couldn't understand why he put up with it. He was a grown man so why did he have to listen to Auntie Sadie and a lot of silly stuff about Miss Blustein or have to serve a customer who was probably a witch in Real Life? I personally would do only what I wanted to do when I grew up and nobody would dare to run my life—so there.

Papa didn't want tea and he wouldn't even look at the cake so it turned out that Miss Blustein sat all by herself, holding a cup of tea to her lips while a piece of cake sat in the saucer in her lap and I was willing to bet a million dollars that she hadn't wanted it in the first place. We all sat and looked at her eat, watching as the crumbs of cake dropped inexorably onto her lap and from there to the floor, so that she sat surrounded by bits and pieces of sponge cake around her pointed shoes, and I felt sorrier for her every minute.

When they left, I imagined Mama's reaction to what had just happened. With her arms folded she would look at her rival and laugh, just laugh. We won, Mama, I told her in in my mind. You have nothing to worry about. I felt as if Mama smiled then. She patted my head.

I began to clean up the mess left by the little tea party.

Auntie Sadie's last words still rang in my ears. "I'll come back," she promised, and the threat was directed at Papa, not at us for a change.

"How come," I asked him as he stared moodily at the floor, "you have to listen to her when you're a grown-up man? Why can't you just tell her to mind her own business?"

Papa shrugged. "It isn't that she doesn't mean it for our good. It just happens that she knows only a shvartz yor. A human being I could consider — her, I couldn't."

I hoped silently that none of the ladies would be human beings; I hoped for a procession of shvartz yor, as Papa called them—hopeless cases.

"You mean, you would marry somebody else just because they say so, Papa? You'd let somebody take Mama's place?"

He brushed it aside. "I have to be practical, Becky, but I'm not crazy. Don't worry about it."

"But *why* do you have to be practical? Why does she have the right to boss you around?"

"She won't boss me around. But why do I have to be practical? Because I'm only one person. Somebody has to be here to look after you and Saul. I can't do it by myself."

"Nobody has to look after *me*. I'm not a baby."

"I'm not a baby *either!*" Simply Simon said.

"So you're not babies. You have to eat? Your clothes have to be clean? Who will do it? Me? You?" Papa's eyes burned into mine, demanding an answer. I couldn't think of one.

We didn't see Auntie Sadie for a few days and I had a suspicion she was mad at us. Not that I cared but I couldn't see how it was our fault if Miss Blustein was a shvartz yor. All I hoped was that she didn't have anybody else in mind for Papa. She'd had her chance, and if she'd gone and spoiled it, well, hooray for her. Now all I had to worry about was whether one of the other ladies was a human being or not. It didn't take long to find out.

The cousins came on Wednesday. It hadn't taken them long to find out that Auntie Sadie had laid an egg. Edna and

Nankie were Papa's cousins, not first cousins, but the several times removed kind, and whenever they came to our house, it meant a party. Except for this time. Nankie had brought "a friend," a lady who towered over both of them, both in height and in width. I couldn't really believe when I looked at her that they were serious about Mrs. Markle. If anything, Mrs. Markle was more of a washout than Miss Blustein. At least Miss Blustein had a certain dainty air about her. At least Miss Blustein had a certain amount of dignity. Looking at Mrs. Markle, I could see any number of good points about Miss Blustein that I had completely overlooked. At least Miss Blustein had nice straight teeth, or at least we hadn't seen them in evidence the way we could see Mrs. Markle's.

As we sat in an uneasy circle in the middle room, Nankie next to Papa, Edna next to Mrs. Markle, I had a brilliant flash of intuition which told me that it wasn't the awkward, big-boned, horse-faced Mrs. Markle who was on display at all. It was soft and round Nankie with her nearly visible set of bosoms showing just above the dip of her low neckline, the always-smiling, pleasant-appearing Nankie, who had never married and now found Papa a tempting target. I gaped at her, hardly listening to the chatter and gabble that flowed over my head, because if Papa liked Nankie, I knew I was sunk, sunk, sunk. Edna, of course, was another Auntie Sadie type, being of one family and very waspish, but Nankie could fool anybody, especially a man, into thinking she was nice. She could certainly be nice, I knew from past experience, but she could also be mean, nasty and cutting.

My heart made large jumps inside me as I stared at her and at Papa, who sat with a small smile on his lips listening to Nankie while horse-faced Mrs. Markle laughed and Edna scrunched herself into a straight line, knees, ankles and feet all pointed one way, and offered acid comments each time Nankie stopped for breath.

"So when I heard Sadie washed her hands, I said to Edna why don't we bring Mrs. Markle here when you're both in the same boat." She leaned forward so Papa could see into the front of her dress, but he looked the other way.

"She just buried her second husband," Edna laughed in a snickery sort of sound. Mrs. Markle smiled and nodded.

"And he left her well fixed!" Nankie slyly poked Papa with a round bare elbow. Papa didn't like being poked or marrying ladies for their money, but Nankie didn't seem to notice. "And her first one wasn't exactly a rich so-and-so but he wasn't so poor either!"

If I hadn't caught on that it was Nankie and not Mrs. Markle who was the candidate in this little party, I would've been amazed at the absolutely wrong things she was saying to convince Papa, but of course I knew, and it all seemed very vulgar and cold-blooded to me. I glared at Nankie when she calmly slipped her hand inside her dress and scratched her bust, all without her eyes leaving Papa's face.

Mrs. Markle spoke for the first time, her voice rich with humor and interest. "You own the store? All paid for? And the house?"

"He's a wonderful provider," Nankie answered for Papa. "A good man. You couldn't find a better one." She nodded and laughed and poked Papa again. "I personally think he's one in a million," she said, but to Papa, not to Mrs. Markle. "And I should know. We were kids together in Kiev, grew up in one house, eh, Jake?" Poke, poke.

"And these are yours?" pursued the relentless Mrs. Markle, jerking her head in my direction. I felt sorry for her. She really thought she had a chance; she really thought Nankie had brought her there to meet Papa, when the fact was she was just a front. It wouldn't do for Nankie to come by herself and say: "Look at me. I'd be a good wife for you." Instead, she brought the most hopeless person she could think of so she would look a hundred percent better than her.

"They're good children," Nankie spoke up and smiled at us and noticed for the first time my tight disapproving expression. Her smile caught on the hook of my frown and came unraveled. Our eyes held and with my heart beating in dull thuds I felt my sudden power over her. A tinge of red brushed her cheeks, and her eyes dropped. "Yes," she said then, in a more subdued voice, "They are nice, fine children. Of course. Their mother was a fine lady." She straightened in her chair a little so most of her bosom was hidden by the folds of her dress, and now, demurely, she smiled at me. "Still," she said, "they need somebody around the house. Somebody who could cook and look after them. Somebody who knows them already, and understands them."

Me, she meant. Somebody like me. You need me. I wondered if Papa realized the real candidate was sitting next to him. But he'd have to be dumb, I thought, not to know. And Papa wasn't dumb.

Mrs. Markle began to talk about her first two husbands and her problems with them. The chair creaked loudly under her as she sat, both feet solidly rooted on the floor, hands creasing the flowered material of the dress across her lap.

"The first one, rest him, died of a heart attack," she sighed. "The other one, in the mental hospital." She gave Papa an appraising look. "How's your health?"

"So far," Papa said coldly, "it's good. I can't complain."

Mrs. Markle seemed relieved but before she could say anything else, Edna leaned forward. "Did we tell you this Mrs. Markle is a cook? She used to work for a caterer. Did you know Hammerstein's? Well, she worked there five years before they went out of business. It doesn't hurt to know it. Some people can cook, some can't."

Nankie suddenly thought of something and poked Papa's arm again. "Did you stop to think how strong is this Mrs. Markle; she could help you in the store? Lifting boxes, you wouldn't have to move a finger?" It was as though she'd forgotten that Mrs. Markle wasn't the real candidate. She smiled into Papa's face. He took a long breath.

"I'll have to think about it."

"What's to think about?" Nankie urged. "This is a golden chance. You shouldn't need to think about it."

In the background, Mrs. Markle listened attentively, smiling, nodding, shifting her body. The chair creaked savagely, the sound spearing into our ears.

"And you want to know how she is with money? It

grows by her; like some people have a green thumb with plants, with her it's money!" Nankie seemed so genuinely eager to convince Papa she had grabbed his sleeve and now held on to his arm, leaning on it with most of her bosom, ignoring my incensed loud breathing.

Papa removed his arm from her clutch. "I'm not ready yet to talk about it," he said. "I'll let you know." He looked directly at Mrs. Markle who seemed to take this as consent, and in her pleasure, she lifted one leg to cross it over the other. The chair jiggled wildly for a moment, then collapsed. There was a stunned silence during which we stared at her as she sat in the wreckage, her legs sprawled apart, large white bloomers leering from underneath the flowered dress. For one moment her expression was blank, then the smile returned. I whirled away grabbing onto Simply Simon and we both fell down laughing. We laughed alone. Crawling on my hands and knees, I dragged myself into the kitchen and sat on the floor until I could stop the convulsions that had taken hold of me. I kept both hands firmly plastered to my face to smother the fresh outbursts that threatened to keep me from thinking clearly and I wanted to think clearly. Because I knew now what had happened. Somehow, she had been given the chair that nobody used anymore, the one that Mama had fallen from a year ago. Somehow—and who else could have done it but Mama?

I wiped the tears that rolled out of my eyes every time I visualized the collapse of the chair, seeing it all in slow motion, the legs flying apart, the blank stare, the just as blank smile following. A fresh storm of giggles took hold of me.

I stood up and leaned against the sink, feeling Mama very close to me. I got myself a drink of water. Mama was in charge of the situation. I had nothing to worry about. But did she know that it was really Nankie and not Mrs. Markle who was after Papa? I wondered why she hadn't done something to Nankie.

Papa came into the kitchen, the remains of the chair in his hands, with Simply Simon right behind him carrying the rest of it. They opened the back door which led into the summer kitchen and tossed the pieces in there. Papa gave me a grim look. "She could have been hurt," he told me curtly.

"I didn't do anything, Papa!" I gave him my most innocent stare. "I hope you're not blaming *me*!"

He turned and walked away from me. I looked at Simply Simon. "Well, I didn't!" I told him. He shrugged. "Neither did I."

I leaned my face to his ear and whispered, "Somebody is helping us, so don't worry. We're not going to get a stepmother!"

He looked interested. "Who is it?" But I wouldn't tell.

Auntie Sadie came in soon after that, carrying a shopping bag. "Well," she said to me. "Don't just sit. Put this in the kitchen." I could see she was still mad over the Miss Blustein affair.

"What is it?" I took it out of her hands.

"You'll look and you'll see."

Papa prudently left us and went into the store. Although nobody had gone in yet, he could always find something to do to keep busy. I tried to imagine them as children and I was sure she'd bossed him around plenty in those days. Poor Papa—nothing had changed for him. Auntie Sadie didn't wait long before she flounced into the store. I could hear her voice all the way into the kitchen. "I haven't got all day and I want to talk to you."

They came into the house, Papa looking on the defensive.

"I hope you're satisfied."

Papa looked at her then. "What? What are you babbling now?"

"You threw away your best chance to get them a good mother."

"Are you crazy or what? What are you talking about? That same one?"

"Yes, that same one. What's wrong, she's not good enough? Eh? You need maybe a raving beauty?"

Papa glared at her, breathing deeply. "Look Sadie, I know you mean well but please leave me alone already. I can't think yet about getting married. I just want peace. And how does it look, talking about another wedding when there isn't even a stone on her grave yet."

"So we can put a stone on her grave. We got enough time for that."

"It should be done first."

"Look, a rabbi you are, you always have to do things by the book? A little less religious and a little more normal wouldn't hurt you. The stone can go on her grave after you're married just as easy."

"The way you talk sometimes, Sadie." Papa gave her a look of utter disgust.

"There's nothing wrong with the way I talk." Auntie Sadie drew herself up majestically. "Now, we'll get down to business. You'll maybe have one more chance. I know she didn't look like much when you saw her, but I think I talked her into doing her hair in a beauty parlor. She's only thirty years old, and she doesn't have to look like that. I don't know why she does it. Anyway, I'll bring her over tonight. Keep those brats upstairs so you can both get to know each other better. You didn't really get a chance before."

Papa threw his hands up, walking away, but she walked behind him, still talking. "I brought over a sponge cake and some kuchen. Over tea with just three of us there"—she eyed me severely—"maybe we can get someplace."

I glared at her. Why did she have to butt into our lives? But then I remembered and smiled. Somebody was making sure that everything would be all right. I could relax and forget it. "Anything you say, Auntie Sadie *dear!*" I cooed in my phoniest, sugariest voice.

Such was her suspicious nature that she merely glared at me and waggled a warning finger in my face. And I hadn't even done anything.


**4** Later, it seemed incredible to me that I had ever worried about Miss Blustein. Miss Blustein with her hair done up was still Miss Blustein, still timid, stealing quick glances at us from under her finger wave, pulling down the skirt of her gray shapeless dress. Miss Blustein was a zero. Even Nankie, I soon discovered, paled in importance when Miss Cohen appeared on the scene. Miss Cohen stood out as The Enemy the minute she arrived.

The really strange part about it was that Miss Cohen wore her hair essentially the same way as Miss Blustein, coiled into a bun at the back. Her dress was a waistless brown and her shoes were more noted for their wearing qualities than for their beauty or glamor. At the first impact, as she entered our house behind Auntie Leah, I had experienced relief. She was no gorgeous movie star type and Papa wouldn't fall in love with her. I pegged her as another Miss Blustein, in fact. But that was just the first impact.

Auntie Leah, ushering her in, turned to smile at her protégé. Miss Cohen smiled back, the unremarkable face on the long slender neck taking on an unexpected glow. Miss Cohen's eyes, a deep brown, penetrated beneath the surface of our combined passivity as if she knew there was a certain amount of resistance to be overcome. Her teeth were even and white, the lips faintly pink, as though she had worn lipstick but taken most of it off.

"Sylvia"—Auntie Leah's voice lifted with confidence— "I want you should meet my brother-in-law, Jake. Jake this is Sylvia Cohen that I was telling you about that comes from my village Kasrilevke, only she's here since she was a little girl."

Miss Cohen stepped forward, her smile widening at Papa, her hand outstretched towards him. Papa seemed stunned by such straightforwardness, his hand rising to grip hers. I stared at their clasped hands, my heart making funny little leaps inside me. Mama, I whispered in my head, do something, do something fast. "I'm so glad to meet you," Miss Cohen said with a smile. "Leah keeps talking about you, and I couldn't help being curious."

Papa didn't know what to say. He nodded, still shaking her hand, not quite smiling but not looking very grim either.

"And here are the children," Auntie Leah said, one hand on Miss Cohen's arm. "This is Becky, she's the oldest, ten years old now. . . ."

The full power of Miss Cohen's smile was turned on me. She somehow extricated her hand from Papa's and held it out to me. I resisted her magnetic joy with difficulty, keeping Mama as a shield between us, but I couldn't do less than shake the proffered hand without looking rude and maybe incurring Papa's wrath.

"Hello, Becky," she said softly. "I've heard a lot about you from your Auntie Leah."

Her hand felt warm and friendly yet I pulled away from her at the earliest moment so our contact was a quicksilver one and said nothing. I was relieved when Auntie Leah continued with the introductions so the full effect of her personality was directed next at Simply Simon. "And this is Saul, just turned nine years old." Auntie Leah beamed.

I watched him, incredulous at his sudden movement towards her as she shook his hand.

"I've heard a lot about you too, Saul," she smiled, and he said:

"How do you do?" just as if he were Little Lord Fauntleroy!

Auntie Leah smiled all around. "Get chairs, Becky," she said, and I hurried to comply. Mama, I thought, you'll have to think of something real fast because I think this one *maybe* is a human being and not a shvartz yor. So you better do something, if you're going to.

I hung over the back of a chair and studied her as they sat and chatted about the weather. No, she wasn't beautiful— in fact, she was plain in a way. With her high broad forehead under its sweep of brown hair and the straight black eyebrows, she didn't look Jewish or any particular religion. If I'd seen her on the street, casually, I wouldn't have known what to make of her. But her smile lit her face with brightness, the eyes coming alive, warmth emanating from her.

Simply Simon had pulled a chair up next to hers, and it didn't surprise me in the least. I knew from the moment he had responded to her handshake that he had turned traitor.

She crossed her knees, body turned towards Papa, and I heard her say in a low pleasant-sounding voice: "I decided, that after teaching school for ten years, I'd had enough."

A schoolteacher! What could be worse than having a schoolteacher living with you? This was as bad as it could get. But suddenly I remembered something Papa had said, and I relaxed. He couldn't possibly be interested in her. He had as good as promised me that he wouldn't get married for ten years. I looked at him, at the way his lips were pointing upwards at the corners, not actually smiling but the next thing to it. He sat listening, nodding, more than ordinarily polite, and I had it in me to remind him of his promise just in case he forgot. Except that wasn't something you did in front of . . . of . . . strangers.

Auntie Leah looked pleased with herself, her arms folded over her broad chest, her eyes going from Papa to Miss Cohen and back again, and I couldn't understand how she could do it. How could she, when I could still, if I closed my eyes, see her and Mama hugging each other at the door on the Friday night of my birthday—the last happy day of my life if I'd only known it then.

"You're a teacher ten years already?" Papa said, in an utterly sickening way. "You don't even look old enough!"

She laughed, throwing her head back, doing it in a graceful gesture so I hated her for it. "What a lovely compliment!" she said, her eyes sparkling. "I didn't know you were so gallant!"

I tried to remember when, if ever, Papa had paid Mama a compliment like that. Never, that I had heard.

"Yes," she continued smoothly, "ten years, and believe me, Mr. Devine, I am old enough." Her voice poured the words out as if she spoke her own true language, English, as if she didn't have to mentally translate everything she wanted to say from Jewish first. I wondered how Jewish she could be—like Betty Greenberg's family? Or real, like us. I decided she wasn't very Jewish after all and it wouldn't take Papa long to find out even if Mama didn't somehow intervene the way she had with Mrs. Markle.

Suddenly she switched the subject, looking at me as if she sensed my hostility, my thoughts like spears stabbing into her mind. "How do you like school, Becky?" she asked me, looking almost as if she cared, not smiling anymore.

I shrugged. "It's okay, I guess." Did she really think I would take her into my confidence? I wasn't a traitor like *some* people in this family.

"Your Auntie Leah tells me you like to read." She smiled at me. "That's very good. I'm sure you must do well at school."

I tossed a quick annoyed look at the beaming Auntie Leah. Blabbermouth! What else did she tell her about me that was none of anybody's business? I pressed my lips together, feeling almost like Auntie Sadie in my rigidity. That shook me for a moment so I unstuck my lips, my mouth coming open. But I did *not* smile. And I wouldn't, even if they held a gun to my head. I could feel Papa's eyes on me, and I knew he was going to be mad at me later, but I knew what I had to do. If I was the only one in this family who could remember Mama, that was too bad for them. That was their problem, not mine. Nobody would be able to say later that I let somebody step into Mama's shoes before she even got cold in her grave. And if there was one thing I knew, it was that Mama didn't want anyone to take her place. Especially not someone like Miss Cohen—a *schoolteacher!*

After a short while, Miss Cohen rose and extended her hand to Papa. "I hope," she said smiling, "that we can get together again very soon. It's been delightful visiting with you, all of you," and she glanced at Simply Simon but avoided looking at me. My heart thumped so loudly I was sure she could hear it. So she knew we were enemies, and would now be on her guard!

Papa shook her hand and seemed reluctant to let go.

"When will you come again?" he asked, so I felt embarrassed for him. To act so eager!

"Maybe next week." She glanced out the window. "I have some meetings with parents coming up, but I'll keep one day next week free."

Papa nodded. "We can talk again then."

I had to shake her hand before she left. There was no way out of it but I kept my eyes on our hands and I didn't wear any particular expression on my face. Papa wouldn't be able to say I was nasty with her. I was polite, that was all.

"Very nice," Papa said to me sarcastically when they were gone. "Would it hurt you to smile? What did she do to you that you acted like that?"

Tears sprang to my eyes. "You promised! You promised, and you're breaking your promise!"

"What are you talking about?"

"You said you didn't want to get married again. You said you couldn't even think about it. But you're thinking about it. I can tell!"

Papa looked at me and licked his lips, and all the steam had gone out of him. He didn't have a single word to say.

When I came home from school the day after that, Auntie Leah sat in the front room, her hands in her lap. She seemed very nervous for some reason but since she was no longer my favorite relative, I didn't care. I thought about ignoring her but habit was too strong in me. She was still Auntie Leah, the jolly one.

"Hi," I said laconically, "does Papa know you're here?" She was sitting by herself.

"Yes," she said, patting the seat beside her. "I didn't come to talk to Papa."

"Then, why?" I slowly sat beside her.

"You, that's why," she said meaningfully.

"Oh." In that case, I didn't think I wanted to sit there at all and made a motion as if to rise but she anticipated me and held me down.

"I want to talk to you, Becky, so just sit."

I knew already what she would say and I didn't want to hear it. It wouldn't make any difference anyway. She couldn't change my mind about how I felt and I couldn't change anything that was going to happen either. Only Mama could do that, maybe. . . .

"Becky. Beckala . . . try to understand why we're doing this. Try to listen with a grown-up heart."

I scrunched my eyes up tight, held my hands into tight fists. I didn't want to listen with a grown-up heart, I wasn't grown up; it wasn't fair for her to ask me to be what I wasn't. I didn't want to be sweetly reasonable, the way she assumed I should be. Her voice was like warm oil, oozing into the dried-up corners of my heart, and if I wasn't careful, it would loosen my hardened emotions. I didn't want them loosened. I liked them stiff that way. It saved me a lot of trouble.

She put her hand on my fist, tried to undo my fingers. "You see, it isn't good for a man to be alone all his life. Try to think about Papa. And another thing, it isn't good for a girl not to have someone to take care of her. Miss Cohen is very nice and I'm not saying just because she's the daughter of my landsman. Everybody likes her. . . ."

"Oh yeah? Then how come she isn't married yet?"

"It's a long story and it isn't your business anyway. Believe me when I say she's the best your Papa could ever find if he looked for many years."

"I don't care about years. I care about right now. I care about Mama!"

She looked shocked. "You think *we* don't? You think you're the only one?"

"Mama doesn't want anyone to take her place."

"Where did you get such an idea? Mama is gone. It doesn't matter to her anymore."

"It does *so* matter to her. And I *know* she doesn't want anybody to marry Papa."

Auntie Leah looked exasperated. She made a conscious effort to hold her temper. She sighed and scratched her head. Then she looked at me, turning my face towards her. I moved my eyes sideways away from her face. "Becky. Do you understand what death is? When someone dies, they are dead. Do you understand that?" I stared at the ceiling above her head. She shook me a little. "Dead people don't feel things anymore. It doesn't matter to them what the living do. Do you understand that?" There was a crack in the ceiling there I'd never noticed before. My eyes traced the crack to its source.

"I'm going to tell you a secret that only you will know. When I die, if I die first, I hope that Uncle Dave will find somebody nice to marry so he won't be alone. It's terrible to be alone. Will you remember?"

I shrugged, not impressed. She could say that now. She wasn't going to die. She wasn't in the least danger of dying for a long time yet. *She* wasn't about to have a baby, as far as I could tell.

"Now, you can be sure, Becky, that your Mama felt the same way as me, only with more reason. Because when you leave small children, you don't want them to be without a mother. You want and hope that somebody will come and be good to them, to take as good care of them as you would."

"Ha! You just said the dead can't feel anything. Now you're saying that they want somebody to take care of their children. Make up your mind!"

Auntie Leah stared at me, her mouth partly open, eyes blinking. She shook her head slightly and leaned away from me, dropping her hands. I kind of still liked her, in spite of what she had done to us, and I hated to see her so confused, so I gave her another chance at me. "If Papa gets married, the person he marries becomes a stepmother." I said this with an air of great finality, as irrefutable logic. She didn't seem to see the significance.

"So?"

"So? Didn't you ever hear about stepmothers? The things they do? I mean, why are they called wicked?"

"Who calls them wicked?" She looked more confused than before.

I couldn't believe that somebody as old as Auntie Leah could be so innocent, so naive. "You mean you never heard about wicked stepmothers? *Everybody's* heard about wicked stepmothers!"

"Maybe in fairy stories, not for really."

"You mean, fairy *tales*. And if they're wicked in fairy *tales*, it's because there really are such things, in Real Life."

Auntie Leah brushed it aside with a gesture of her hand.

"Miss Cohen never did a mean thing in her life. Why should she change just because she becomes a stepmother?"

"Well, gee whiz, she's even a *schoolteacher*! She could do anything." As far as I was concerned, the proof was right there, plain for anyone to see. "Anyway, I don't see why Papa has to get married so soon. Why can't he wait?"

Auntie Leah looked suddenly hopeful. "Well, nobody said they're going to get married right away. How long do you think they ought to wait?" I could see she was holding her breath, waiting for my answer.

"Well, what's wrong with them waiting about ten years?"

On the other side of the wall, in the store, something went crash, and I knew Papa had been listening.


**5** When people die, I wrote in my scribbler, they're not really dead. They are somewhere. I tried to think where that somewhere could be. During the Seders at Pesach when I couldn't find Mama in any of the corners of the room, Auntie Leah had leaned towards me. Sometimes, she seemed able to read my mind.

"Even if you can't see Mama," she had said then, "Mama is with us. You remember that." She had tapped herself on the plump bosom. "Here is where she is, in the heart."

I had stared at Auntie Leah's bosom, wondering if it was true. Was Mama really in the heart? But how could she be? She was too big to fit into such a small space, even one the size of Auntie Leah's. I looked up at the ceiling, all the four corners of it, but there was no sign of her and Auntie Leah kept looking at me, tapping her chest ominously, as though she were sending me an important message. I shrugged. Unless Mama could make herself awfully small, Auntie Leah had to be wrong. But she could make herself invisible, so maybe she had been there after all.

It was hard to know what to believe. I bit the end of my

pencil, staring at the words I had written. One day Auntie Leah says Mama is in the heart, then another time she says she is dead, gone. Both times, she is absolutely serious, and Auntie Leah doesn't lie, does she? But she can't be right both times. Once she wasn't telling the truth. Which time was that?

If Mama really was in the heart, I decided, it wouldn't be Auntie Leah's. It would be mine. After all, who was a closer relative? I looked down at myself, trying to feel the extra weight inside me. I felt the same as always. Yet, she must be with me, I thought, because I sometimes can hear her whispering.

I heard her whispering later when Miss Cohen knocked at our door. She didn't whisper words, just a hissing sort of sound inside me. I opened the door, knowing in advance that it would be Miss Cohen. The hissing inside me said so.

It was a shock to see her. She had taken some pains with her appearance, her hair curled loosely around her face and she wore a filmy feminine kind of dress which made her look kind of pretty.

"Hello, Becky."

"Hello."

"May I come in?"

I stepped aside and pulled the door wider. "Papa is in the store. I'll get him."

"Wait." She caught my arm. "If he's busy, I can wait. Please don't disturb him."

I felt awkward, not knowing what to do and wished Simply Simon was around. He never was, when you needed him.

"Let's just sit and talk," she said, smiling, and walked into the room towards the chair. I watched her silently. I have to be polite, I told myself, so Papa won't be ashamed and Mama won't turn in her grave. *If* that's where Mama is. I looked down at myself, in case Mama, having abandoned the grave and climbed into my heart, should think I wanted to be polite. I didn't really.

"Would you like some tea?" It would be an excuse to

escape those brown eyes on me.

"No thank you. Why don't you sit here beside me?"

I was trapped. I pushed the chair back a few feet before I slid into it, facing her.

"You don't like me, do you?" She smiled uncertainly.

I stiffened, heat rushing into my face. It wasn't the kind of thing you'd expect an adult to say. It was more a child's remark and I felt she had violated something, a code of sorts.

"It's all right, Becky," she said, surprising me again. "I do understand. As a matter of fact, I'd be rather disappointed if you accepted me right away. You must love your mother very much!"

I held my breath. My heart was being squeezed so tightly. It beat in solemn strokes, rising upwards, pushing something ahead of it into my throat. I clenched my teeth together so it couldn't get out. I was afraid I might vomit.

"How do you like school?" The question, so impersonal, hung in the air, giving me a chance to swallow. She waited, her eyes bright and interested.

"I don't like school. I hate it. And teachers too." I looked her straight in the eye. If she was going to be so understanding, let her understand that.

"Oh?" Her smile wasn't as firm as before. "Any reason?"

"They pick on me, that's why. They're mean and they give kids too much homework."

"Oh. Yes, homework. I remember I used to feel the same way about homework, and I don't suppose I cared much for teachers either." She laughed suddenly, throwing back her head in the same gesture she had used before, completely natural. "I had a teacher who was so mean . . ." She threw a quick glance at me, her eyes mischievous.

"What did she used to do?" I was curious in spite of myself.

"Oh—terrible things. I got strapped once, for talking!"

"You didn't!" A schoolteacher? I couldn't believe it.

"Oh, I was far from perfect, you know. But look at me now—a teacher myself! When I was your age, I'd never have

116

believed that I would turn into one of them!"

"Well, I sure won't!"

"Nobody knows anything for sure," she said gaily. "Why, you could be anything you wanted to be! What would that be, I wonder?" Her eyes gleamed with speculation. "A model? A movie star? Hmm . . ."

I looked at her. Well, she must think I'm dumb! As if she could trick me into giving myself away! I wouldn't tell her anything.

"I don't know."

She smiled gently. "Well, you have plenty of time to make up your mind."

There was an awkward pause. I wished that I had gone and told Papa right away instead of being trapped with her. I stood up stiffly. "I'll get Papa now," I told her, and left. Papa would be furious with me if I spent an hour talking with *his* company, instead of letting him spend the time with her.

Papa was kneeling behind the cooler, straightening it up when I stopped beside him. He glanced up at me.

"She's here," I said.

"What?" Then a light came into his eyes and he rose to his feet. He began to remove his store apron. "Why didn't you let me know right away?"

"I am!" I couldn't help being angry with him for acting so happy. He was like a stranger when he looked like that. He went into the house but I stayed in the store so I wouldn't have to see them greet each other and hold hands, and gaze into each other's eyes like a couple of . . . of . . . I didn't know what. Besides, I didn't want Mama to see them either, and she would if she looked out through my skin.

Just to pay Papa back for what he was doing to Mama and me, I helped myself to some candy from the glass case . . . a whole handful, and it served him right. I stuffed some caramels into my mouth and as I chewed on it and felt it sticking to my teeth so I could hardly pull them apart, I leaned on the counter, listening to the soft murmur of their voices from the house. The more I listened the more I felt Papa owed me something, so I added licorice sticks to my loot and buttons of peppermint pasted on cardboard and several melting bits of chocolate. I chewed, sucked and drooled, the sweetness disappearing down my throat, and told myself that it served him right that I was eating up the profits. And I would eat up a lot more. So there.

The sun came through the big window on the Boyd Avenue side of the store, gleaming in bright angled lines across the ledge of the window, where cigarettes were displayed, and onto the wooden floor that needed some sweeping up, and then up the side and top of the counter where I stood. A finger of sunlight crept up my bare arm, leaving a warm scar all the way to my shoulder. It flashed in a dazzle of gold on the cans of vegetables on shelves behind me. Half blinded by it all, I went into the house, past Papa and Miss Cohen who sat talking together earnestly, and without even looking at them, I got my coat off its hanger, shoved my arms through the sleeves, and went outside.

What had I seen out of the corners of my eyes? Papa leaning towards her, his hands in his lap, Miss Cohen very composed. They hadn't jumped guiltily apart, the way lovers in movies always did. I decided they weren't real lovers, not yet.

I sat on the front steps. The rough splintered wood jabbed me so I was careful to have enough layers of cloth between me and the step and wondered what she thought about our house. Did it look poor and crumby to her? After all, she was probably used to better things, nicer furniture, for instance. Well, it was good enough for us, and for Mama. It would be plenty good enough for someone like *her*.

I walked over to the gate which hung open, and leaned on it. It creaked maddeningly, a sound I liked. I wondered how Miss Cohen would feel about it if I swung on the gate like this, and it went: squueee—eak, squueee—eak. Would she go out of her mind? Mama had always come to the door and yelled at me. Why can't you act like a lady? Ladies don't do like that. Then I don't want to be a lady, I want to stay a kid forever, I used to say to myself. I wouldn't say it out loud, of course.

I leaned across the gate so my head hung down and let it swing back and forth, the blood rushing to my head, a sickening dizzy feeling coming over me. The sidewalk looked close. If I reached out with my hand, I could touch it. If Papa married her, would she say: Why can't you act like a lady? That was exactly the kind of thing you'd expect a school-teacher to say. Would she say other things too, like: You're too young to know. When the time is right, then I'll tell you? Or: Go away now and play outside. I haven't got any time to talk to you. What was the use of going outside to play? I didn't have anybody to play with. I didn't have any friends who lived close enough to us, and nobody wanted to be bothered with me. Not even my own mother.

Papa loved me. I was sure of it, surer than I had ever been before. Mama had loved me too, but she'd never had time for me. I wished we were rich. Rich people seemed to have more time to spend with their families, and they did things like go for rides in their car. I didn't really care about a car. I didn't care if we never owned one. They were ugly and they smelled bad.

What was going on in the house? Were they still talking? What did strangers have to talk about anyway? Were they talking about me? The edge of the gate bit into my stomach. I straightened up, my head feeling light as the world swam before my eyes. Mrs. Wurster appeared in front of me so suddenly, I was sure she had materialized out of the air. But of course, witches could do that sort of thing with their eyes shut.

"Hallo, Becky!" I was surprised she knew my name. "What are you doing?" She looked almost pleasant . . . for her anyway.

Anybody could see what I was doing. Nothing. I looked at her, waiting for the next question.

"Is your father busy?"

"He sure is busy. Horribly busy."

She became conspiratorial. "What kind of food does he like to eat? What's his favorite supper?"

"Why?" It wasn't any of her business.

"Oh, I just want to make him something special, a special meal you all like to eat!" Her protruding eyes seemed about to pop out of her head at me.

"Frog soup," I said with relish ... "with lots of pork and bacon and ham!"

She reared back, staring at me as though I had grown another head, as though I'd turned into a monster. Maybe she would turn me into one, I thought, my heart pounding at my daring, but all she did was turn and scuttle back across the street to her house. I wondered why she didn't use her broomstick. If I could fly on one, I'd never walk anywhere. I watched her for a minute, thinking. Why did she want to make something special for Papa? Was she going to put a curse on him, or what? Or maybe she meant to do some magic that would get him to marry her. Imagine being married to a witch, imagine having a witch for a stepmother! I shuddered, then walked over to the skinny elm tree on the boulevard in front of our house. I touched the rough bark and looked down at the frowzy grass. Suddenly I remembered the grave Simply Simon and I had made for the little frozen bird. I looked down to see if the bird was still there. I couldn't find the spot; grass grew all around the tree.

With a stick I dug in the approximate place where we'd buried it, stirring up the earth under the tree. I didn't really think about the bird as I dug. I let me mind go pleasantly blank, just digging away.... I turned a clod of earth over and there it lay in the shallow grave, a hunk of something stiff, ugly. Bones! I got to my feet and kicked the clumps of earth back where I'd taken them from. Hide it, hide the dead thing. It was ugly, ugly! Death was ugly!

The front door opened. Papa beckoned me in with a jerk of his head. I walked quickly away from the tree. I didn't want to think about it anymore. It was only a bird. It wasn't human!

Miss Cohen hadn't left her chair. As I walked in, she smiled faintly at me. My heart began a dull thudding. I felt as though hands were at my throat, strangling me. Were they going to make an Announcement?

"Where is Saul?" Papa wanted to know.

"I haven't seen him for hours." I shrugged.

They *must* be going to make an Announcement, I thought, or why would Papa want to know where Simply Simon was? So she had won. Well, she wasn't going to win with me.

"Sit down," Papa said. "We should get to know each other better."

Why? He couldn't fool me. He was going to marry her and she would be my stepmother. With Mama in her grave, looking like . . . No! Mama was in my heart. What was she thinking? Looking at Miss Cohen, her rival, what did Mama think of the whole thing?

Miss Cohen didn't look like a wicked stepmother. In pictures that I had seen in my storybooks, they had slanted eyes that shone with triumph, and thin narrow faces and wide collars that came above their sleek black hair. But even if she didn't look like one yet, that was understandable. She hadn't married Papa yet.

Wicked stepmothers usually got rid of the unwanted child by poisoning it or something. Or maybe she would try to lose us in the woods. I had never seen any woods; I didn't have the faintest idea where we would find woods in the city, but I was willing to bet five million dollars that Miss Cohen knew where they were.

I couldn't find the triumph in her eyes. They looked sad in fact, or was it scared? I couldn't think of a single reason why she should be afraid. *She* wasn't going to have a stepmother. Anyway, she had Papa on her side. I had Mama. Maybe Mama had power . . . maybe she had more power in some things than Papa did. Look how she got rid of Mrs. Markle!

I thought again of the little brown bird and how it had changed. I didn't want to imagine Mama . . . Anyway, I reminded myself, she wasn't in the grave, remember? She had escaped from everybody that day to come and visit me; she couldn't very well crawl into the ground after that, could she? Besides, I thought, you know she's really in your heart like

Auntie Leah said. That's why she could go out and do things, and one way or another, she would get rid of Miss Cohen.

I hoped Mama wouldn't hurt her. It wasn't her fault if she wanted to marry Papa. She just didn't know. Probably it seemed all right for her to marry a man and cook for him and his kids as long as she hadn't ever known Mama. She might even be a nice person for all I knew. Auntie Leah liked her. . . .

"You're very quiet," Miss Cohen said. I couldn't think of a thing to say.

"Would you like me to come down and give you some help with your schoolwork?"

"No thank you," I said stiffly. My voice sounded prim to me but I wasn't going to give her any extra excuses to come to our house. Anyhow, I knew something would happen to her if she tried it. I suddenly became convinced that Papa wouldn't ever be able to get married. Mama would see to that.

"Oh, I wish you'd let me, Becky! You'd be surprised how much easier work is when you understand it better."

The store bell tinkled and Papa excused himself. Now I was stuck there and would have to be polite again. Why didn't that dumb brother of mine show up so at least I wouldn't have that job all to myself?

I sat on the edge of my chair, feeling her eyes on my face. It made me uncomfortable.

"Becky, I wish we could be friends. . . ."

It was a heartrending cry. I felt sorry for her, but what could I say? It wasn't anything personal. I wished I could explain but I was sure she wouldn't understand about Mama. You were supposed to hate your enemy, but I couldn't quite hate Miss Cohen. "Can't we be friends?"

"Sure, if you want to." They were only words. If Mama wanted to make something out of them there was nothing I could do about it.

Papa returned quickly so I knew he'd gotten rid of the customer as soon as possible. "Maybe Miss Cohen would like some tea?"

"No," she said. "Thank you. I think it's about time I

was leaving anyway; I didn't mean to stay so long." She rose, clutching her brown handbag.

"So soon?" Papa's voice drizzled with regret. They walked to the door together while I sat, my toe wound around the chair rung. I felt like a spectator in a movie house watching a film. They didn't seem like real people to me.

"I don't want to overstay my welcome. . . ."

"Maybe the next time, you could have supper with us? Nothing fancy but . . ."

"Perhaps next time. Thank you very much."

"When will you come again?"

"Should I come tomorrow?"

"Good. Then tomorrow you will stay for supper?"

"I'd like that very much."

"Don't forget."

"How could I possibly forget?"

I went to the side window and looked out over Powers Street. They were hard to listen to for any length of time. I looked at the dried ruts where wagon wheels had bitten deep and piles of horse dung where they had been dropped by passing horses. The soft voices went on and on, seemingly forever. I glanced over my shoulder at them. They were shaking hands.

"After a while," Papa said, "they'll get used to it. Then it will be better."

"I hope you're right," she said.

I looked out of the window till I heard the door close. Then Papa went back into the store without speaking to me. Already, without even moving in, she had come between us.

**6** Simply Simon sat whittling on a stick, chips flying as though he didn't have a care in the world. I sat, my chin on my hands, and watched him, wishing we could trade places. For one thing, he didn't have Mama in his heart, listening in on all his thoughts, and for another, he didn't have Papa mad at him. How did I ever get into this, I wondered? Why did it have to be me?

It irritated me to see him so cheerful.

"Just you wait! When you have *her* for a mother, things'll be a lot different. She won't let you do *that* anymore!" I had to lower my voice so Papa wouldn't hear me. He'd been in the kitchen for a couple of hours already, cooking a fancy supper. When I'd offered to help him, to get back in his good graces, he'd said curtly:

"Never mind. Just stay out of the kitchen."

What did he think I'd do? Poison her or something?

"She's not that bad," Simply Simon said, brushing all the bits of wood together. "She seems pretty nice to me."

"Oh, that's *now*. That's just until she gets into the family. Then she'll show her true self to us. That's when you'll have to watch out." A thought occurred to me.

"Besides, she's a schoolteacher!"

The door opened and Auntie Sadie barged in. I looked up. She seemed in her usual humor: bad. "Where's Papa?"

I jerked my head in the direction of the kitchen. She marched in, standing just inside the doorway, her back to us.

Papa said genially: "Hello, Sadie. I didn't see you around here lately."

"Don't tell me you missed me."

"So you want to be mad."

"Mad? Who's mad? I just came to find out for myself if what Leah says is true. She brought you Cohen and it's practically a shiddach? From her I don't believe it. From you . . . maybe."

"It's true."

"I don't believe it." Auntie Sadie's back arched indignantly. "I don't believe it! *Her?* After all the trouble I went through, you should get married again, mine you don't like and hers you do?"

"What's that got to do with? Is that what's important? Whose I marry is more important than that it should be with a mensh?"

"Why did it have to be Leah's?" Auntie Sadie was almost in tears. "It could have been Nankie's even, I wouldn't mind, but Leah's so she can have her nose in the air over it, and I can't keep my head up?"

"Why can't you keep your head up? What difference does it make? Sadie, you're impossible. Nankie's was like something should be in a cage. Should I marry just anybody to keep you happy?"

"That's not the point. I'm your sister. How's it going to look for me?"

"I don't care how it looks. As long as I don't have a shvartz yor for a wife, I don't care."

"Are you calling my friend Blustein a shvartz yor? That's the thanks I get. Always, I try my best for you, and who says thank you?"

"Sadie, I appreciate. Believe me. But please, let me make up my own mind. I'm the one who has to live with her, and if you think it's easy to decide to get married again, I can tell you, it isn't."

Auntie Sadie abruptly changed the subject.

"What are you making?"

"A roast. With potatoes and gravy, carrots. Nothing fancy."

There was a long and heavy pause, then Papa's voice added unconvincingly: "Would you like to eat supper with us?"

"No. I didn't come here for an invitation. I only came because I couldn't stand her putting her nose in the air over her shiddach. I understand she's an old-maid schoolteacher."

I could visualize Papa's face; I could imagine the purple color it was turning. But he didn't say one word, and I was positive I could hear him breathing heavily. Suddenly, Auntie Sadie stood beside me.

"This house," she said with deep satisfaction, "looks a mess. I never in all my born days saw such a mess. Like ten galoots had a party here." Then she walked grandly out the door, her head held majestically high.

By the time Miss Cohen arrived, we had straightened things up enough so it didn't look like any galoots had held a party there.

Supper passed quietly and pleasantly, and then Papa said: "If you're finished, Becky, you can clean off the table. Saul you help her."

Miss Cohen started to rise. "Oh, let me wash the dishes."

Papa said: "No. No, Becky can do it. She's good around the house. You're a guest here."

She allowed herself to be led out of the kitchen. I knew she hadn't really meant it anyway. She could have argued with Papa. I was tired of doing the dishes all the time. "Come on, slowpoke!" I took it out on Simply Simon. "Get the stuff off the table!" I didn't want to spend the whole evening in the kitchen.

He brought a few things and grinned at me, dropping them onto the counter beside me. "You can get the rest," he informed me. "I'm not a girl, and anyway, I want to get to know Papa's girlfriend better."

"Papa's girlfriend!" I hissed. "Don't you dare call her that in front of him. He'll kill you!"

Simply Simon pranced out, leaving me everything as usual. Well, this would show her, I thought. This would show her that I could handle everything myself. We didn't really need her. What were they talking about anyway? What kind of plans were they making without me? I felt sad. Life always had to get so complicated. I didn't know why. If only Mama hadn't decided to have another baby!

The dishwater was cold as ice, leaving a coating of

grease on the plates and cutlery. It made it almost impossible to do a good job on the dishes, but I did the best I could and put them away.

They were discussing the grocery business.

"You're right of course, Jake. Still, you shouldn't be forced to carry customers on your books indefinitely. *You* have to pay the suppliers; the wholesalers don't give *you* credit."

"That's true," Papa conceded, "but if you ask them for your money, they go someplace else and then you never collect."

"There must be *some* way." Miss Cohen's brows puckered in thought. "Surely something could be done!"

Ho-hum, I thought. It certainly wasn't the way it would be in the movies. I could just imagine Robert Taylor and Barbara Stanwyck talking together about deadbeat customers. Mama, you have nothing to worry about. She's just a visitor here and Papa is giving her an earful about his troubles. You heard it a million times; now it's her turn.

She glanced out the window and jumped up. Papa moved a split second later.

"I didn't know it was getting so dark out!"

"I'll walk with you," Papa offered, "so you won't go home alone in the dark."

I thought of the times in the past Mama had gone to a show by herself, or visited relatives and came home late. Papa had never worried then that Mama was walking alone in the dark. Strange, I thought, and felt something twist inside me.

"Certainly not!" Miss Cohen said. "I'll just walk up to the bus stop. The bus will take me right home!"

She began pulling on her leather gloves, smoothing them against each finger. I watched, fascinated, to see how it was done, a finger at a time. Someday, I would have leather gloves and would perfect the ritual of pulling them on so they smoothed out like that. I might do it in front of a lot of people, like reporters, after I became famous.

"Everything was delicious. Thank you very much. You are a good cook!"

Papa looked modest. "Only so-so. We were glad you

could come. Come back again soon."

She laughed. "Well, I want to show you I can cook too. You'll have to come to my place, all of you!"

Papa shook his head. "Thank you, but you shouldn't bother. First of all, you're a busy lady, and second of all, I would have to close down the store."

She opened the door. "Well, we can discuss this further. There's no point in talking about it right now. Goodbye Becky, Saul. I'm glad I could spend the time with you. The more I see you, the better I like you!"

I knew that was true of Papa and Simply Simon, but I was sure she didn't mean me too. I had a feeling that every time she looked at me, she got sick inside. I could be very difficult, and intended to be. In fact, if they were giving out prizes for being difficult, Mama once said, I would win without any trouble. And that was when I gave *Mama* a big pain. I flashed Miss Cohen a big smile. But I kept my fingers crossed behind my back.

"Aren't you just great, boy!" I hissed at Simply Simon when we were alone.

"What did I do now?"

"Practically kissing her hand, you're so crazy about her!"

"I did not! Anyway, she's nice and I like her. And I bet you do too!"

"No I don't. At least, I don't hate her but she wants to marry Papa and if we don't watch out, she will."

"Well, what's wrong with that? Anyway, if Papa wants to marry her, there's nothing we can do to stop him."

I threw myself onto the chesterfield. "Maybe we can't, but . . ." I bit my lip, I had almost said "but Mama can" and that was something I had no intention of giving away.

But if you're going to do something, Mama, I thought to myself, you'd better hurry up and do it. Because, judging by the way Papa acted, he is really serious about Miss Cohen and if you wait too long, it will be too late.

**7** In May, Papa and Miss Cohen informed us that they were going to be married. We sat across the table from them and inside me something twisted and turned, trying to stab me to pieces.

"Well," Papa said. "can't you say something? Do you have to sit like a dummy?"

I looked at him. "What should I say?" I was surprised my voice came out so calmly, considering how I felt.

Papa looked like he was about to bite my head off but Miss Cohen held her hand up as if to stop him from speaking. "Leave her alone, Jake. I can understand how she feels. It will take her time to get used to the idea. I won't rush you, either one of you."

"You could say: 'Welcome to the family!' " Papa said coldly.

I said woodenly, "Welcome to the family."

She smiled. "Good enough. I'm sure someday you'll mean it."

She rose from her chair and before I realized her intentions, she had kissed the top of my head. It was the lightest of kisses, the gentlest of touches, and I burst into tears. I wished . . . I couldn't put my wish into words. Mama would know.

There was silence around me as I sat with my head bent, my hands covering my face so nobody could see me, and I knew she still stood beside me. Then she moved away and I knew when she no longer stood there; an emptiness had opened up beside me. Papa said: "Becky, go to your room."

Still covering my face, I stumbled out of the kitchen, through the hall to the stairs. Then, sobbing, I ran up the stairs to my bedroom and closed the door. I wiped my eyes. Why was I crying exactly? I wasn't sure. My door opened and Papa stood there. I stared at him, frightened. What was he going to do?

"Sit," Papa said, pointing to my bed. I obeyed, my eyes fixed on his face. He pulled my chair around to face me and sat on it.

"I'm not an educated man," he said, leaning forward. "I

didn't go to school here, so maybe I don't know all the right words to say, but I understand this much. You need a mama and a mama is what you're going to get. Understand?"

My mouth felt dry; my tongue seemed to have swelled double its size. If only I could tell him!

"Do you think it's easy for Miss Cohen, a teacher, to come to our house and do what she's doing? Bringing up somebody else's children is no great pleasure. Think about it. Miss Cohen is going to sacrifice a lot. And the way you act, it's as if you think you're doing her a big favor!"

"It isn't me!" I tried to explain. "It's Mama! She doesn't want Miss Cohen to take her place!"

"Don't talk foolish. What do you mean, Mama doesn't want. Don't you know that Mama is gone, she should rest in peace? Don't talk silly!"

Papa frowned at me. "Where she is," he said, speaking slowly as if he thought I was an idiot who didn't understand, "she doesn't care anymore. Get that through your head."

I shook my head stubbornly. I knew what I knew.

"Now listen to me." Papa tapped my knee with one finger. "I want you should listen carefully. When a person dies, they're gone. Do you hear me?" I looked down, unable to bear his burning eyes. I bit my lips till I could feel the taste of salt on my tongue. Papa's voice went on . . . "To me, Mama's memory is holy. I wouldn't think of getting married again if it was only me. I wouldn't care. I could be alone the rest of my life. What I care about is what Mama cared about. You. Saul. She wanted the best for you, and so do I. Let me make you understand the way it was. . . ." He seemed to be talking more to himself now than to me. . . .

"When she died, I wanted to die too. I didn't want to live. I wanted to be buried with her." I stared at him then, shocked. He'd stopped looking at me; his eyes were on his hands as they lay limply together in his lap. "But I had to think about my children. I couldn't die and leave them orphans. What would happen to you, eh? You'd have some life, wouldn't you, with Auntie Sadie?"

I shuddered. Auntie Sadie! Ugh!

"So what happens? I make myself live. I do my best and

all the relatives, they do their best. You think it's easy? I can't be Papa, Mama both. I'm tired all the time. Why am I telling you this? So you'll understand why I let them talk me into this. We're lucky to have someone as clever as Miss Cohen, still young and nice, want to be a mother to you. We should thank God!"

Papa took a deep breath, his face wrung out, eyes as terrible as they were on that day, that dreadful day.

"God took Mama and the baby away from us," I heard my voice say dully. "Why couldn't He let them live?"

"I don't know why," Papa said tiredly. "But it happened and we have to get over it. Hating God isn't the way. Mama loved God. Do you think she would like you to talk like this?"

"Mama made Cousin Nankie's lady collapse in the broken chair!" I suddenly remembered with a note of satisfaction. Papa's eyebrows went up. So he'd never thought of that! "Mama doesn't want anybody to take her place!" Papa turned white, eyes blazing.

"I'll tell you what Mama wants!" His voice sent ominous shivers through me. "When the nurse let me in to see her after she was in bed, she told me: 'If anything goes wrong and I don't come back, I don't want you should be alone. The children need a mama and you need a helper.' Then Mama made me promise to get married again. She must have known. I didn't believe her, so I promised. She wouldn't lie quiet till I gave her my promise. So now you know. Are you satisfied? Mama didn't make the chair fall. It was an accident, pure and simple."

I held my breath, unable to pull my eyes away from Papa's. There was a thudding inside my head, beat, beat, beat, beat. I finally shifted my gaze away, blinking fast. Papa rose to his feet and walked over to my door. With his hand on the knob he turned and looked at me.

"Becky, Miss Cohen is going to need a lot of help from everybody in the family, to feel at home. I'm counting on you because you're a girl and the oldest. It's up to you."

He went out then, leaving me with my mixed-up, upside-down emotions.

# PART fOUR

**1** It would be a small wedding in June. Funny. Weddings in June sounded so romantic. They sounded like love, sweethearts gazing into each other's eyes, flowers and hearts and cupid's bow. This wedding wouldn't be anything like that.

It was Auntie Sadie insisting we hold it in her house because it was bigger than ours, and Papa consenting, thus losing hold on the reins. Since it was Auntie Sadie's house, it would be her wedding arrangements, her telling the others what to bake, what to cook, who should get the photographer and when, and Rabbi Berg consulting with her on the time and the date for an interview with the couple. As far as anyone could tell, Miss Cohen was merely an inconvenience to the entire affair and ignored as much as possible.

The only thing Miss Cohen was allowed to do was choose her attendant. Only one, Auntie Sadie specified, so it wouldn't look like too much fuss. One was nice, but more than one, who do you think you're fooling? Miss Cohen had smiled, very calmly I'd thought. If it were me, I would have thrown the whole family out of the house. But she had a lot of self-control.

"Two," she smiled. "Not one, but two."

Auntie Sadie frowned. She hated being contradicted.

"Why two? Eh? Who is it going to be, this two?"

Miss Cohen smiled at me. "Who *could* it be? Becky and Saul, of course!"

Papa nodded his approval and I knew Auntie Sadie had lost that round. It became important for some reason I couldn't explain for Auntie Sadie to become as frustrated in her plans as possible. All she could do was shrug her shoulders.

"Okay," she said with pretended indifference. "I should care? If you want them, you can have them. Okay by me."

I had never been an attendant and it sounded very glamorous and exciting. All the same, I kept aloof so she wouldn't think I was eager for the marriage. Papa, keeping an eagle eye on me to make sure I behaved the way he wanted, pushed me forward but I always hung back. No matter what he'd said about Mama, I wasn't taking any chances.

Primly, I called her Miss Cohen even though Simply Simon had taken to calling her Sylvia. It sounded too chummy to me, too friendly and accepting. I couldn't utter her name. It stuck in my throat like long spaghetti.

"You don't think two will be too much?" Auntie Sadie would ask at odd moments as though it still rankled with her. "After all, it isn't like you're a young couple getting married. Maybe it wouldn't look right? What do you think?"

"It will look right," Miss Cohen assured her. "This *is* my first wedding." She stressed the fact none too subtly. "And my *only* one, God willing, so I'd like it to be just right. If *you* don't mind?"

There was irony in her voice, but Auntie Sadie was too immersed in plans to notice. "Let it be like that then," she said magnanimously and passed on to the next point. "Now about your dress."

"Which will be white."

Auntie Sadie girded her loins for battle. "White wouldn't look right, with the children right there at the wedding."

"Believe me, Sadie, I'm perfectly qualified to wear white. Even with the children there."

"You want everyone should laugh at you? What are you, a silly young girl, eh? You can wear any color and still be the bride."

Miss Cohen had a glint in her eye. "I know that as well as you. However, I prefer to wear white."

"Please, please," Papa said, leaning between them. "Let's not argue. Sylvia will wear whatever she likes; she's old enough to make up her own mind. Don't forget this is her wedding, not yours, Sadie. I don't want to hear any more arguments about it or we'll just go to the Rabbi and get married without any fuss."

Auntie Sadie reared back as though Papa had struck her. "Who's arguing? What does it matter to me? She can wear green for all I care. Or purple. Arguing!" She took several deep breaths. "As if I'm arguing. If I care that people shouldn't laugh behind our backs, it means I'm arguing. Is it for my sake? No. It's so nobody can laugh at my brother, they should say he looked like a fool at his second wedding."

Papa put his face in his hands. He could have been praying, crying, or counting to ten. Miss Cohen gazed at the wall above our heads. She wasn't smiling anymore. I decided that this time, Auntie Sadie had gone too far. Now Papa would give her the heave-ho, right out of the house. I waited expectantly, hopefully, but nothing happened, except I was sent to the kitchen as usual to make everybody some tea. It was very disappointing.

The days leading up to the wedding were filled with feverish activity. We saw only the fringes of it, most of the actual work taking place at Auntie Sadie's. But we would be made aware of what was happening by her suddenly bursting into the house and collapsing on a chair, moaning: "If I see one more cherry or nut I'm going to scream!"

Since she lived only four blocks away, on Burrows Avenue, we were treated to this kind of hysteria regularly. "The blintzes!" she wailed. "They're driving me out of my mind!"

When Papa, feeling guilty at how hard she was working, said: "We can do without blintzes, Sadie," she stared at him aghast.

"Are you crazy? What kind of wedding is it with no blintzes?" She made it sound as though nobody was legally married unless there were blintzes on the table.

Auntie Leah, who was responsible for the whole thing in a way, lived on the other side of Selkirk Avenue closer to Auntie Sadie's than to us. As the campaigner whose candidate had won, she was anxious not to be left out of the plans. Consequently, she was there nearly every day to get in on the arrangements and to put her veto as often as she thought necessary. "I like roses," Auntie Leah said. "Sylvia should have roses at her wedding." She folded her plump arms implacably across her chest.

"Roses cost too much. What's wrong with lilacs, they smell so nice and I have plenty in the yard, they should only last till then? And the way it's so cold out the last few weeks we'll be lucky if they don't freeze. And irises from my brother-in-law the florist, he'll give them half price if he has any."

"Irises? Whoever heard of irises at a wedding? Lilacs and irises is a combination? For your daughter you'd have them?"

"A daughter I haven't got, but a brother I have, and for his second wedding, lilacs and irises are very nice. I told him and he didn't complain.

"Since when do you ask a man? Everybody knows weddings are for the bride, and when you got married, five, six years ago, I suppose you had lilacs and irises?"

"No. I got married in the winter and you know it. We had to have roses and gladioluses, and Morris's brother, the florist, gave them to us as a present. And there's nothing wrong with lilacs and irises."

"We'll be the laughingstock. Nobody has lilacs and irises at a wedding. Not even the poorest schnook. You want Sylvia should look like she married a schnook?"

Since it was my father's name and reputation being dragged into the muck, I yelled: "Hey! I'm gonna tell Papa what you said!"

Auntie Sadie and Auntie Leah stared at me in consternation and anger. My presence till then had gone unnoticed.

"Why aren't you home?" Auntie Sadie shrilled at me inhospitably. "You go home, Becky, and do some studying. Look at that. She hides in corners and we talk and nobody even knows she's there."

I hadn't been hiding in corners and I didn't sneak in either. I used the front door and nobody had ever told me you had to knock to visit your own aunties. After all, *they* never knocked at *our* door.

I went home, highly insulted, trying to decide whether I should turn stool pigeon and tell Papa that they'd called him a schnook or hold it over their heads to use as blackmail in future dealings with them.

I felt sorrier for Miss Cohen than before. She had been pushed into the background and couldn't even choose her own flowers. I liked lilacs but it did seem awfully cheap to use flowers that grew in your yard. As for irises, I didn't know much about them except for one thing: If Auntie Sadie liked them, they must be ugly.

The wedding would be on a Sunday, with final exams slated to begin the Monday after. How was I supposed to study with all that was going on? Miss Cohen came over every day now. Although she wasn't Papa's wife yet, she had managed to make herself indispensable to him by taking over his bookkeeping, most of our suppers, and then helping me with the dishes. I supposed she was trying to gradually worm her way into our lives so that soon we wouldn't be able to do without her.

I hunched over my books, reading the same sentence over and over again, making hardly any sense out of it. I'd be lucky, I thought grimly, if I didn't have to stay in grade four another year with her standing in the kitchen, baking a batch of cookies, making all the clatter connected with it. Simply Simon kept up a running commentary with her, further distracting me, and sneaking some coconut when she looked the other way. I knew what went on in there better than I knew what was on the page in front of my eyes.

I tried not to notice but if I raised my eyes and looked into the kitchen, I'd see him licking the big mixing spoon (she had brought one with her when she couldn't find Mama's) and they'd exchange a smile, a secret smile. They were friends already and I didn't know how or when it had happened, I was always left out of everything. But I wanted it that way, I reminded myself.

It drove me crazy to see him standing beside her that way as if she were Mama. I never thought my own brother could be such a traitor, going over to the enemy's side even before the wedding. The way I figured, I'd probably start being nice to her after two or three years, if then. But certainly not before the wedding!

I gathered my books in a sudden angry gesture and stomped out of the room and up the stairs. It gave me a feeling of triumph, power. She couldn't ignore it; she would have to be aware of her failure with me. No matter what Papa said, no matter what he told me about Mama's last words, I knew what I knew. Mama didn't want anybody to take her place!

I spread my books out on the bed, but I couldn't concentrate. Why did Papa have to get married *now*? Why not in August? Or September. Of course, I couldn't blame Miss Cohen for that. She hadn't been consulted either. The time was set at a family conference which was held at our house without her presence. Papa, busy in the store, had no idea what was going on. I was the sole representative of the family most directly concerned, and my opinion didn't count.

"When do you think?" Cousin Edna had said, squinting at a hangnail. "When should it be?"

"What difference does it make? The sooner the better," Auntie Sadie said with feigned indifference. "We should get it over with before summer anyway."

Cousin Edna yawned. "Yah . . . Nankie and me will be going to Chicago maybe the first week in July. . . ."

Uncle Morris, susceptible to suggestion, yawned loudly too. His mouth closed with a sharp click of dentures, and Auntie Sadie gave him a dirty look.

"Who's got a calendar?" she asked. "We can have it the second Sunday in June. Okay by everybody?"

"Why don't you ask Papa?" I said. "Maybe it isn't okay by Papa?"

"Let's see," she said, ignoring me as if I were a buzzing fly and scanning the small calendar somebody, Cousin Edna I guessed, had fished out of her purse. "MMM—hmmm. We can have it on the fourteenth of the month. That gives us enough time to make arrangements. Okay?"

Auntie Leah shrugged, Cousin Edna nodded, and both uncles yawned, scratched and agreed. I was furious.

"How do you know it'll be okay by Papa?"

Auntie Sadie deigned to notice me now. "By your Papa it'll be okay, Miss Nosy Parker, because Papa left all the arrangements to me. If he wants me to do it, it has to be when the time is best for me. Your Uncle Morris and me are going to Los Angeles to visit with his relatives like we always do and we're going July third. Auntie Leah and Uncle Dave are going to Philadelphia to see her sisters, and the cousins are going to Chicago. Do you want your Papa should go to a Rabbi and get married or should he have a nice wedding so you can see it? Now go get me a toothpick. I got something stuck in my teeth."

I huffed out of the front room, banging kitchen cupboard doors in futile rage. I got her a toothpick and told her mentally what she could do with it. Nobody cared what I thought. I wanted the wedding to be held sometime in the summer so it wouldn't be too soon and to give Papa a chance to change his mind.

The plans moved on, gathering momentum like a tornado, with Auntie Sadie in the middle. On the sidelines, the rest of us merely looked on. I thought this was the most ridiculous thing of all.

Papa hadn't minded in the least being told when it would be. Any time was fine with him. Now, later, he didn't care. Miss Cohen hadn't objected either. She'd only said: "Good."

It appeared as though I was the only one who had objections. I flicked through my books, trying to soak up bits of information, things I hoped would stick with me in case they came up in exams. If I didn't pass I'd look stupid in front of Miss Cohen. She'd think I was a real dumbbell.

There were loud voices downstairs. There, I told myself. That's what I mean. Stuff like that! Auntie Sadie and Uncle Morris coming over whenever they felt like it, night or day. I ran down to see what it was all about.

Auntie Sadie leaned against the back of a chair, gazing

at us wildly. "I'm fainting," she said dramatically, her hand going up to her forehead. "The smell of food makes me sick. I think I'm going to have the flu!"

"Sit down," Papa said, pushing her into the chair. "You walked all the way here, sick like that, to tell me you're going to have the flu?"

"How else would you know, dummy, when you haven't got a telephone?"

"I don't need a telephone. It costs money and it isn't worth it."

"If you had a telephone, I could talk to you and not have to walk all the way here when I'm sick and falling off my feet."

"I haven't got time to stand here and argue with you. If you want to argue, argue with Morris. He's got more time than me."

"Why should I argue with Morris? Morris got a telephone. You don't."

The store bell tinkled and Papa fled to the store. Miss Cohen was rinsing the baking things, and a sweet smell of cookies filled the air. Auntie Sadie went into the kitchen, her fainting spell apparently past. "Well, you almost ready for your Big Moment?" Her tone was condescending.

Miss Cohen smiled. "Yes, just about. I still have a few of my things to pack up and bring down here. We want to keep everything as calm as possible for the children's sakes."

Her eyes strayed to my face as she spoke. For a minute, our eyes held, the I turned and went back upstairs. She really meant it. Holy Toledo! The things that went on, I thought. No wonder I couldn't concentrate. I leaned over my books again. But I didn't see the words on the pages.

". . . for the children's sakes . . ." she had said. I gazed blindly at the book. It would be nice to have a telephone. I'd never thought much about it before. . . . But it was still none of Auntie Sadie's business. If Papa wanted one, it would be up to him, not her. Anyway, what right did she have to use that nasty smug tone to Miss Cohen? It burned me up. Miss Cohen should have ignored her, instead of answering her so politely. I sure wouldn't be polite if I was in her place. I tried to imagine what it must be like to be Miss Cohen . . . a wedding coming up, a family . . . me . . . Simply Simon. I gave up. If I were her, I'd quit trying, especially with Auntie Sadie around.

I thought some more about a telephone. If we had one, I could pick it up and dial Betty Greenberg's number, and say:

"Hello, Betty? Guess who this is!" She'd never guess, of course, so I'd tell her: "This is Becky! What did we have to do for geography?"

And she would tell me, very surprised that I had a phone and was just like them, one of the well-to-do kids in the bunch. But we wouldn't get one. They cost money and Papa said they weren't worth it.

The wedding drifted back into my mind, not that it was ever far away at any time. How many girls could go to their own father's wedding? Not many, I was sure. No one in the school, as far as I knew.

The dress I would wear hung in my closet. All I had to do to see it was open the closet door. A gleaming silk of pale yellow with butterfly-cap sleeves and small diamonds marching down the front of the bodice. They weren't real diamonds of course, but they sparkled like diamonds when you held them a certain way and they caught the light and reflected it back. All the beautiful colors . . . blue, green, red, purple . . . flashed into my eyes. I'd hold my breath with the beauty of it all. The skirt had tiny pleats all around and when I spun on one foot, the skirt whirled out, flaring like petals, in a glamorous swirl of silk.

Miss Cohen had chosen it and brought it home for me to try on. I remembered my reaction when she'd taken it out of the box and held it up for me to see; my heart had pounded with sheer joy to own something as beautiful as that. The dress had been too long, so she had shortened it, and with the extra material, she had covered a headband which she stitched tiny pearls onto, and it belonged with the dress. When I tried it on, dress and all, I couldn't believe my eyes. I didn't look like myself but like a movie star, like Shirley Temple, almost.

Papa had nodded approvingly and then Simply Simon tried on the blue blazer and white pants she'd brought for him, with the white shirt and black bow tie. I grinned at him. He looked so elegant, like a well-dressed midget or Little Lord Fauntleroy. We'd pranced around like a couple of idiots in our outfits and laughed and giggled and it had been fun, I remembered. Until the thought hit me: It was for the wedding.

I described what was happening for the girls at school, and from the way they listened, their eyes shining, I could tell that they envied me, especially about the dress.

"Oh you lucky fish!" Marjorie screamed. "It sounds absolutely *gorgeous!*"

"Imagine going to your own father's wedding!" Betty giggled. "I mean, whoever *could?* I wasn't even born yet!"

"Well, I hope not!" Denise Borvier, a girl who had been transferred into our room a month before and was now one of the crowd, snickered. "It sure wouldn't look right!"

"You lucky fish!"

I listened to their wisecracks with mounting resentment. "Who's a lucky fish? You didn't think so when my mother died! So what if my father is getting married again? It wasn't my idea!"

Betty frowned a little. "I know, Becky, but just think: You're getting a new mother now. Isn't that swell?"

"She'll never be my mother. Just because she marries my father, doesn't mean she's going to be my mother. She'll be his wife, and that's all." I gazed defiantly around the group of faces watching me. "You don't think I'll ever call her . . . Mama?"

The subject dropped right there.

It was Friday, and Simply Simon and I were on our way home from school. Rain had threatened off and on during the afternoon and now a few drops fell. We walked faster, almost running, not even halfway home yet. At the first intersection, we slowed, approaching Shaeffer's Grocery. A baby carriage stood beside the store's entrance. I never could resist looking into baby carriages. I didn't resist now, twisting my head as we passed, glancing in to see the baby, the cute little baby that would be smiling up at me.

. . . There wasn't any cute little baby in the carriage. My heart pushed itself into my throat, strangling me as I clutched Simply Simon's hand. We both stared at the . . . thing . . . that leaned its huge head against the tiny pillow, staring impassively at us. Rain dripped down on us . . . on it . . . my heart thumping heavily in the vicinity of my chin. I started to run, still holding Simply Simon's hand.

We dashed headlong across the street, faster and faster, trying to outrun the image we carried in our minds, the monstrous thing with the huge white face. I wanted to vomit, I wanted to cry, and my side hurt with running so I had to stop. We stood together, panting, and leaned against a picket fence.

"What was it?" he whispered, his face almost as white as that . . . baby's. "What was the matter with it?"

"I don't know! I don't know! Oh the poor thing!" I had looked into the carriage, hoping to find my lost baby sister, which had become habit with me by now, and instead I had found a monster . . . the staring black eyes had burned their way into my mind and I knew I would have nightmares about it from now on. "Don't talk about it anymore! I want to forget it."

We walked slowly on, rain falling intermittently.

"Did you notice it was leaning?" he said, unable to keep from talking about it. "Like it couldn't hold up its head?"

"It must be sick. Anyway, I told you not to talk about it. What an awful thing to happen to a baby!"

"If I didn't see it with my own eyes, I wouldn't believe it. Did it make you feel sick to the stomach too?"

I stopped and glared at him. "Can't you understand English? I want you to shut up!"

Miss Cohen wore a blue apron around her waist, looking cute and unschoolteacherish, with a big bow at the back. She was preparing our Friday Night Supper as calmly as though she'd been doing it for ten years or so. Looking at her, I told myself by this time next week, she'll be doing it for real as Papa's wife. The wedding was two days off.

The blabbermouth couldn't wait to tell her. "D'you know what we *saw*, Sylvia?" he began the minute we walked in. I whirled on him in fury.

"Can't you keep quiet? I told you not to talk about it!"

I had a glimpse of Miss Cohen's startled eyes staring at me, the stirring spoon still in her hand, dripping large globs of gravy all over the floor, as I ran out and up to my room.

I stared out of the window at the rain. Thrumming drops beating on the roof directly outside of my window were also falling on that baby, unless the mother had taken her baby home by now. I pressed my face against the cool glass. The rain beat inside my head too, beat against my brain, against the baby's brain. I had thought every baby was born beautiful, and now I knew sometimes they weren't. I saw the misshapen head, like a huge watermelon, or a very large pear, and I thought of Mrs. Hodnik's baby, Stella, with the round face, laughing blue eyes, wispy blond hair, the baby teeth like white blisters on the pink gums. That was what babies looked like, usually.

How did it feel to be the mother of that baby? I blew on the cold window, forming a mist with my breath. With one finger, I drew a picture of a baby in the mist . . . small round head, two dots for eyes, a dot for the nose, and an upcurved line underneath, for a smiling mouth. I drew one hair out of the top of the head and a tiny bow near its tip. My baby sister, who hadn't lived.

Why, I wondered, did she die while this other, awful-looking creature lived? How did mistakes like that happen? Every baby I'd ever seen had been beautiful, perfect, until today. Was the baby we saw a mistake that should have died, but didn't? Should ours have lived? Or maybe, ours would have been like that if she had lived. Did the mother wish sometimes that it had died, or even that it had never been born?

I pulled out my scribbler and slid into my chair in front of my dresser. With the stubby pencil gripped between my thumb and fingers, I began to write, filling page after page.

. . ."Sometimes," I wrote, "living is worse than dying." For the first time I understood this. Death, I decided, was something you got used to, like Mama dying and it hardly hurt my throat at all to think about it anymore. But I was sure a person could never get used to the sight of that baby, day after day, especially its mother.

**2** Sunday morning, June 14, 1937, Papa's wedding day . . . I awoke with a feeling like panic, and sat straight up in bed to be greeted by blinding sunlight streaking through my window. Papa had pulled the blind up and now stood silhouetted against the window. "This is no time for sleeping," he said. "Get up and clean up around the house."

I blinked at him, still sleepy, not quite grasping the fact that after today, many things would be changed. I waited till he left my room and listened to his footsteps going down the stairs; then I flopped back against my pillow. But I couldn't go back to blessed oblivion. Suddenly my heart did a little dance. It was today! The wedding, the excitement, the glamor, all of it. Today! I leaped out of bed.

Birds sang out there. I let the happy sounds pervade my senses. I could see a horse and wagon on Powers Street. Clip-clop, clip-clop, the horse's hooves sent up dust clouds. Both man and animal perked along. It was that kind of morning. I dressed quickly, in yesterday's clothes, and stole a peek at the yellow dress. I loved yellow, the color of the sun, of dandelions and buttercups. Yellow meant happiness, joy, good things. I wondered how Miss Cohen had known that yellow was my favorite color, or had it just been a lucky guess?

My mind nibbled at the problem, so delicate, that I worried with at odd moments. The problem: what I would do when Miss Cohen became Mrs. Devine. What was I going to call her? What? How? I supposed I'd have to say Sylvia sooner or later, even though it lodged in my throat at the moment, but I couldn't imagine myself saying it. It was like an admission of defeat. I envied Simply Simon the ease with which he'd gone from Miss Cohen to Sylvia so long ago. It was a fact that he hadn't seemed in the least troubled by it. One day he'd said her first name and that was that. My pride wouldn't let me. It meant giving in, accepting her . . . public-ly. I knew I'd have to do it but I couldn't face it just yet.

I looked into Papa's room. There stood the trunk. Some men had brought it to the house last night, grunting, panting, as they'd carried it up the stairs. Papa had paid them, and they'd left, and the trunk had taken up residence in the bedroom, immutable proof, if any were needed, that Miss Cohen actually intended to marry Papa and move into this house, this bedroom, that bed.

I tiptoed in. This was the bed where Papa and Mama had slept together so many years. Tonight Miss Cohen would sleep in it. Probably right there, in the very spot where Mama had lain. I touched it lightly, so as not to disturb a sleeping ghost, then turned and went out of the room.

Now it began to feel true, as if before it was just a maybe. Papa could still change his mind before but now it was too late. She would live in this house with us.

There was a feeling of unreality throughout the morning and early afternoon. Everything I did was with a sense of "the last time," almost as if I was going to die. We ate lightly, by ourselves, just the three of us. We would never be a family to ourselves after today, I thought. I felt an edge to the silence where we moved softly, scarcely stirring up a whisper. Simply Simon polished our shoes. Papa had merely pointed at them and there had been no words. I dusted and tidied everywhere just to keep busy, because when I looked at Papa, he seemed to me so tragic. I put our books away out of sight, straighten-ing papers, looking for things to do to ward off the moment that we were hurtling towards, Papa's last chance. Yet in the background, I felt time moving inexorably into the distance, bringing that other time, the moment when we would have to start getting ready.

Papa cleared his throat. The impact of it was like that of a pistol shot. We both jumped, staring at him, but he kept his gaze firmly upon us. "Before you put on the good clothes," he said without any particular emphasis, "I want you to wash real good. Especially the neck and ears."

I felt my face grow hot. It sounded like criticism. I touched my neck; was it dirty? We avoided each other's eyes, embarrassed, and went to wash up. My hands shook as I splashed water all over my neck, feeling it slide down inside my undershirt. I began to feel a pain in my stomach, a twisting, stabbing pain, the familiar kind connected with Mama. She was reminding me that she wasn't happy about Papa getting married today.

The pace quickened. Now that the time to get ready had arrived, time telescoped. We dressed and admired each other, gave the house a last-minute inspection. When we next entered through the front door, it would be with Papa's new wife. I whirled on one foot, to see my skirt spin out around me, and readjusted my headband with the pearls. The pain in my stomach subsided now that we were actually on our way down the steps with Papa locking the front door.

It was a beautiful day for a walk. The sun touched everything, turning it to gold. My diamonds sparkled and flashed and when I stopped to get a good look at the different colors, Papa and Simply Simon went on ahead so I had to run to catch up. Running made me warm so I began to perspire inside the collar of the dress. I put a finger between my throat and the collar and scuffed my shoes, the new ones Papa had bought me, shiny black with a strap across the front. I stopped to wipe the dust off the toes.

At Auntie Sadie's, my stomachache came back. I knew this was the end. We would stay till it was all over and I really didn't know how I felt about it, even now. I stopped in the darkened, cool hallway of Auntie Sadie's house, holding my stomach, watching Papa disappear down the end of the hall where the men's voices could be heard, laughing in sudden gusts. Simply Simon peered into all the rooms and then some of our younger kid cousins came out of one and a game of tag started. I felt strangely abandoned.

Although it was still early, there were quite a lot of people there already. I peered into the living room, which looked different with all the furniture taken out of it. The shiny dark brown piano had been removed to a far corner of the adjoining dining room. I could see it from where I stood because there was a wide archway between the two rooms. The piano, I noticed glumly, was closed and locked. That was just like Auntie Sadie; she was the stingiest person with a piano that I knew. I loved to touch the keys, to hear music come out of them and pretend I was a great pianist. Naturally, she would make sure that we couldn't. It was going to be used during the ceremony. I wondered where she kept the key and decided it was around her neck, inside her dress.

"Don't touch anything" were Auntie Sadie's first words to me. "And stay out of the living room." Those were her next words. Her sharp thin face and quickly moving eyes that took in everything, even my thoughts, barely stopped before she went on to supervise elsewhere.

"Can't I even look?" I said to her disappearing back, and when she was out of sight, I put my head around the entranceway. It all seemed so strange, like being in a house for the first time. There were bridge chairs lined up in rows, like in the Palace Theatre. In front of the fake fireplace, a canopy had been set up. It stood on four poles, with a velvet cloth edged with gold fringes stretched over the top of them. I wondered what it was for but there was nobody that I knew sitting in the bridge chairs that I could ask. . . .

I looked around the room and noticed the vases massed with lilacs and big ugly purple things which I knew immediately must be irises. What else could they be, looking exactly the way I'd expected. One thing was sure. I'd never let Auntie Sadie do any arrangements for *my* wedding. *If* I ever got married, which I doubted very much.

I withdrew from the living room and looked at all the people. Some of them were once-in-a-blue-moon types who sat stolidly fanning themselves with doubled-up newspapers, watching everybody come in. Some of them were every-Yontiff people, whom we had to visit on the special holidays. Then there were the ordinary relatives. The everyday people.

"Hey boy! You look spiffy, Becky!" My cousin Cecile

looked sweaty from running around and playing games with Simply Simon and all the little kids. She stared at me, popeyed, her curly brown hair falling in tangles over her forehead. "Are those *real* diamonds?"

"Are you nuts? Of *course* they're not real. D'you think we're millionaires or something? They're only fakes. But they sparkle just as good." I pulled her into the living room and stood in a shaft of sunlight so she could get the full effect of the flashes. She moved closer and touched them, her hair tickling my nose.

"Oh, they're beautiful," she breathed. Her blue hair ribbon, which matched the ruffled dress and socks, bobbed up and down. She was younger than Simply Simon, and ordinarily I wouldn't speak to her as an equal, but this was an out-of-the-ordinary occasion. I moved a bit to give her some more dazzle.

"I told you not to go into the living room, didn't I?" Auntie Sadie shrilled at us.

"Holy Toledo! We're not doing anything!" I was insulted. "Can't we even *stand* here?"

"Out, out!" We were unceremoniously shooed away, and deposited like so much trash near the kitchen door. *Some people*, I thought. Give them a little power, and they sure get carried away. Cecile looked as disgusted as I felt.

"I bet she even thinks this is her wedding!" I said out of the corner of my mouth so only Cecile could hear. I didn't stay mad though, because it took one second for me to realize that some wonderful smells were coming out of the kitchen, and every time the front door opened, someone else came through the hall carrying a pot, pan, or bag or box with food inside. We were caught in a crossfire of greetings, even one or two meant for me.

"Nu, Becky? Soon, eh? You're excited?"

"Sure, I'm excited," I said in a bored voice so Cecile giggled, but it was wasted on the grown-ups because nobody waited to hear my answer anyway. Somebody pinched my cheek.

"You look like a bride yourself."

"Give a look, Geitle, what a picture. Where did you get such a nice dress?"

"Where's Papa? Did he come with you?"

"Where do you think?" someone answered for me. "With the menner, they're all drinking pretty good in there!"

I looked up at them as they burst into a staccato of laughter. Holy Toledo, I thought again. I'm getting out of here.

"When's it going to start?" Cecile asked me, as if it was up to me.

I shrugged. "Ask *her*. She's running the whole thing." But Auntie Sadie shooed us away again farther into the kitchen among all the backsides and sweaty armpits and bumping elbows where things were being unwrapped and unpacked and set out on platters. They mixed, sliced, mashed, arranged this and that, or stood beside the stove and stirred things that bubbled, hissed, seethed and steamed, adding to the already high humidity.

And they talked in high voices. "You put a little spices in, and mmmmaaa—*maaa*! Like you never tasted!"

"You gotta gimme the recipe!"

"Where he pinched her, he should be ashamed! I told her, if it was me, oy, would there be screaming!"

"Where did he pinch her?"

"Don't ask!"

"A baby in nine months . . . mark my words. To the *day!*"

"I believe you. After all, a schoolteacher!"

"Mmm-hmm. And younger she'll never be." A baby! They're talking about Papa and Miss Cohen! I hadn't thought about it. Of course it might happen. . . . No. I wouldn't think about it. Not after what happened to Mama. I didn't want to ever think about a baby again. An unwanted image flashed into my mind, the apparition of the baby in the carriage in front of Shaeffer's. No! I walked quickly out of the kitchen, down the hall towards the front door and stood looking out. The big door was wide open, but the screen door kept out the flies while letting in a lovely cooling breeze.

I wondered what was taking Miss Cohen so long. I

wished she'd get here already so it could start. It was boring just standing around with Simply Simon playing with the boys in one of the bedrooms and Papa with all the men in the card room.

What if Miss Cohen changed her mind? What if she thought it over and decided she didn't want to marry Papa? After all, I had done everything I could think of to discourage her. Maybe now, at the last minute, she couldn't go through with it. It would be my fault, and Papa would look like a fool. He'd be shamed; he'd be mad at me. We'd all look like idiots. After all the work and everything Auntie Sadie would have a fit!

Her clothes . . . they were at our house. Well, she wouldn't get them back. It would serve her right! Maybe she was lost. Did she know the address? I stood, biting my nails. Oh my God, the Rabbi was coming up the walk. And there was Cousin Miriam. She was going to play the wedding music on the piano. There were some other people coming too, I knew them vaguely. Holy Toledo. How many people were there going to be at this wedding?

I turned and went back to the kitchen. The smells made me hungry. It seemed like years since we'd last eaten. We wouldn't have supper till the ceremony was over and Miss Cohen wasn't even here!

The sounds of jazz came tinkling through the air, cutting through the sounds of conversation like a smooth ribbon. Cousin Miriam had managed to get the piano opened. I pushed through towards the end of the dining room where the piano stood. Cousin Miriam was pretty with her dark hair in a smooth roll around her head. She smiled at me and let her fingers run over the keys. "How's it going?" she asked.

"Not bad," I said, feeling shy. She usually ignored me but now I was important. I looked at her red lips, shaped into cupid's bows, and cheeks blushing with rouge. I knew she had lots of boyfriends. I envied her. Not only for being old enough to do all the things she could do, but for knowing how to play the piano too.

"What would you like to hear, anything special?"

I shook my head and as the expert fingers flew over the keys, voices were raised in greeting. I looked towards the commotion and saw Miss Cohen framed in the entranceway to the living room. My heart stopped for a fraction of a second as I stared at her, thankful that she hadn't changed her mind.

Miriam whistled softly, then went into a shortened version of "Here Comes the Bride." Miss Cohen hadn't seen me yet so I could look at her in private. The dress with short sleeves and scooped neckline was almost white, I could see, and she wore a matching hat covered with tiny white flowers and a short misty veil. I forgot for a moment that she was still the enemy—a schoolteacher. For a moment my heart leaped with happy anticipation. The next minute I was yanked away from the piano and Simply Simon hung from the end of Auntie Sadie's other hand. We were hustled out of everybody's sight into a vacant bedroom.

"Stay there. When we want you we'll let you know." The door was shut in our astonished faces.

"Boy!" I said, "Some people!"

The door opened again and this time it was Miss Cohen. She smiled and closed the door behind her. "Well," she said. "Here we are. Now let's see how you two look."

She inspected us and out of her small white purse extracted a comb which she ran through Simply Simon's hair. I watched her, feeling strange, mixed up, half glad, half excited, and half resentful. There was another half somewhere, and it didn't know how to feel exactly . . . afraid?

"Where is your yarmelke?"

Simply Simon put his hand in his pocket, and pulled out a white satin skullcap. She placed it on the back of his head, then pointed to his shoelaces, which were untied. While he tied them she turned to me, adjusted my head band, straightened my hair beside my face, then smiled.

"You look fine! Now come here, Becky." And she bent over a box which stood open on the bed. It contained flowers . . . a small nosegay of red and yellow baby roses for me, a boutonniere for Simply Simon, and a beautiful corsage of mauve orchids for Miss Cohen.

"Would you please pin this on me?" She held out the corsage. I'd never even seen one before but I took it out of her hand with the pin and fastened it to the shoulder of her dress. I tried hard not to stab her with the pin.

"How does it look?"

"It's beautiful!"

Auntie Sadie poked her head through the door. "Are you ready? We can start anytime. Everybody is sitting in the living room, waiting."

"Not yet," Miss Cohen said. "I want to give them their instructions."

She nodded. "I'll wait here by the door. Let me know when you're ready."

Miss Cohen whispered her instructions, her eyes going from my face to Simply Simon's face. We nodded slowly, listening, and inside I felt a tightening in my chest. This was it. This was really it. This was going to be the end. Miss Cohen opened the door. Auntie Sadie looked at her and nodded, then scuttled off. We listened through the open doorway. All we heard was a waiting silence, then the wedding march crashed out of the dining room.

Miss Cohen touched our shoulders pushing us out into the hall. I clutched my nosegay, holding it in front of my heart, glancing sideways at Simply Simon. He didn't have anything to hold on to and kept his arms stiffly at his side.

The hall was a million miles long. The music came muffled to our ears. We walked, agonizingly slowly, in time to the music, each step taking us closer to the entrance to the living room. Now we were there and we stopped. There was a rustling of starched collars and silk collars as heads turned towards us. My perspiring hands held on to the nosegay, which wafted a sweet smell to my nose. I felt as if I could faint, but I held to the sight of Papa at the end of the aisle between the rows of chairs. He stood under the canopy with the Rabbi, looking at us, nodding a little in encouragement. We started down the aisle to Papa, and having reached him, we parted, the way Miss Cohen had said, and stood on each side of him.

The music changed to "Here Comes the Bride." I looked up in the direction of the doorway and in a moment she stood there looking beautiful, the veil hiding most of her face giving her a mysterious air. It surprised me that she looked beautiful. I remembered the way she had looked the first time we saw her and I had dismissed her as another Miss Blustein. How could she have changed so much?

Now I looked at Papa, and was shocked by his expression. It was so plain. It was so obvious. Papa was in love with Miss Cohen! I hadn't expected that; I hadn't counted on him falling in love with her. He only wanted someone to help him, he'd said. He couldn't be father and mother both, he'd said. And now, he was in *love* with her. He wasn't *supposed* to!

Miss Cohen walked slowly towards us, keeping in time to the piano thumping out the melody, and nobody even breathed. Then we all turned to face the Rabbi who began to read in Hebrew. It didn't take long at all. I hadn't known what to expect but I didn't expect it to take just a few minutes. The whole thing was very unspectacular, until somebody placed a brown paper bag on the floor and Papa stamped on it. There was a grinding crunch, like glass breaking . . . and it *was* glass. I was very surprised, but everybody laughed and yelled: "Mazel tov!"

They pounded Papa on the back and it was all over. Papa kissed her on the cheek and they were married. Papa and . . . and Miss Cohen. Only she wasn't Miss Cohen anymore. She was now Mrs. Devine.

The photographer arrived. There were shrill cries as people went into groups to have their picture taken. I watched from the sidelines as Papa and Miss Cohen were pushed this way and that way by the relatives who tried to pose them and pose with them. I had to keep reminding myself . . . not Miss Cohen. She wasn't Miss Cohen anymore. She was . . . Sylvia. I said it to myself. Sylvia. I had to get used to the feel of it on my tongue because I knew I would have to call her that sooner or later. I would have to say it out loud, where she could hear me. Sylvia.

Finally, some of the women remembered the food and

the dining-room table was set. With all the ladies helping, it didn't take long till everything had been transferred from kitchen to dining room. Soon, I promised my empty stomach, we were going to eat. A hand touched my shoulder. "You disappeared so fast, I didn't know where you'd gone."

"Well, Holy Toledo. You should see all the people around you. I wasn't going to push."

"Come," she said. "Papa wants to have a family picture taken."

We went into the living room. Cousin Cecile stood at the piano, thumping noisily on the keys, smiling happily. Out of the corner of my eye, I saw Auntie Sadie descend on her, wrath in every step. I was glad at that instant it was her and not me. The thumping stopped immediately. When I looked back, the piano was closed and locked and Cousin Cecile had her lower lip extended a city block. Auntie Sadie's irate back marched from the scene.

We had our pictures taken, my stomach feeling as if it had a permanent hole in it. I smiled and smiled for the camera with just my lips, and inside I growled with hunger. Finally we could join the others at the table. It was a relief to sit down, a plate in front of me, and a vast store of goodies to choose from—as much food as I had seen in one place in my life up till that time.

Everything tasted wonderful. The women in our family were superb cooks, and each one had outdone herself in honor of the occasion. Nobody paid any attention to me and I ignored all the talk, laughter, and toasts. I was glad not to hear "Don't eat so fast." Or "Don't eat so much." I intended to eat till I burst.

It had to end. Sylvia tapped me on the arm.

"We're leaving now, dear. You have some studying to do for tomorrow's exams. Remember?"

I had all but forgotten and didn't appreciate being reminded just now. The party would go on for hours. Nobody looked ready to call it a day. I didn't think it was fair that we, who were the main reason for all the celebrating, should have to miss most of it, but Papa agreed with Sylvia. It was time, he said, to go home.

We said our good-byes, and the four of us went out into the cool June evening and walked the four blocks home. Anybody looking at us would think we had always gone for walks together. I was sure nobody could tell we had just had a wedding in our family.

**3** Afterwards, when I thought about that afternoon, I couldn't remember hearing the whisper of Mama's voice, only the intermittent pains in my stomach which could just as easily be hunger, and I couldn't help wondering about that.

I was supposed to be studying for my exam. Sylvia had sent me to my room with my schoolbooks and now I sat reviewing the events that had just taken place. Before it had been a jumble of faces and voices but now my mind separated them into compartments marked "then" and "now."

Then. That was when Mama died. Everybody was at our house then. There were tears, real heartbroken tears. I could still feel Auntie Leah crushing me to her breast, smothering me. The top of my head felt wet. The cousins wept against each other's shoulders, consoling each other. Uncle Dave squeezed my arm so hard that I'd winced. When I looked up at him, his face had a tight pinched look to it as though someone had placed it in a nutcracker. Auntie Sadie wailed like a fire truck. Cousin Hinda tiptoed around the house, whispering to people as though somebody was asleep. People I hardly knew came, wearing solemn expressions, to fill the house with their voices; they left with solemn expressions, and in between the coming and the going discussed politics, the Depression, Europe—especially Germany—and what was happening there, talking about everything except the reason they had come. That was then.

Now, this afternoon, they had slapped Papa on the back, shouting "Mazel tov!" raised their glasses of wine saying "L'chayim!" kissed Sylvia, hugged her, welcomed her. Just as if there had never been a Mama, as if they hadn't cried over her just about six months ago, as if they forgot she'd ever lived. How could they do that? How could they forget Mama so completely? Today nobody had given Mama a thought except me.

I looked at her chair beside my dresser and tried to see Mama sitting in it. Sometimes I could, but tonight I couldn't. I wondered if the wedding had made her go away, so far away she would never come back. Did she feel unwanted? But I wouldn't forget her. Never! My eyes felt heavy as I looked at my open book. Exams tomorrow and I would fail. Mama help me! But she had gone away.

I saw Sylvia as she had looked standing in the entranceway to the living room in her white dress with the orchid pinned to her shoulder where I had placed it myself, and heard again the in-drawn breath and the thumping piano playing "Here Comes the Bride," saw the expressions in the eyes that followed her approach towards Papa. I saw Papa standing beside me, his eyes on Sylvia with the look I had never seen before.

There was a quiet knock at my door and it jerked me erect. "Come in," I said.

I knew it would be her. She smiled and I saw that she'd changed out of her dress into something blue. She held her corsage to me as she sat on my bed. "I thought you'd like this," she said.

I took it, looking at the velvety softness of the petals. "Don't you want it?"

"They die so quickly. I could press it in a book, but I always feel a flower is meant to be enjoyed while it's fresh and lovely. So I thought . . . here."

She pinned it to my dress. I hadn't changed out of my dress yet; I wanted to hold that feeling of glamor it gave me as long as I could. I looked down at the orchid corsage on my shoulder. It was so beautiful, encircled with tiny pink blooms.

"Would you like some help? I can ask you questions, and you can give me the answers."

She picked up the book and looked at the open page.

"All right now," she began briskly, sounding like Miss Harrison, "Give me the names of . . ."

I sighed. I wasn't in the least interested in studying but now I had to concentrate. I lowered my face to the flowers and inhaled deeply, then let my mind stumble through answers that would satisfy her.

"All right," she said finally, "Let's go downstairs for cocoa and then you can go to bed." She pulled me to my feet, her grip warm, and we went downstairs together.

When it was time to go to bed, we said good night and Simply Simon walked around the table and kissed her. I could have killed him for that, the show-off. I knew I couldn't . . . kiss her . . . yet. It would mean completely giving in. It would mean being a traitor to Mama.

"Good night, Becky," she said, a slight smile on her lips. I replied stiffly and went up to bed.

"You little rat!" I hissed at his closed bedroom door before I went into my own room.

I hung the dress in my closet, and carefully removed the corsage, pinning it on my pillow. It would give me good luck.

I didn't mean to hurt her feelings, especially after the way she helped me study and all, but I still had to think about myself. My pride wouldn't let me give in so quickly and easily. I'd feel, first of all, like an idiot, a dummy that didn't know her own mind. I knew I wouldn't be able to stand myself if I kissed her the very first night she moved in with us . . . and besides, how would Mama feel?

With my head covered over, hiding from the Black Dark, I closed my eyes, inhaling the aroma, so delicate, of the blooms near my face. I thought of Papa and Sylvia in bed together tonight, and wondered what it felt like to lie in bed with a man when you had never done that before. Would Papa put his arms around her? Or would they lie stiffly apart, embarrassed? I imagined them lying apart with Mama coming and getting between them. After all, she saw him first. Would I let somebody else have my husband? Of course not.

Strange how she didn't come to the wedding, as if she had gone away at last, convinced that she wasn't wanted. But the pains in my stomach—hadn't that been Mama? I didn't know.

Mama stood there in her white robes. I could see her as something white in the distance, coming closer. Oh I was glad! I ran towards her, my arms outstretched. Mama! You're still here! I thought you went away! But Mama didn't move. She looked angry. I stopped running. Mama spoke. You like her. You want to kiss her, don't you? I stood and stared and shook my head. No Mama. You'll always be Mama. She'll only be Sylvia. It has nothing to do with me. Papa is the one that wants her. I can't do anything.

Mama didn't believe me. Yes you can. But you don't want to. Suddenly Mama's hand came up; she had something sharp in it, that glinted as she moved . . . a knife or something. A long thin knife. I couldn't believe Mama would use it on *me*. I stood paralyzed. Don't Mama. No don't. Her hand came down again in a long slashing movement, the knife stabbing me in the cheek. I yelled, falling back, a white-hot pain searing me. Mama laughed, and crumbled at the edges . . . crumbling away into darkness until there were only her eyes, and then they were gone too.

Papa was shaking me and shaking me. "Becky, get up. Time to get up and go to school."

I looked at him, unbelieving, but the sun shone into my window, and that was the proof. I sat up slowly and suddenly Papa bent and peered at my face. He reached a hand out and touched my cheek. It felt tender and sore to his touch. I winced away from his finger.

"What's this?"

I put my hand on the spot, letting my finger run down along a roughness there. Mama, I thought, remembering. Mama had done that. But I couldn't tell Papa. I couldn't ever let him know.

"I don't know," I lied. Then Papa stooped and picked something off the floor. It was the corsage with the pin stuck in the stem. It looked old and wilted now. I stared at it. How had it gotten down there? Did Mama throw it in a rage?

"What's this doing here?" Papa asked.

"I had it pinned on my pillow. I wanted to keep it there. For luck."

Papa twirled it between his thumb and finger. "It was pinned on the pillow?"

"Yes."

"That's where you got the scratch from. When you come downstairs, I'll put peroxide on it. Now hurry up, Sylvia is making breakfast." He walked out of my room, still holding the corsage, and went into Simply Simon's room.

I looked at my face in the mirror. A thin red line. I could see Mama's face, see her hand coming down with the knife in it. I wondered what Papa would say if he knew the truth, but I was glad he thought it was the corsage. Grown people sure had funny ways of putting things together in their minds, and how easily they convinced themselves they were right! Well, it was all the better. I started to dress for school, my mind darting ahead to the exam.

It seemed very strange to see Sylvia in the kitchen first thing in the morning. Of course I knew she had to go to school too. She would go right up till the last day of June, and then she would be finished, because they didn't allow any married teachers. I didn't know why but that was the law.

"Becky." She looked over her shoulder at me. "I'll put something on the scratch in a minute." Papa must have mentioned it to her.

We ate breakfast in silence. As a rule, nobody ever said much in the morning. It wasn't a written rule but one we always followed. It took me about an hour to wake up in the mornings even after I was dressed and walking around. Sylvia looked at us anxiously and I supposed she thought we were doing it on purpose.

We kissed Papa good-bye and with Sylvia between us, we went off down Boyd. The bus stop was one block down and that's where we left her.

"Good luck, dear," she said, and lightly patted my shoulder. I'd been afraid she might try to kiss me and was relieved when she didn't.

"Thanks," I said and, with Simply Simon a step ahead

of me, ran across the street. We turned down College. It was much too beautiful a morning to waste in school, especially on exams. Simply Simon crossed the street to the zigzag lane. I watched him disappear, heard the metallic thunk! as he kicked a can in front of him. Thunk! it went, then thunk, again, but quieter. He had turned and was already out of sight.

I stopped a moment, staring at the spot where he no longer stood, and felt a strange yearning inside me. Overhead a bird sang a high plaintive theme. It filled my head, my brain, till I thought I'd burst, and I knew a perfect instant. I held still and everything around me faded. I was no place, I had vanished into thin air, become the air, the sky, the trees and the bird.

But it didn't last, couldn't last. I turned and ran along College, ran as fast as I could, faster than the wind. I was wide awake, alert, alive, I had to talk to the girls. I had to tell them everything. They would want to know all that had happened.

The exam wasn't too tough after all. It was old stuff that we had taken before. Besides, I had studied for it. Going home, I walked on tiptoe and reached for low branches, just missing with my fingertips. I picked a blade of grass and chewed on the sweet end of it and thought about summer holidays, a mere two weeks away. What would they be like this year, I wondered?

Papa had lunch ready for us. Sylvia would take over in July, but for now she ate her lunches at the school where she taught across town. It was nice, just the three of us like before. Nice. Well, I didn't really mind her of course but she was after all a stepmother.

I touched my cheek, what Papa had called a scratch, but what I knew wasn't just a scratch. A stab-wound. I looked at it in the mirror over the sink. Was it my imagination, or did it seem redder than before, longer, more of a gash? It was growing. Mama was reminding me what could happen— what had already happened—if I ever forgot about her. I hurried to go back to school for the second exam, arithmetic.

I was thankful when the week was over, because then we had free time. We could read or sit out in the playground and watch the boys play baseball. I preferred to read. Each day was like a prelude to the holidays, a rehearsal, and it made school seem almost enjoyable.

At home in the late afternoon, I went up to my room. I hadn't touched my scribbler lately. So much had happened and there hadn't been time. Besides that, I needed a safer hiding place than the blanket box. She could find it easily if she decided to clean it out. I thought of various other places but they were all so accessible. Finally I made up my mind. I'd hide them in my schoolbag. I could hang it by its strap on a nail in the corner of the closet. I never used the schoolbag anyway and my clothes would hide it.

I took the latest scribbler out. What would she think if she read it? Would she think I was silly? Or would she like what I wrote? One thing was certain, she wouldn't like what I wrote about her the first day I saw her. She had been just another candidate then. I marveled at how much had happened in just over two months. I hadn't really expected Papa to want to get married again and he had broken his promise to me. Not for ten years, Papa had said. You couldn't trust anybody, not even your own father. Not even your own *mother*! Hadn't she made Papa give her a promise while she lay dying and didn't she go and change her mind? And now she was back inside me, listening to all my thoughts and threatening me.

Auntie Sadie came over the day we got our report cards, the last day of school. I didn't show it to her because it wasn't that good and unless I had 100 in everything, she would say: "So? What are you showing me? You passed, that's all."

That was all I cared about anyway, that I had passed to grade five. But Auntie Sadie wouldn't be interested anyway. She just wanted to poke around and see how we were getting along. Snooping, in other words. "What's this?" She lifted the lid on a pot on the stove. Sylvia was just coming down the stairs, having changed into a cotton dress.

"Hello, Sadie." She looked at Auntie Sadie, who still

held the lid in her hands. "Will you stay for supper? It's nothing much, I'm afraid, just something light, but you're welcome . . ."

Auntie Sadie put the lid back on. "No, no. I have my supper cooking on the stove. I didn't come to eat. Everything is all right here?"

She raised an eyebrow and jerked her head in my direction. I knew she meant, How are you making out with the monster?

"Everything is fine," Sylvia said. "We're getting along very well, the four of us."

"Hmm," Auntie Sadie said, as if she didn't believe her, and I caught her staring at Sylvia's waistline and pretending she wasn't.

"She's not pregnant yet," I said, trying to keep a straight face and failing. It was the first time I'd ever said that word out loud and it rolled strangely on my tongue. I'd heard the big girls on the playground use that term when they talked about women having babies.

"Becky!" they both said, but in different voices; Sylvia's laughing, Auntie Sadie's shocked.

"Well, you looked!" I accused her, "and that's just as bad!"

"Wait till I tell your Papa! He'll give it to you!"

I shrugged. Let her tell, the old tattletale. Papa wouldn't care anyway. He might even laugh. He was a new kind of Papa lately, and anything might happen. He hadn't thrown a customer out of the store in such a long time, I was sure he'd forgotten how.

Papa came in then, wiping his forehead. "It's getting so hot already," he said, "my customers are leaving for the beach."

Auntie Sadie gave him a thorough inspection. I waited for her to tell Papa I was cheeky but instead she said: "Well, you *look* all right."

"So believe your eyes. If I look all right, then I must be. When are you and Morris leaving?"

"In a couple days. You need anything? You got whatever you need?"

"A million dollars might help. Or maybe some new customers. Otherwise, nothing," said my new kind of Papa glibly.

Auntie Sadie sniffed. She had no sense of humor.

"Well, I have to go. Good-bye. You should have a good life and be well. We'll be back, if God spares us, in September . . . or maybe the last week in August. We'll see. . . . Anyway, take care."

"You too. Have a good summer, and write sometime, let us know how you are."

"Kiss Auntie Sadie good-bye," Sylvia said, so I had to put my lips on the dry skin that felt like the rind of a lemon and even smelled like it. When she finally left we sat down to eat.

For a change, the store bell didn't tinkle, and then I remembered, everybody went away for the summer. The beach, or the states, but somewhere. It would be quiet for the next while.

I'd never seen the beach, but I knew what it was like because Betty had told me all about it. There was a big lake, she said, very huge, like the ocean, only I'd never seen that either. You looked far out and maybe on a clear day, you could see a soft blue line on the other side. That, she said, was land. I tried to imagine a soft blue line being land but I couldn't. I didn't think she was outright lying, but you never knew what was true and what wasn't unless you saw it for yourself.

The lake, she said, was cold as anything when you first went in, but after a while you got used to it and it felt warm and cozy. I pretended to be interested and said: "Oh, isn't that nice?"

I didn't want Betty to think I was so dumb that everything she said impressed me. Just because they had a lot of money and everything, who cared about things like that? They were empty-headed nothings. Oh, Betty was okay I guessed and I liked her, but when she started talking about the *beach*, where they went every summer, well, who *cared*?

The city was good enough for me. After all, I was no snob.

# PART five

**1** I sat on the wooden veranda steps and looked at the stars. It was a warm night, and in the dark I could see our elm tree standing on tiptoe, trying to touch the telephone wires that were strung past the houses on Boyd. Each leaf seemed to tremble with the effort, although it would be years before they came even close, I thought. I wished summer could last forever, always calm and quiet, with the flower-laden breeze touching my cheeks, and murmurs from inside the house touching my ears.

Then Simply Simon came out, letting the door slam behind him. "Guess what?" He dropped down beside me.

"Guess what? They're going over the customer accounts, and Sylvia says we should be making more money." He scratched a mosquito bite on his ankle, his bare knees in the short pants looking bony in the dark.

Quick resentment ran through me. I took it as criticism of Papa. "Why? Isn't Papa making good enough for her? It was good enough before!"

"No it wasn't," he said in reasonable tones that only made me mad at him. "We lost eight customers last month. The ones Papa used to holler at the most."

"Well, who needs *them*? Anyway, they always come back."

"Some of them didn't though. And you know what she said? She said the customer is always right. Even if he isn't."

"That's crazy. How can they be right if they're wrong? That doesn't make sense."

"Don't ask *me*. That's what *she* said."

"What did Papa say?" I could just imagine what he'd say to that.

"He said he'd try it and see if it worked."

"What?"

"Oh you know, be nice, smile at them, even when he

*165*

wants to murder them."

"Ho, ho. I can just see that."

"Sylvia says when you're in business you have to hide your real feelings. That's the way to make money."

"That's the same as telling a lie!"

"Well, that's the way you have to do it anyhow, even if it is like telling a lie."

"You know what I think? I think she complains too much. Look how many years Mama lived with Papa, and *she* never said things like that. If it was okay for Mama, it's plenty okay for *her*."

"Mama always told Papa that she shouldn't yell at the customers. Plenty of times!" he reminded me.

"Well, that's different!" I said hotly. Of course Mama told him things. She had a right to. She'd lived through lots of things with Papa that Sylvia couldn't even imagine. Anyway, what did she marry him for if she felt that way? The whole thing was her idea in the first place, and now here she was, complaining about this and that. She could just get out if she didn't like it. "If I was a customer in a store," I said firmly, trying to convince him, "and the owner started yelling at me, I would wonder what I did to get him so mad. I would think there must be a good reason."

This struck Simply Simon as so funny he went into a fit of laughter. "You! I can just see it, boy! I'll bet!" he gurgled, so I had trouble not joining him.

"Yes I would! You don't have to believe me. I don't care!" I started hitting him and in a minute, we were pulling each other's hair. I jumped up and ran down to the gate and leaned on it. "Go away. You make me sick," I told him.

The screen door creaked open suddenly and I saw Papa silhouetted against the light from the middle room at the end of the darkened hall. He stuck his head out and looked at me. "Go to Mrs. Hollis and ask her if she can pay something on her bill," Papa said. "You know the address?"

I nodded. She lived two blocks down Powers Street going north. I'd been there on several occasions before. I stood stiffly beside the gate, looking at Papa's shadowy form silently. I hated, hated, hated to ask people for money. Like a beggar. Even if they owed it to us, I felt like like a beggar, a charity case, begging for money. I turned reluctantly and went through the gate and down to the corner.

Walking along the rose-scented street, I blotted out the reason I was going. Actually, I told myself, The Princess was on an errand of mercy. Here she comes, beautiful and brave. I held my head high so my servants and bodyguards wouldn't know I was afraid of what the enemy would do to me. Because when I stepped into their lair, I would be alone. I couldn't bring anyone with me. . . . She walks silently, in her ermine robes and the slippers on her feet gleam with gold and jewels. Her hair streams back in the wind, her eyes look straight ahead. People turn to stare at her. They know who she is and they've heard of her great beauty. They want to see if it's true. They fall in piles at her feet. It is true! They gasp in amazement! It is all true! Their eyes pop out of their heads, because they will never forget the sight they have seen. The beauty of The Princess will stay in their minds forever.

I arrived at the apartment block where Mrs. Hollis lived, with the big sign NO PEDDLERS, NO DOGS on the double glass doors. How about kids, I wondered. Are kids allowed? The hall was well lit, that was one good thing. I went in and pounded up the steps, rehearsing what I would say.

Hello, Mrs. Hollis . . . my father . . . uh . . . would like to know . . . Well, Holy Toledo! It was our money, wasn't it? I wasn't asking for a handout. I only wanted money *she owed us*. Mrs. Hollis never paid unless you made a special trip and asked for it. *Well, the hell with her.*

I clumped up to the top of the building, stopping at each landing to get my breath. People who owed you money always made sure they lived on the third floor so you could drop dead of heart failure trying to collect it. It wouldn't do her any good though, 'cause here I was, whether she liked it or not.

I knocked at the door, my heart pounding like hammers. Someone must have been expecting me, I thought, because the door opened immediately and a heavy man with a hairy chest glowered at me. I could see the hair clearly because it showed through the holes in his undershirt.

"Yeah?"

"Could I speak to Mrs. Hollis please?"

He yelled over his shoulder. "Helen, the door!"

I had a whiff of sweaty armpits as he turned, his arm upraised, and moved off. I choked a little, holding my breath, and stepped backwards. Mrs. Hollis poked her head out of an open doorway in the small hall, the rest of her following, then stopped when she saw it was only me. Her hand dropped from the mess of red hair she had been smoothing.

"It's the storekeeper's kid," she said, with a note of disappointment in her voice. Her husband gave me one disinterested glance and went away. I was relieved and moved closer to the open door.

"Mrs. Hollis ... my father ... uh ... says, couldyou paysomethingonyourbillplease?" It's our money! I'm not begging you! You owe it to us!

She seemed to be thinking it over. "Just a minute. I'll see."

She left me standing in the hall. I leaned against the side of the door, prepared to wait. The last time I had counted up to 250. I wanted to see if she would beat her record. By 135, though, she was back, a new speed record, I told myself. She held out a five-dollar bill.

"I want a receipt," she told me. "And you tell your father to make sure he marks it off the bill."

She produced a piece of paper torn off a brown paper bag. She scrawled the words "Paid, $5.00" across it. "Sign this, just to be sure." She handed me a pencil and I wrote my name underneath it.

"Don't forget to give the money to your father."

"I won't forget."

"And don't lose it. Stick it in your pocket. I won't pay it again if anything happens."

"Okay." I backed away almost into the middle of the hall. Her breath pursued me. I couldn't wait to get down the stairs and out into the night. I placed the money in my pocket and kept my hand over it all the way home.

I had a wonderful feeling of success. My mission carried out, Papa would be pleased, even if she did owe close to fifty dollars. I wondered if it was possible for Mrs. Hollis to ever be completely paid up. I doubted it. Tomorrow she would probably come into the store and buy seven dollars worth of groceries and charge that too. She did it all the time, especially after I'd collected some money from her. As if, having paid a little, she could now afford to buy lots more.

Papa had said every little bit helped, and this was sure a little bit. I squeezed the five-dollar bill inside my pocket. It crinkled into an insignificant ball.

**2** All the summers of my life had followed a familiar pattern. The only important considerations were whether the library would be open and whether the sun would shine so I could wander along Powers Street, or rain fall so I would lean my head against the rusty window screen in my room, a prisoner in my own bedroom. I had no reason to believe that this summer would be different as I sat at the table eating lunch.

Business was so slow that the bell didn't ring at all while we ate. Papa dipped his spoon into the custard Sylvia had made for dessert and said, "The customers must have dropped dead."

Sylvia put down her spoon quickly, looking at him, as if she had been waiting for him to make that remark. "Jake, why don't we close the store for two weeks and take the children to the beach?"

For a moment, there was a stunned silence. We all stared at her, with Papa staring hardest, as though he'd been kicked under the table.

"Oh boy! The beach!" Simply Simon said, looking at Papa hopefully, afraid to say too much and really queer it.

Papa, the spoon still in midair halfway to his mouth, said, "Close the store?" in a voice that made it seem as if he had never heard those words spoken before. "And take them to the beach?" on an even more incredulous note.

"Yes," she said firmly. "Why not? You said yourself that business is at a standstill. So why don't we close altogether and give the children a good time?"

Papa lowered the spoon to his dish, then held his hands out, palms upwards. "It costs money, no? Do you know what you are saying?"

I held my breath. Of course it cost money! Sylvia must be crazy. Still, I dared to hope as I watched her face carefully for the tiniest change of expression. It became more eager, if anything. "Of course I know what I'm saying! You're forgetting, Jake, I am a woman with means. I have money!"

My heart leaped. I hadn't known that Sylvia was rich! I glanced towards Simply Simon to see if he appreciated the significance of what she'd said. He did.

Papa's face became stony, stubborn. "Your money is your money. I wouldn't touch it."

It was time to take a hand. I couldn't let Papa snatch away our first glimmer of hope without a battle. "Oh please please please!" I grabbed Papa's arm. "Please, Papa, let's do it!"

Simply Simon took his cue from me and grabbed Papa's other arm. "Please, please, Papa! We want to go to the beach!"

"It'll be the first time!" I urged. "The first time, when we go back to school, that I'll have something interesting to write about when we have to do our compositions!"

Papa looked at me crossly. "What are you talking?"

"Our compositions," I explained, "that we have to do in September, the My Vacation composition!"

"So? This is a reason to spend so much money, money that we haven't got?"

"It's a very good reason!" Sylvia laughed. "Especially when we do have the money! Don't forget that we share everything."

"You earned it. And you saved it. I don't want to touch it."

"Well, I *do!*" She was just as stubborn as Papa. "Anyway, it isn't only the children. You need a holiday too. When was the last time you took a week off?"

Papa sulked and refused to answer.

"I don't think you ever did take a holiday, Jake. Now please don't be so stubborn. Anyway, let's say that it's my money. Then I have the right to spend it any way I like. And this is how I want to spend it. I go to the beach every summer and I want to go again this year." Papa remained silent, staring past all our heads. "Besides," she said, a desperate note in her voice, "if what's yours is mine, then why shouldn't it work the other way around and what is mine is yours?"

"That's different," Papa said, sounding like Simply Simon when he was on the losing end of an argument.

"Please, please, please," I kept up the pressure. "We want to go to the beach. Can't we go *please?*" I could drive anybody crazy if I wanted to. I knew I had this magic power. Able to keep it up indefinitely, reducing grown-ups to gibbering idiots. Everybody we knew went somewhere for the summer, and if we couldn't go too, then I would see to it that Papa would regret it. His eyes would roll and he'd froth at the mouth and still I wouldn't stop nagging. So he might as well give up.

"I've been teaching ten years," Sylvia said, "and I've managed to save something of my salary, a little bit here and a little bit there. It's no fortune, but it's enough."

She rose and went to the cupboard where she kept her purse and brought it to the table, opened it and fished something out. "What's this?" Papa looked at the thing she held out to him.

"My bank book."

"I don't want it. It belongs to you."

Sylvia dropped it in front of him. "Will you please take a look? If it were the other way around, I would at least give you the courtesy of looking."

Papa, looking very henpecked suddenly, sighed and picked it up. We watched, hardly daring to breathe as he opened up the little book. He kept his face blank, the way he did when he looked at my report card when it was the best one I ever had. It probably irked her the way it had irked me, I thought, watching her out of the corner of my eye. Now Papa lifted his head and looked right at her.

"Well?" she said.

"We'll have to get them bathing suits," Papa said.

We were delirious with joy.

The way we went, a week later, we must have looked like immigrants, like refugees coming to a new land. We packed our belonging onto the truck Papa rented for the trip. He had to rent the driver too. Papa and Sylvia sat in the cab of the truck with the driver (Papa next to the driver) and Simply Simon and I sat in the back on top of our boxes, holding them down as we bumped and lurched over the gravelly highway which was little more than a dirt track. We waved happily to everyone we saw on the way, and laughed joyously if they waved back. All our sheets, pillows, blankets, pots and pans, dishes and cutlery were in the boxes: everything we could possibly need, because Sylvia had wrinkled her nose in a cute way and said: "We can't use *theirs!*"

Who knew, she explained, what kind of food had been cooked and eaten on the utensils that belonged to the cottage? Pork and all kinds of chozzerai, she said, were probably made on their dishes. The food we were going to eat was packed in cartons surrounded by ice. Sylvia had been busy with the preparations all week, cooking roasts, chicken, and all kinds of delicious smelling things, enough to last most of the two weeks of the wonderful holiday that lay ahead of us. I felt the sun and the wind in my face, and told myself it was going to be nothing but fun, fun, fun!

The beach was strange. For one thing, it was dirtier than I had expected. I had visualized it as a sort of Garden of Eden . . . a Paradise where angels sported. . . . It turned out to be the opposite: a slummy sort of town with mud streets and dingy cottages in rows. But worst of all, as I found out the minute we arrived at our cottage, was the foul-smelling shack out in the back, which would serve as our bathroom. I'd had to go almost since we'd left home, and the lumpy ride had only served to intensify my need. While Papa and Sylvia and Simply Simon and the driver unloaded our stuff in the large yard which held a series of identical cabins, I went hunting for the *"facilities."* There weren't any inside, I soon discovered, and when I had to finally whisper my distress to Sylvia, she smiled. "Oh Becky, you'll find it out in the back. Go quickly!"

I'd been shocked. To have to go outside to the bathroom seemed to me a step backward out of civilization. But I was in no condition to complain. I ran around to the back and walked along a narrow crooked boardwalk. Hidden among silver birch and maples, the weathered outhouse looked almost romantic, with its peaked roof and moonshaped hole in the door.

The notion vanished as I approached it and opened the small creaking door. Spiderwebs draped themselves in all the corners, and directly in front of my eyes lay the small bench with the hole in the middle. I couldn't believe it. Was *this* the kind of thing Betty Greenberg took as a matter of course? I held my nose, stepped inside, and closed and locked the door. It took great courage to stay there even for a minute. I imagined spiders sidling up to me in the dark or hanging suspended in front of my nose from long silk threads. I groped around me for paper, afraid my hand would touch something crawly, found the paper, and finally was able to escape.

"Sylvia," I told her irately. "It stinks in there!"

She looked up from her labors cleaning the shelves in the smallish cramped kitchen and smiled. "In that case, dear," she said calmly, "we'll have to clean it up." And as reward, she gave me the job of doing it.

Lake Winnipeg made up for everything. As I looked at it I was sure it was as big as the ocean. I stood on the rough gravelly road and squinted into the sun. There was a vast blueness above and a second, landlocked sky below. Bits of white cloud flowed along the ripples, as though they had fallen in. I went closer, down through the scrubby grass to the sand, and leaned on a slender birch. Heads bobbed close to shore and shrieks of laughter came from far out in the water.

I wondered if Betty could be down there somewhere. Wouldn't she be surprised if I were to walk up to her and say: "Hi!"

I turned and went back towards the cottage and was met partway by Simply Simon. He had been sent to find me. There was still a lot of work to do to get the place livable, and both Papa and Sylvia were busy washing floors and cupboards and everything.

"Holy Toledo!" I said. "It looks like we're cleaning up for Pesach!"

Papa pointed to one of the boxes. "You can put your clothes away," he suggested, and that was the end of the holidays for me on that first day at the beach.

The cabin had two bedrooms and a kitchen and a screened-in veranda. Simply Simon and I were going to share one of the bedrooms. When I tried to complain that I didn't want to sleep in the same room as a *boy*, Sylvia said: "You'll take turns undressing. I'm sure it will work out just fine. This is the best we could afford."

She made me feel like a rat for complaining when I had nagged so hard for this holiday at the beach. I closed my mouth up tightly and didn't argue about it anymore.

It felt good to finally be finished cleaning up. Everything smelled of soap and water and drying wood. We ate roast beef sandwiches and Papa arranged for ice delivery for the ice box, which was cleaned and smelled sweet. Afterwards, I went outside and stood on our walk in the big yard. It looked more like a park with all the old trees scattered throughout. I counted eight cottages in the yard, sharing the trees, the grass, the gentle wind blowing in off the lake, the birds that sang with different voices here than in the city. I approached what I decided would be my tree and touched the gnarled trunk, which was bent and twisted so it almost touched the ground and looked a thousand years old. I could imagine myself sitting in the crotch of the tree with leaves for a roof, reading one of my library books, Louisa May Alcott or Booth Tarkington. I wished I'd had the foresight to bring some books, even *Tabitha's Promise* which I'd already read about five times.

I climbed my tree, an easy thing to do with its main trunk so close to the ground, and went as high into the leaves as I dared. I felt secret, hidden, like an unseen watcher. I climbed down again and went into the cottage.

"Can I put my bathing suit on now?"

Sylvia stood in the kitchen, arranging our dishes on one of the top shelves, making it look like home, while Papa lined a lower shelf with paper. She looked airy in her cool chiffon dress with outsize flowers, her legs bare underneath, her feet in sandals. She didn't look like anybody's mother dressed like that, but Papa still looked like Papa. He even had a shirt on, buttoned to the neck and clipped with a dark blue tie.

I wandered outside again, so that I wouldn't be too handy in case there was something for me to do. I walked back to the clearing where I had first seen the lake, imagining the time that lay ahead of us stretching into forever. The sun shone with brilliance, bouncing off the water into millions of skimming sparkles. The breeze smelled tantalizingly of water and seaweed.

In my bathing suit that came halfway to my knees, I felt terribly exposed, half naked. It didn't matter that other kids at the beach were as bare as I was, I still felt very conscious of all the areas of myself which were usually hidden suddenly open for anyone to see.

Sylvia carried a blanket and some of our towels in her arms and Papa carried the newspaper that he'd brought with him and hadn't had a chance to read yet. I noticed that although he still wore his shirt, he had made one concession to the informal beach life. He had removed his tie and unbuttoned the top button of his shirt.

Simply Simon and I walked on ahead of them using the well-worn path through weeds and long grass, dodging the swarm of insects that rose to greet us at every step. We darted around other families spread before us on blankets on the sand—around couples, babies and small children building sand castles at the water's edge—and finally found a spot we could call our own. Sylvia spread the blanket on the ground, and we helped her, straightening out the corners.

Our ears were assaulted by noise. It was a teeming laughing place with gaudy color, wide beach umbrellas and picnic baskets on the sand. Shrieks and yells bounced, magnified, off the undulating water. Everywhere I looked I saw brown bodies, red bodies, and like ours, white bodies, the giveaway that they had just arrived at the beach. The white ones looked pale, sickly, and I didn't want to be one of them. I wondered how long it would be before we were the right color for the beach.

"You can go in the water now," Papa said, "but stay together and don't go too far. I want to see you both." He settled himself comfortably beside Sylvia and opened his newspaper. She rummaged through a brown paper bag she had brought and arranged the towels on the blanket beside her.

"And come out, when we tell you to," she added, "without arguments."

We ran, laughing into the sun, to the water's edge. The water looked on fire from the sun, so I ran confidently in, my feet splashing silver spray ahead of me, and stopped as the first drops landed on my skin fiercely cold. I screamed and leaped back, suddenly remembering Betty's description of the lake. I hadn't imagined anything could be that cold. My skin puckered with goosepimples. I hugged myself, staring incredulously at Simply Simon, who had run past me into the water and was now way out, with half of his body underwater.

"Wait for me!" I shrieked, and made a valiant attempt to step into the water and ignore the cold, the way he did. Simply Simon turned and grinned, wading back towards me.

"Come on, you big sissy!" he yelled, waving his arm. His voice had a strange sound—as if it had left his mouth and traveled far away before it returned, jumping in a wide arc towards me. I stared at him, wondering how he had done that.

There were waves of cold coming up from my toes to my knees and I marveled at all the people I could see, bodies glistening, swimming or playing in the lake. I hoped Betty was right, and you did get used to it after a while because otherwise, the whole thing was a gyp. I put my other toe in gingerly.

Suddenly I was wet from head to feet, and Simply Simon was laughing and turning to run through the water away from me, the spray from his hands settling all over my skin. "Simply Simon, you stupid idiot!" I shrieked at him and forgot to be cold in my rage and desire to get my hands on him. I was up to my waist in water before I realized that it wasn't as cold as all that! I couldn't get close enough to splash him back and get my revenge, and anyway, he was wet already and he wouldn't care. But just in case, he dodged behind some boys, keeping them between him and me and then a ball landed in front of me, splashing me in the face. In a minute, we were all involved in the game.

Once in a while I'd look towards shore to see if Papa and Sylvia wanted us. They looked very far away, as though they were on an island and I was viewing them through a telescope, tiny figures on a scrap of white, surrounded by other tiny figures, yet alone and self-sufficient. They didn't need anybody, not even us, I thought, feeling abandoned. Then the ball would bounce off my head and in a minute I was back in the game, having a wonderful time. Wasn't that enough for me?

When Papa did wave us in, we didn't want to go, but we went. We dried off on the towels, a breeze bringing a shiver to our skins. The sun beat down efficiently and soon we were warm again. Sitting on the edge of the blanket, I looked around me at the other sunbathers, wondering if any of them could be Betty. Mostly, there were little kids or babies, grandmothers or parents. I couldn't see anybody who looked remotely like Betty. It was very disappointing. Where could all the girls my age be? There were plenty of boys for Simply Simon to play with, I noticed. He had always been a lucky fish that way. Somebody must be taking good care of me, I thought sarcastically. Somebody was punishing me, no doubt. Mama.

We went back to the cottage and ate a light supper of

cold cuts and salad which we took outside and ate on the grass, picnic style. Later, I leaned on the gray slat fence and watched people go by, wondering where they were going, and making up stories in my head about them. There was nothing else to do. I looked down the street where groves of fir, pine, spruce, birch and poplar massed outwards towards the sky in ever-receding spires. The road wound on and on and disappeared around a bend. I wondered what was at the other end, and decided to explore.

At the bend, the road straightened, then continued on, partly hidden by dense mysterious undergrowth. As far as I could tell, it just went along the same way, leading nowhere. I'd hoped for adventure and was disappointed. The whole holiday was turning into a zero. What was so great about the beach? At home, I'd have gone to the library and taken an armful of books out and read them at the park. Or I'd go see a show at the Palace Theatre, or for long walks to the City Limits, about 20 blocks from Powers Street going west. Come to think of it, there was always a lot to do at home in the summer. Except for the lake, what was there to do here?

But the air smelled different, and the sounds were different; I appreciated things like that. The lake, now out of sight, spoke in fluid tones, a rhythmic pulsing language of surf washing over the shore; the shrill cries of birds above me mingled with the voices that came from the water, voices robbed of resonance by the torpid air. I walked back along the path, happier.

Papa and Sylvia sat on the veranda looking as if they'd always been together. Always and forever. There had never been Mama, never been a time when "four of us" included not her but Mama, my mother. She had never gone to the beach, neither she nor Papa were people who would go even if they had money. But of course, they didn't have money.

I wondered how Mama felt, seeing them sit together like that. I knew how I'd feel . . . I'd hate it. I supposed she felt the same way even if she did want Papa to get married again. I'd have to be very careful and not have any thoughts that would make Mama think I liked Sylvia at all . . . even a tiny bit. It made me feel mean. I didn't want to hurt my own mother, but at the same time, I couldn't go on being nasty to Sylvia forever. Mama would have to understand. I wished I didn't have to be so mixed up.

"We were waiting for you." Sylvia smiled, getting up. "Come, we're going for a walk into town."

Papa rose too and went inside. In a minute, he came out, his tie firmly in place under his chin, his suit jacket buttoned up.

In town we walked along a wide boardwalk. There were booths on both sides of it, with rides and shooting galleries where a person could win all kinds of prizes, big stuffed teddy bears or dolls with beautiful painted faces. I lingered at each booth, gazing at the dolls and plush animals and the fantastic variety of things worth winning. I knew it was no use nagging Papa for money to try for one of those prizes, and when I looked around, they had gone. I had to run to catch up to them.

Behind the boardwalk were grocery stores as small as ours, and small cafés, a barbershop, drugstore, ice cream parlor and a horrible-looking hotel which looked more like a glorified boardinghouse. Gaudy neon signs flicked on and off, and crowds of people jostled each other. They overflowed the sidewalks, moved sluggishly through stores and cafés, over boardwalks and against booths, onto the rides, into the dance pavilion which vibrated with loud music, between the buildings, where couples hugged and kissed shamelessly. I stared goggle-eyed till one young romeo stopped kissing long enough to growl at me: "Beat it, kid!"

Papa walked along beside Sylvia, looking neither to left nor to right, missing everything that I found interesting, and Simply Simon and I snickered whenever we caught sight of another one of those passionate embraces. Personally, I thought lovers were disgusting, and I couldn't see why they had to do anything as sickening as that and why they had to do it in public.

Suddenly, Papa did a very uncharacteristic thing. He walked over to the window of the ice cream parlor and bought us all ice cream cones. I stared at his back. He still looked like Papa, wearing Papa-type clothes, but inside them, he was a stranger to me. I could imagine Betty's father strolling along the boardwalk with her and buying her an ice cream but this man who held out a cone to me, was this my father?

I blamed Mama now and whispered to her in my mind. You see, I told her, it's a new kind of Papa, one you would never recognize. And it's all your fault, Mama, because you never made Papa take us to the beach. You never had *money of your own.*

Back at the cottage, with night black as velvet pricked with tiny sparks of starlight, we prepared to go to bed. But first we had to take turns going to the bathroom. Sylvia stood on the walk leading to the outhouse, which now reeked with disinfectant that she had instructed me to pour into the hole in the seat. I had also cleaned away the spider webs, but, even though Sylvia held a flashlight, shining it into the hole in the door while I sat inside, I still could feel the beady eyes of insects watching me from their hidey-holes. I did what I had to do as quickly as I could, and rushed out, taking my turn with the flashlight at arm's-length beaming into the small room for Sylvia's benefit. When she came out, she looked as if she'd been holding her breath. We waited for Simply Simon, who made loud comments from inside. "Why does it have to stink in here?" he demanded. "I'd rather go somewhere in the bushes!"

Life at the beach was far from ideal, but I had to admit it was different. Our beds felt damp as we slid under the covers and Simply Simon giggled as he reached his arm across the narrow space between our beds and poked me in the dark. I moved away from the edge, shaking his hand away as though he were an insect, and rolled closer to the window, open onto the night with only a black screen between us and the big yard.

I looked up and saw strange shapes silhouetted against the utter blackness. Trees moved out there, leaves swished and whispered to each other, and waves broke against the shore farther away. The sounds were muted, hushed. They painted a picture in my mind, silver and black, black and silver. It was a lullaby, a sleep-painting, a landscape of dreams. My eyes closed, and still I saw them, the moving shapes, and heard the sound they made, and suddenly . . .

. . . the sun glimmered through the branches of trees, knocking against my eyelids, making them open. I stared, and for an instant, I was nowhere. I frowned. The room was small and bright with morning. I let my eyes roam over the ceiling, and saw cracked plaster where I hadn't seen any before. The gray painted chest of drawers against the wall at the foot of my bed, and the identical bed at my left, with Simply Simon curled up asleep under the blanket, brought me back. We were at the beach. Of course. How could I forget?

Millions of birds sang outside the big window above my bed. I sat up and looked out of the window at the sun-drenched yard and knew it must be very early. The quality of sunlight edged in gold was different somehow.

I dressed quickly before Simply Simon woke up and caught me at it, then tiptoed out past his bed and through the door. Today, I told myself, was Monday, July 13th, and we had another 13 days left of our beach vacation. I didn't want to waste any of it.

I hurried to the outhouse and was surprised to find that the smell hardly bothered me. I must be getting used to it, I thought. Anyway, it was cleaner than it had been. I didn't linger, in case the spiders were watching me, and they could be boy spiders, for all I knew. I hated the feeling of being spied upon.

There were washbasins at the back of the cottage on a sort of stand. It took me a minute to find my source of water, the big tank right alongside the stand, with the spigot in its side. I finished washing up, and dripping turned to look for a towel. I knew there must be one hanging from the line where Sylvia had left them after we'd come back from swimming. I grabbed one off and wiped my face, neck and arms. Then I tossed it back over the line to dry.

It was nice being the only person awake in the whole world. I could pretend as I poured milk into a bowl of corn flakes that I was the only person alive, that there was nobody else but me. I always wondered what it would feel like. What would I do? First of all, I would help myself to as much sugar as I wanted. I turned the sugar bowl over my corn flakes and dumped a mountain of sugar into it. Papa would kill me if he saw me do a thing like that. "Don't you know," he would say, "that you'll get a big worm in your stomach from too much sugar?"

But I never let that worry me. It sounded like the kind of thing parents said just to scare you. It wasn't really true. I stirred the sugar into the milk and corn flakes, feeling it scrunch against the bottom of my bowl. For once I'd have enough sugar. I raised the spoon to my lips. Next, I thought, moving the sickeningly sweet food around in my mouth, I would take all the money I could find. It would all be mine, and I could spend it on anything I liked. I rubbed my finger over the rough wood of the table and looked at the closed doors, Papa's and the room where Simply Simon still slept. The kitchen felt closed in, small. I glanced towards the window on the side where it opened onto the view of the cottage next door and for a moment I wondered who lived there. Then my mind returned to my fantasy.

I wouldn't need money, I reminded myself, because there wouldn't be anybody left to buy things from, you see. I could just help myself. I could take all the dolls and plush toys and other prizes from those booths on the boardwalk. It wouldn't be stealing. It would belong to me, the only person left alive!

I made myself finish my breakfast, even though it tasted awful. The sweetness was cloying; great mounds of sugar lined the bottom of the bowl, undissolved; which was a good thing because I didn't want any of it. I went outside when I heard the sounds of stirring from Papa's room, so I could hold on to my feeling of being special and alone. I climbed the climbing tree and, safely hidden among the leaves, pretended that I lived in the jungle, far away from civilization, and my only companions were the wild jungle beasts.

I half sat, half leaned along one thick branch and looked

down, feeling the branch bend under my weight. I knew it wouldn't break because it was too solid, but I needed the element of danger, the belief that it might, to give me a feeling of adventure.

A door slammed. I lifted my head and saw Simply Simon going towards the outhouse. Good luck, I told him silently. Then my name was being called. Papa stood on the veranda, looking anxiously along the sidewalk. He didn't think of looking up into the tree. I watched him, feeling absolutely nothing. Sylvia joined him a moment later, a bathrobe tied around her. Their voices came to me thinly. "I can't find her," Papa said worriedly. "She doesn't answer."

Sylvia put her head through the doorway. "Becky!" Her voice sounded high and wavery, not cool the way it usually was. "Becky, where are you?"

I watched them, like a spectator at a movie watching actors perform on the screen. What would they do next, I wondered? What were they supposed to do? The director would tell them to rush off and find me. Or maybe he would tell them to shrug and say: "She'll come back, all by herself. She's all right." I was curious.

"I can't understand it," Papa said, his eyes moving outwards. "Where could she go? To the water?"

Sylvia put her hands on Papa's shoulders soothingly. "I'm sure she didn't go far," she said. "You know how Becky is, she likes to go for walks. . . ."

They turned and went inside. I was disappointed. That wasn't the way it should go, I thought. If it had been Mama, she would have fainted. She would have screamed and run outside to find me. She would have been sure that I'd drowned; she would have rushed to the lake, screaming my name and running up and down along the beach, maybe grabbing people and begging them to go and save me. For all Papa seemed to care, I could have been a dog that got lost. They were lovers, that was all. What were they doing inside anyway? A vision of them hugging like the young couples did between the buildings along the boardwalk loomed before my eyes. I scrambled backwards towards the fork of the branch, then slithered down to the ground, jumping the last two feet and landing hard, hurting my ankle. I picked myself up and limped up the steps of the veranda and into the cottage.

"Did somebody call me?" I hollered loudly because I couldn't see them, so they must be in their bedroom.

Papa came right out, a stern look on his face. "Where did you go? From now on, I want you to tell me before you leave this house. Understand?"

I rubbed my ankle. "I only went for a little walk," I said. "Holy Toledo, what is this, a jail or something?"

Papa humphed, and went back into the bedroom. The door closed firmly behind him. Well, I thought. Well! Now I know what he thinks of me. Now I know!

I sat down, my arms folded across my chest, glaring at their door. I would stare so hard that my eyes would burn a hole right through the wood. That would teach them not to shut doors in my face. Simply Simon came in then. "Hey! We're supposed to go to the store for Sylvia. I've got the money and a list. Come on!"

I turned and glared at him, but he was busy tying his shoelaces and my fiercest expression was lost on him. "Hurry up then, slowpoke!" I jumped to my feet, forgetting for a minute that I'd hurt my ankle. We took our time walking to the store in town and by the time we got there, I felt much better. It was going to be another marvelous hot day, and nobody could stay mad on a day like this. Besides, my ankle had stopped hurting.

Later, I even forgave Papa and Sylvia, although they didn't appreciate it because they hadn't known I was mad at them in the first place. We put on our bathing suits still damp from the day before and walked down to the beach. There weren't as many people around because all the weekenders had gone back to the city. Simply Simon and I waded into the icy water, our teeth chattering, wishing the water was as warm as it looked.

There were fewer people in the lake too, and the boys with the beach ball had gone away. It wasn't as much fun when all there was to do was splash each other, and dip down, pretending to swim, our feet never leaving the ground. I looked across as far as I could see. I squinted against the brightness and saw where the water touched the edge of the sky. I had a feeling that this lake reached all around the world, that there wasn't any other land except what lay behind us. Straight ahead, blue sky faded into blue water and as my eyes ran along the edges, I saw something faint, a line of deeper blue, floating above the water level. Land. Just as Betty had said. Land at the other side of the lake. I wondered if there were people there looking at us, and seeing nothing but a faint blue line too and wondering if there were people here who wondered if there were people there . . . I gave up and bent my knees so my body was hidden in the water, and looked around at the scattered swimmers.

A wet arm came slicing towards me, propelled by what looked like a storm churning up the water behind it. I backed away as a dripping head surfaced and the water stopped churning. A woman, wet hair plastered to her face, blew water out of her mouth and nose. As she stood, wiping her face with her hands, oblivious to me, I had a very close look at her bulging bathing suit top, because the wide shoulder strap had come loose off her shoulder exposing her right breast. I stared at it in fascination, marveling at the way it seemed to burst out of her skin. I remembered Cousin Nankie with her deep neckline. Women were shaped funny, I decided, staring down at my own flat bathing suit. I hoped I'd never have to look like that, so big and flabby.

The woman didn't seem to know or care that it showed, and because an opportunity like that wouldn't come again in a long time, I took a good look at her out of the corner of my eye. The pink tip was a lot bigger than mine. I wondered what it felt like to have them right under your nose, practically. Did she look at them a lot, and how come it didn't bother her that her strap was loose? That reminded me of an expression I'd heard from some of Papa's customers. Now I understood what they'd meant by "loose women," who did bad things. I looked around quickly to make sure there were no men around to see her, and moved out of her range of vision so she wouldn't guess I'd seen her if she happened to look up.

With a whoosh, she flattened herself on top of the water, and kicked a storm right into my face as she swam away. I shook by head, wiping away the drops, but I couldn't wipe away what I had seen. So that's what they looked like. Every woman—even Mama—had big ones like that. And so did Sylvia, I remembered, and . . . and . . . everybody. Except, come to think of it, Auntie Sadie. She was as flat as a board, and look what a mean type of person she was, while Auntie Leah, jolly happy old Auntie Leah, had bigger ones than anybody else I knew. I wondered if that meant anything. I wondered what kind of person I was . . . the big type, or flat. Only time would tell, but from now on, I made up my mind to examine myself in the mirror carefully. Just to see what kind of person I would be.

I turned to find Simply Simon, who was some distance away, pretending he was a great swimmer. "I'm going in now," I said. "Coming?"

The sun dried us as we sat shivering, wrapped in towels. I felt sleepy, lethargic, as though the lake breeze was blowing my brains away. I lay on the blanket and let the sun cover me with its hot hands. Sylvia, sitting beside me, leaned over and cast a shadow, and I felt the brush. She was trying to fix my hair while I lay on my stomach, my head to one side. I kept my eyes closed, seeing the naked breast in my mind, and knew if I opened my eyes, I would see the fullness of Sylvia's dress hanging over me. I tried to imagine Sylvia without her clothes on, but I couldn't. It seemed very dirty to me to even try. But I bet Papa could. They slept in the same bed. I didn't see how they could stand it. People were such . . . pigs! They got married and saw each other in bed. I would never!

I turned on my side and, through my squinted-up eyes, saw Papa reading a book. He never went anywhere without his books, either in Yiddish or Hebrew, and he'd had the foresight to bring his whole library, just about. My eyelids felt heavy. Somebody covered me with towels. The waves made lapping little noises. I visualized them going out, away from the shore, farther and farther away. It was a very peaceful idea.

**7** After a few days, it was possible to believe that we had always lived at the beach, always lolled on the sand, tiptoed to the water's edge hoping to catch it by surprise so it would forget to be cold. We felt as though it was quite ordinary to walk the mile and a half to town for our needs, have our ice delivered to the cottage by horse and wagon (the same as in the city, except that it was a different horse, a brown one here, a black and white one at home) and spend hours and hours together. After a few days, the lazy life became our way of life.

If it hadn't been for Mrs. Hanover it wouldn't have been quite as interesting, although it wasn't her so much as her baby, Jennifer. Besides them, our next-door neighbors, there was only Johnny, the storekeeper's son, who made life bearable by giving us some diversion from the leisurely life. He went swimming with us, showed us where an old hoot owl lived in a hollow tree, and led us through some trails that he said the Indians had made a hundred years ago.

But my favorite person was Jennifer, who was eight months old, and had beautiful big blue eyes, a wisp of light brown curls and dimples where it mattered. She had small spears of teeth peeping through her gums and a laugh that turned the world into a rainbow of colored bubbles. I called her Jenny-Wren, and she liked it. I could tell.

"Please!" I would beg, "Please, Mrs. Hanover, can I take Jenny-Wren for a walk in her carriage?"

Mrs. Hanover would rub her light blond hair and wrinkle her nose, and while I waited, breathlessly, would appear to be thinking it over very hard. Then she would laugh and shrug. "Oh, go ahead. But be careful, and not too far. It's almost time for her nap." She would light a cigarette and take a deep drag on it, looking at me through the smoke.

It was always almost time for something, for her bath,

for her lunch or supper or nighttime bottle, for her bedtime. It seemed to me that Jenny was regulated right up to her diapers, and her mother never had time to enjoy her. But I made up for it by doing things that would make Jenny happy—sharing my ice cream cone when nobody was looking, or taking her in a carriage where she could see the lake.

With Johnny showing us places at the beach that only he knew about, and Jenny-Wren in her carriage bouncing happily, I didn't mind the long lazy days or the less-than-perfect way of life here.

"Hey, d'you wanna see where the rich people live?" He scratched the side of his leg with his bare left foot.

"You mean, they live in a special place?" Of course, why wouldn't rich people live fancier than the rest of us, even at the beach?

"Sure. Come on. I'll show ya!"

We strolled down the graveled path.

"Doesn't that hurt your feet?" I couldn't see how anybody could walk on stones without limping.

"Nah. I'm used to it. Who wants to wear shoes?" He leaned on the carriage while he lifted one foot to show me the dirty underpads of his feet, rough and leathery. "I don't need shoes. See that? Hard as a rock. Feel it. Go ahead, feel it, you'll see."

"It's okay. I believe you. It looks hard as a rock all right." I wouldn't touch his foot for a million dollars, but he wasn't offended and put his foot down.

We passed ditches where wild saskatoons grew, and strawberries, raspberries, and many other promising delights which weren't quite ripe yet, and alas, wouldn't be even in two weeks. Between the path and Lake Winnipeg dense shrubbery murmured mysteriously as a breeze stirred their leaves. Scraggly pine shot straight up at the path's edge, guarding a tangle of underbrush, strange and fascinating to my city eyes. I glanced into interlocking growth, rampant with life, positive that if I stood still long enough, I would see rabbits, chipmunks or even a wolf stare out from between the thick branches.

"We're almost there," he said now. "The White Way. That's what they call it. Know why? Because they have special sand brought in for their beach. Special white sand every summer. Honest."

"No kidding." I couldn't believe anything so extravagant.

"Cross my heart and hope to spit." He spat into the bushes. I looked at him with distaste. Sometimes he didn't seem quite respectable enough for me, but I bit back the quick reprimand that ached to come out.

Up ahead where the path curved slightly, where the trees parted in cultivated clearings, I glimpsed the outlines of a house, a solid-looking house with gables, shutters and the wide chimney at the bottom of the house which promised a real fireplace inside. Manicured shrubs nestled close. Soon other details became apparent—diamond-shaped windows, several chimneys, a fan-shaped decoration over the big front door—a sprawling structure surrounded by trees so it could only be seen in sections. And beyond, in a thicket, another style of mansion appeared, and farther down, still another. This was The White Way. Without even asking, I knew one other thing; there would be no smelly little outhouse in the back and no pump for water on the corner of the street for the use of all the residents, with a rusty handle that squeaked horribly when it was pumped up and down.

He grinned. "Well, here it is: where the rich bitches live!"

I gasped, ran around in front of Jenny and clapped both my hands over her ears. "You watch your language, Johnny! That's not a nice word, and you know it!"

"So what? It's what they are, isn't it? My mother calls them that. What's wrong with it?"

"Your mother shouldn't call people names. Especially when they're her customers. Anyway, just because they have a lot of money doesn't mean there's anything wrong with them. They're just as good as you are, and I have a rich friend that's very nice. So there." I looked at the houses in awe. They were grander than many houses I had seen in the city on my way to school, grander-looking than the house Betty lived in. "Do they ever come to our beach?"

He gave me a disdainful look. "What for? Why would they come to our lousy beach that's full of sharp stones and not much sand when they can be by themselves over here without bums like us hanging around?"

He picked at a mosquito bite on his elbow, and I looked at him quite frankly, at his once-blue shorts, now an indeterminate color, frayed at the edges, his striped jersey pocked with snags, hands and feet dirty. I looked down at myself in my none-too-clean cotton dress, sandals on my bare feet and two spots of black on my knees where I had knelt in the grass. We did look like bums, I thought, both of us. "Let's go back," I said quickly. If Betty Greenberg came out of one of those beautiful mansions and saw me looking like a bum, she would never be my friend again. I turned the carriage around and headed back up the path at high speed. Johnny had no choice but to follow me. "What's your rush? Wait for me!"

Back at the cottage, after I returned Jenny-Wren to her mother, I went inside and changed my dress, then spent a futile fifteen minutes scrubbing my knees at the washstand in back. The dirt seemed to be painted on, so I finally gave up. For the next few days, I avoided Johnny as much as possible, not only because he looked like a bum and didn't care, but because he called rich people *"bitches"* and I hoped to be rich myself one day.

Now I looked even harder among the bathers, in case some of my friends might actually be somewhere in their midst, and I spent long minutes scanning the distant waters along the shores of the lake in the general direction of The White Way, but I didn't see even the specks that I assumed would be swimmers at that distance. In town I looked for them playing the penny ante machines on the boardwalk, or buying ice cream at the window of the ice cream parlor, or in the drugstore, reading the latest movie magazines at the newsstands. If they were here, as I felt sure they must be, they were making certain nobody in the ordinary part of the beach saw them.

It was disappointing in a way, but at least I still had my favorite person, Jenny-Wren, who crowed with delight when I crawled around on my hands and knees with her in the grass. I was curious about her father, whom I hadn't met; I wondered what he looked like. Jenny's mother was very pretty, with her wide-apart eyes and nose that turned up adorably at the tip. I compared her to Sylvia and realized that Sylvia was really quite ordinary. Also, Sylvia's skin had a dark tinge which was in direct contrast to Mrs. Hanover's. It gave me secret pleasure to realize that Sylvia was nothing special.

Jenny's father would be, of course, tall and handsome with broad shoulders and kind eyes. He would lean protectively over his family and never let sorrow touch them in any way, and he would give them anything they asked for. I could hardly wait for the weekend when he would come out of the city to spend the two days with them. I was sure Jenny-Wren missed him terribly and couldn't bear the separation.

"Jenny-Wren," I told her comfortingly, as she reached for the grass at the edge of her blanket and tried to put it in her mouth, "when your daddy comes he will pick you up and throw you in the air and catch you. Won't that be fun?"

Jenny gurgled and examined the grass in her clenched fist, as though she didn't care whether he came or not. I took it away from her before she could stuff it into her mouth, and as I expected, she burst into loud wails. It took all the faces I knew how to make to get her laughing again.

Sylvia looked down at us, a funny look on her face. "I need you to set the table, Becky," she said then. "Will you please go inside?"

"What about Jenny?"

"I'll take Jenny to her mother." Sylvia leaned down and picked Jenny up, wrapping the blanket around her. I waited hopefully for Jenny to set up another loud wail because I was sure she loved me more, but to my intense disappointment, she didn't mind at all. I went into the cottage. Babies were fickle, I decided. They didn't care who handled them.

When Sylvia walked in a few minutes later, I was busy

washing my hands in the basin on the counter. "I'll bet her father looks like a movie star," I said, trying to imagine which one he would resemble the most.

"I don't think so."

"I'll bet he's tall, dark and handsome, and very strong."

"He's actually short." Sylvia cut up some lettuce for a salad.

I reached into the cupboard for the dishes. "What do you mean, short?"

"About the same height as Mrs. Hanover." She began to hum the tune "Happy Days Are Here Again."

I didn't believe her. "How could she marry somebody the same size as her? When I get married, my husband will be at *least* six feet tall. I won't even look at somebody shorter."

She stopped humming, and laughed. "I think by the time you're ready for that step, Becky, you'll have other standards." Her hands were red with tomatoes as she sliced them onto the lettuce.

"I don't know what you mean, and anyway, how do you know Mr. Hanover is short?"

"Because I saw him the day we arrived. He's quite ordinary-looking, but pleasant, and that's a lot more important than being handsome. You'll find out someday."

Maybe not, I thought. Maybe to Sylvia he was ordinary, but to Mrs. Hanover and to me, he'd be dashing, handsome. I said: "Huh."

"It's character that counts, Becky. A man's character, not his looks. Do you know what character means?"

"*Sure* I do. Who doesn't know that?" But I pressed my lips together. Of course she was wrong, but I knew better than to tell her. You couldn't see character and it was a person's looks you had to live with. Which just showed how much she knew. Boy!

I looked sideways at her and wondered what she had seen in Papa to make her want to marry him. Papa certainly had character, but how did she know that? It didn't show on a person. Papa wasn't handsome or dashing and he certainly wasn't tall but with Papa it didn't matter, because, well, just because. Anybody who didn't like Papa could just go and jump in the lake.

What made people want to marry other people? How did they know, just to look at each other, that they wanted to be together for the rest of their lives? It was one of those mysteries, those questions without answers that used to make Mama say: When you're old enough to understand, I'll tell you. Mama had always thought that she would be here when I was old enough to know the answer to so many questions.

I found out for myself about Mr. Hanover on Saturday morning. He was the exact opposite of tall, dark and handsome, I discovered when I peeked out at him through my bedroom window. He had a short stocky figure, almost what you would call plump if he was a woman, and his blond hair was slicked back from a high forehead. My first disappointment passed though when he turned his head slightly and I could see his face. It was round and smiling, and the blue eyes brimmed with laughter. So it was all right then, I thought, because Jenny loved to laugh and she learned to be that way from her father.

I liked his character immediately. I would base all my standards, I decided, on whether a person was nice like Mr. Hanover or not. I ran out to be there so I could be introduced to him along with the others.

"Oh, here's my helper." Mrs. Hanover smiled so I became paralyzed with shyness in an instant. I felt my face turn red-hot and couldn't meet his eyes.

"Hello, there!" he said, but immediately looked away. "Where's my pumpkin pie?"

"She's tucked in her crib, napping, George, don't wake her! I missed you." She kissed him on the mouth, right in front of us.

"Did you? That's good, because I wanted you to miss me. Are you sure you don't have a lover on the side?" I listened raptly, as though it were something in a movie, both of them blond and romantic like that.

"As a matter of fact," she said, her eyes flicking at me,

"I have two. One of them is a darling man, Mr. Devine, who lives next door—" I recoiled in horror—"and the other is the iceman. He comes every day, and is much handsomer than you!"

"My father," I gasped, "is *not* your lover, Mrs. Hanover!" I was outraged by the lie and they both burst out laughing. I realized at once that they had been joking for my benefit because I had been so unashamedly listening to their private conversation. I blushed and ran into the house past Papa who stood at the window, facing East and praying, his Tallis draped over his shoulders. It was Shabbas. I ran into the bedroom and shut the door and hid my face on my cool pillow. Sylvia and Simply Simon, who had been out there with me, now knew what a stupid idiot I was, as if it wasn't bad enough that I had made a fool of myself in front of Mr. and Mrs. Hanover. Why did I have to be so stupid?

In the evening, I walked Jenny-Wren along the path in the direction of town. I wanted to see the Giant Weeping Willow Tree, which was the last sight at the end of the row of cottages on our street before one came to the open road leading to the boardwalk and all its attractions.

I stopped the carriage and looked at the tree. It was very old, very deep and green. Strands of ribbonlike tentacles spilled out of its heart, covering the yard like a silky coverlet of green lace knotted in delicate patterns. I imagined it bowing to me, each breeze lifting the wisps to float upwards and bend again. It watched me in its secret heart, its green eyes very high up and hidden, eyes that could see into your mind. I stared up as high as I could, but still couldn't find the watchful eyes that stared so coolly, so greenly down from their lofty place close to heaven.

Somewhere Mama sat, just as coolly and greenly looking down at me. Up in that tree maybe. It seemed an appropriate place to sit in judgment. If Mama judged me then she judged me from the top of the tree, her eyes the eyes of the tree. It seemed to frown. The tree bent over me menacingly. I backed away, pulling the carriage away from the edge of the path, then it straightened and smiled, and its arms beckoned me closer. Mama had gone, leaving the tree and me. I was held, hypnotized, unable to stop staring upwards. Jenny whimpered, reminding me that I wasn't alone. I stared around me. The sky had faded to a pale rose with smudges of purple and blue. It took a long time to grow dark in the summertime.

I leaned over Jenny, who now stared up at me with her large blue eyes unsmiling. She kicked off the blanket and waited. I covered her again. Laughing, her knees working like pistons, she kicked it off again. We played this game many times.

I looked off towards the boardwalk. Strings of lights were looped over the carnival part of it and farther away; they were like necklets of diamonds flashing against the mauve sky. They moved in slow circles and I could almost hear the shrieks of pretended terror from the people on the rides. I turned the carriage around and headed back to the cottage. That was the last time I visited The Tree, even though I passed it many times before the holiday was over. Each time I glanced sideways at it, afraid of the eyes, afraid Mama might be hiding in the topmost branches.

**4** The ride home on the back of the truck was a lot different from the ride two weeks earlier when we had it all before us. Simply Simon and I sat on the boxes, staring somberly at the retreating countryside, the sun beating down on us. "Boy, it's hot," I said.

"Yeah." He stared out of the side, leaning against the back of the truck, jiggling and bumping like me.

"I'll bet it's nice and cool in the lake right now."

"Yeah."

"Lucky fishes."

"Yeah."

"Is that all you can say? Just yeah?"

"Yeah."

When we were almost home with the city limits in view, I said: "Well, anyway, we did get to spend two weeks at the beach!"

"Yeah!"

I gave up. We got home in silence, and in silence began to recognize landmarks on Powers Street. The most surprising thing, when the truck stopped in front of our store, was that it had shrunk so in our absence. We climbed down, stretching our cramped bodies as Papa and Sylvia stepped out of the front of the truck. The street shimmered in the heat, ruts dried and crumbling into powdery dust. It looked deserted, as though everybody had gone away when we had. I felt a trickle of perspiration glide down from under my hair and along my neck. I swiped at it with the back of my hand.

Now came the hard part, helping to unload the boxes. When Papa unlocked the front door, everybody grabbed something and carried it into the house. It seemed airless inside, suffocating, and opening a window didn't help much. I headed for the bathroom just for the pleasure of flushing the toilet, and the luxurious feeling it gave me to see the clean water surging up from the depths of the toilet bowl. At least, there was one good thing about coming home!

It was Sunday, July 26th. I saw by the calendar, and with a pang realized that summer was half over already. I opened the box that contained my clothes, and the first thing I saw was my bathing suit. I looked at it a long time. Probably, I thought, I'd never wear it again.

In the evening, the street came alive with the first cooling breeze. All the way down Boyd Avenue, men in undershirts and women in loose cotton dresses sat on verandas or on their steps, or in chairs on the lawns, fanning themselves with folded-up newspapers. Children played catch on the boulevards, or tippy-stick, and on our corner, Simply Simon and two other boys played kick-the-can with a lot of noise and yelling. Voices carried a long way in the dying light of day, as if they rode the breeze, but I couldn't hear what they were saying.

Papa opened up for business right away so I could see the light from our store window reflected onto the sidewalk, and I imagined Papa and Sylvia straightening out the stock on the shelves. They had been as good as strangers when we had left for the beach, married three weeks, but now, after a two-week vacation, they seemed more married to each other, more familiar. It wasn't anything I could pinpoint exactly. I couldn't say it was because of this or that. All I could figure was that more time had elapsed.

Papa came out, holding an ice cream cone. "You want?" he asked me. I wanted!

The memory of the beach began to fade after the second day at home. It became dimmer as I walked to the library to get new books and dimmer yet as I sat under a big oak in Peanut Park, reading. By the beginning of August I could hardly remember what Mrs. Hanover looked like, or Johnny, or any of the casual people we had met there, like the iceman and the storekeeper.

I began writing in my scribbler again just to try to figure things out, but instead asked myself a lot of questions, such as how could I forget experiences which, at the time they happened, were so important to me? And would I always do that, go to different places and then later feel as though it had all been a dream? For instance the Giant Weeping Willow Tree and Jenny and the lake in the morning and again in the evening when it turned silver and black and the lights of the town visible from a distance as diamonds. They were all lost and gone forever to me, just as Mama was. Except that Mama was always there, a shadowy presence.

Simply Simon leaned over my shoulder. "Guess what!" His eyes were two exclamation points. "We're gonna have a telephone!"

"Who said so? How do you know?"

"I heard them talking. Sylvia said it'll be good for business. And she said we should deliver!"

"Well, we *do* deliver, don't we?"

"Not us. Somebody else. She said we should get a boy with a bike."

I didn't mind *that*. It would be just lovely never to have to pull a wagon loaded with groceries again. "I guess that's not a bad idea," I said slowly, "*if* we can afford it. Can we?"

He shrugged. "Well, look at all the things . . . We went to the beach, didn't we? And she did buy new dishes last week. I *guess* we can afford it."

"She's pretty smart, isn't she?" I had to admit what was true.

"She should be, she's a schoolteacher."

"What's that got to do with it? You don't have to know about being a storekeeper just because you're a schoolteacher. Besides, she isn't a teacher anymore. She had to quit her job."

"I know. We sure are lucky, aren't we? I mean, we're lucky that if Papa had to marry somebody, it was her."

"I still miss Mama," I said quickly. "Why did she have to die?" I didn't want to say it but it just popped out of my mouth. Simply Simon stared at me, but not any harder than I stared at him, my hand over my mouth. It was as if I couldn't hear praise for Sylvia without those words jumping out.

"I don't know," he said, answering my question. "Auntie Leah said God called her because He wanted her with the angels."

I shuddered. Maybe, I thought. Maybe she was with the angels. Maybe she wasn't.

"Do you believe in Heaven?"

"Sure. Don't you?"

"I don't know," I said. "I want to believe in it, but I don't know."

A week later, the men came to install out telephone. It was exciting to have strangers in the house, tools bulging out of their pockets. It was exciting to watch them as they drilled holes and strung wires from the telephone pole to my window, and alongside it and down to the kitchen roof and along the wall. My window was wide open and one of the men straddled my windowsill, his head on the outside. Luckily, it was a beautiful warm day. I wondered what Auntie Sadie would say when she got back from L.A. and found out we had a telephone just like everybody else. Wouldn't she be surprised!

When they left, the phone stood on the big desk, a tall black contraption, elegant, with the receiver hanging from the a clip on the side. I looked through the phone book beside it and wondered if our name would be printed inside but of course it wasn't, yet.

I sat all day trying to get the courage to dial Betty Greenberg's number but managed to convince myself there was no use trying because she probably wasn't even in the city. She was probably still at the beach and there was no sense wasting time phoning somebody who wasn't even home. Not only didn't we use it but nobody phoned us either so I wasn't sure it worked at all. But when I mentioned that to Simply Simon, he said: "That's where you're wrong, 'cause Sylvia used it already. She phoned the fruit wholesale company as soon as those men left." And I hadn't even been downstairs yet!

Papa leaned on the counter, printing a sign in crooked letters and black ink. It read:

BOY WITH BIKE WANTED
TO DELIVER

If business didn't improve now, I thought, it wouldn't be our fault. I leaned against the counter, watching Papa place the sign in the window, and let my eyes roam around the store. Everywhere I looked, I saw little differences, new ways of doing things. Cans were stacked in pyramids, displays were prettied up. It wouldn't be long now before we were a going concern. There was a creak behind me as someone came down the steps from the house. I turned and Sylvia beckoned. "Can you give me a hand? I could use some help with the books."

For a moment I wasn't sure what she was talking about. Library books? But she smiled, pushing back her heavy hair which she'd lately had cut shorter, giving her a younger, pert appearance.

"What I need," she explained, "is somebody to look over the accounts with me, and when we find one who hasn't paid anything for two weeks, we put her in a separate book."

It sounded like a lot of extra work for nothing but I wasn't doing anything anyway. I followed her into the house where she had drawn up two chairs at the big desk and stacked a pile of dog-eared scribblers near the telephone.

There was also a new scribbler with her handwriting on it, open in front of one of the chairs. She pointed to the other chair. I sat down warily, finding that it was too close to her, much to close.

"Just read me the names from that scribbler, Becky dear, and the money owed and the date." When she smiled I could see that her teeth had a faint yellowish cast to them and that there were quite a few freckles sprinkled across her cheeks. She was chewing on Sen-Sen, a violet scent coming from her breath. I cleared my throat, looked at the first name on the page.

"Mrs. Cocker," I intoned, "$26.78, July 30th . . ."

She nodded, but didn't write. "Next?"

When we were through with that, she drew some envelopes towards her and addressed them to the delinquent customers, and slipped bills inside. I watched her curiously.

"Just little reminders," she explained. "People think we don't really care if we don't at least ask for it."

"Won't they be mad?"

She shook her head. "I'm being very polite in my notes. There's no reason for them to be mad."

I remembered how I felt about asking people for money. "Well, anyway," I said, "it isn't as if they don't owe it to us. We're not beggars!" I was glad I wouldn't have to go to Mrs. Hollis's place ever again.

In less than a week we found that it paid off and now even Papa agreed that the new way of doing things was more businesslike than before. The case of Canterovitch, for instance.

Papa had said firmly: "No. You don't send a letter to Canterovitch. His father was a shochet, and it isn't nice to do that to a shochet's son. You want we should lose them as customers altogether?"

"Believe me, Jake," Sylvia had pleaded, "you won't lose the Canterovitches. And even if you do, at least you won't be out more money than you are now. Look at that amount, $78.56!"

Papa had looked and shrugged. "Don't I know? I know.

But this way, maybe she'll pay. If you get her mad and she stops coming in, what then?" But he had given in, as I knew he would because he let Sylvia run everything. He had stopped being one hundred percent the boss.

It wasn't until Mr. Canterovitch, black moustaches twitching, stormed in several days later that I conceded she might have been right. Clutched in his hand was Sylvia's note, and for a minute I thought he was going to punch Papa right in the nose. He shook the notice in Papa's face. "What is this? What is it about?"

Fortunately, Sylvia was right there to take the blame and before Papa could open his mouth to explain, Sylvia said: "It's your bill, Mr. Canterovitch," and she smiled fearlessly (which didn't mean a thing because Mr. Canterovitch, who looked tough, wouldn't hit a lady). "We thought you may have forgotton about it. Your wife hasn't been in here for two weeks."

Mr. Canterovitch switched his gaze from Papa to Sylvia, his mouth open like a fish that's gasping for air. "What? She hasn't paid?" His eyebrows drew together like two black firecrackers about to go off. "I give her enough money to pay with and she doesn't pay? This I didn't know." I had a feeling I should be sorry for Mrs. Canterovitch. I leaned my elbow on the counter, curious to see what would happen next.

"It's not unusual, Mr. Canterovitch," Sylvia said in a soothing voice. "It happens quite a lot."

"Not to me, it doesn't. Nossir." He pulled a black wallet out of his jacket pocket, unsnapping the flaps in angry little pops, and removed a handful of dollar bills from the pouch inside. He snapped them onto the counter, one by one. "My wife will hear of this, you can believe it or not. She will hear." The way he said it made me shiver. "And she will come back and buy from you. I guarantee it, personal."

I would have liked to follow him home and find out what he was going to say to her. I was sure it would be plenty and worth hearing, but had to content myself with making up my own version, which included a black eye. When Mrs. Canterovitch came to our store the next day (just as he promised she would, although he didn't specifiy when) I gave her a thorough inspection, but couldn't find any visible bruises. But then, maybe because she weighted about three hundred pounds they wouldn't show.

"If this keeps up," Papa said almost gleefully, "we might even start to make a living from the store." My respect for Sylvia began to grow.

My admiration for the new delivery boy had already grown beyond acceptable levels. He was very handsome in a blond, rugged sort of way, a fact I verified every time he rode up on his bicycle to make a delivery. Papa would have killed me if he'd caught me staring at a "shaygets," which was a word I hated because it was said in such a mean way. I'd watch him prop his bike against the wall of the store and pretend I was working by piling cans on top of each other in a corner just so I could look at his square chin and dimpled cheeks. His teeth were so white and his hair was so wavy, he reminded me a little of Mr. Hanover. He was very polite to Papa and I was sure he'd never say anything like "bloody Jew," like other ones did. I would hurry to open the door for him as he carried out a box of groceries and Papa even trusted him to make collections for us.

"Thanks," he said, and my heart did funny little flip-flops, and I'd hear his voice say thanks over and over, and see his eyes look at me as he said it, and each time, my heart did the same funny flip-flops, though not as strong as at first, until finally, I'd forget what it felt like till he came back from the delivery and I'd run to open the door for him and he'd smile and say: "Thanks" and then it would start all over again.

What did he think of me, I wondered. Was I pretty? Of course he was older, about fourteen, and besides, he wasn't Jewish. Was it a sin to like a shaygets? I supposed it was but I couldn't help it, even if Papa would murder me if he knew. Just the same, I ran into the house and upstairs to my room so I could take a good long look at myself in the mirror. But it was no use. My eyes had a sparkle to them, I could see, but I still looked like myself. I hadn't changed.

The telephone downstairs rang, its harsh strident tone something I hadn't yet been able to grow accustomed to, and as I ran to answer it, it grated on my ears like a scream, a shriek of pain. It was an alarm that meant: come quickly, right now. Don't wait or it will be too late. When I reached the desk, panting and gasping, Sylvia was there ahead of me, speaking quietly into the mouthpiece.

I'd hoped to answer it with: "Hello, Devine's Grocery," and maybe it would be for me! So far, nobody had made any calls to me, which wasn't surprising because no one even knew we had the phone yet, but still I felt disappointed.

"I think," Sylvia said at supper, "that we should start looking around for a carpet for the front room."

Simply Simon and I were aghast. A carpet! Only rich people had carpets. Everybody else had linoleum like ours, worn out in the heavy traffic areas so you couldn't see the pattern of leaves and squares anymore.

Did that mean we were getting rich? We didn't *look* rich, and we certainly didn't act rich with Papa and Sylvia both working in the store. I always imagined rich people lolling around on fancy furniture, with a million or so servants to wait on them hand and foot. Rich people never had to do a thing for themselves, so we could hardly be rich, I decided. But then, what were we?

Papa nodded. "If you think so, that's a good idea. Maybe before Yontiff."

Yontiff meant autumn, to me. It meant school, with the summer over and winter ahead. I hated to think of Yontiff when it was still August. This year, it would be on September 6th, a Sunday, which was a gyp because it meant we'd only have one day away from school this time. Nothing depressed me more than being reminded of school when August was more than half over. I pushed all thoughts of it out of my mind as quickly as I could.

I spent a long Wednesday afternoon at Peanut Park, not with a book but with a new scribbler which I'd begged from Papa.

"Why do you need it?" he had asked, unconvinced.

"What do you do with your scribblers?"

"I just need it, Papa. Please can I have one, please?"

"All right," he said. "Take." Papa gave in easily nowadays. "But I still don't see what you need a scribbler for in the middle of summer."

"Thank you, Papa!" I'd grabbed one and gone.

It was a glorious, beautiful day, not too hot, even though the sun beamed almost continuously down on the mud-caked street with its ditches on each side padded with tall grass and weeds. I strolled along, watching the white ever-changing clouds above me, confident it wouldn't rain. At the park I found an unoccupied tree with a long shadow and made myself comfortable, stretching out on the long soft grass, and opened the scribbler to the first page. I thought I'd like to write a story, the way real writers did, and it was going to be about a family going to the beach. . . .

Somewhere high above me a bird soared and wheeled, uttering its cry. I heard it dimly but my mind was busy preparing my words, shaping them inside my head before I wrote them on the nice clean page. Louisa May Alcott didn't start with "Once upon a time," and neither would I. I already had my title: "The Princess and the Baby."

The shadows grew longer, a breeze came out of nowhere and ruffled my hair, fluttering the bottom of my dress. In my ecstatic furious scribbling, I hardly noticed when the sun hid its face behind buttermilk clouds. I looked up as I felt the first spattering of rain; I leaped to my feet, scrambling to get out of there before the clouds opened up. With my scribbler clutched to my heart, I ran all the way home, racing the rain. It gushed down in a torrent. I was sopping wet when I flung the door open and ran into the house, gasping for breath.

Sylvia shook her head. "Take off your shoes, run upstairs and change. And take some towels with you."

In a few minutes, I stood naked in the middle of my room, wiping myself dry. I had a good feeling inside, connected somehow with what I had written. I changed into dry clothes, then curled up on my bed and read what I had written. I still liked it, seeing my words as though someone else had written them, uncritical, pleased. Now I leaned over it to complete the job. It was a story, a real made-up story about real people, except that none of the things I'd written had happened. That was what made it so different and wonderful to me.

I had a feeling of accomplishment such as I'd never had before. I felt lucky. After all, how many others had this magic power, to make up what was altogether from my head, to put words on paper. I would be a writer someday. This I knew as surely as I knew that I was plain. I would never be beautiful and it didn't matter.

It wasn't till Sunday that Sylvia mentioned the subject at all. We were doing the dishes. Papa had eaten in a hurry, and under a strain, and had hardly spoken at the table. But now with just the two of us there, she said in a casual way, "What were you doing that day in the park?"

Instantly on guard, I said just as casually, "Nothing. I just sat under a tree. That's all." Well, I *had* sat under a tree. It wasn't exactly a lie.

"You took a scribbler with you. Did you bring it back?"

"Oh. Sure. I brought it back. I guess."

I became very busy drying a plate. I dried it over and over again until she took it out of my hands and put it away.

"Well, you don't have to talk about if if you don't want to," she said. "I'm not trying to pry into your business. If you ever feel like telling me anything, though, will you remember that's what I'm here for? Will you do that?"

I shrugged. "Holy Toledo! I can't think of anything. Honest!" I took a cup and shoved the wadded-up dish towel inside it, turning it around and around. "I mean, I don't know what you want me to tell you."

She laughed then and without warning, kissed me. I stiffened, unable to defend myself from such attacks. We finished the rest of the dishes without referring to the subject again. When the last dish was put away, Sylvia said: "Becky, this afternoon we're going to have some company and I'll need your help, so don't go away."

Before I could ask her who was coming, Papa came into

the kitchen and I was surprised to see he had changed into his Shabbas suit and a white shirt and dark tie. Sylvia removed her apron and looked at him. "Please, Jake," she said, "try to be calm. Don't upset yourself."

Papa nodded and didn't quite meet her eyes.

"I wish I could go with you," she continued, in a worried way, "but I don't think it would look right."

Papa checked his shoes to make sure they were polished, then looked at me.

"If she was older . . . But . . . " He looked up at the kitchen clock standing on top of the cabinet near the ceiling. "I have to go now. The Rabbi said half past two."

"Where are you going, Papa?"

"To the cemetery. I won't be gone long."

"Why are you going to the cemetery?" Just the mention of that place gave me goose pimples.

"To put a stone on Mama's grave. . . ."

His passing glance just barely touched my eyes and I had an instant of looking into his haunted face as he turned and went out. The door closed behind Papa. I stood and stared at it. Papa was going to put a stone on Mama's grave. I had a vision of Papa bending over a grave with a stone in his hand, a small white one, which he then dropped onto the ground. What would he do a thing like that for? I turned my questioning eyes towards Sylvia and found her watching me, a gentle expression on her face. It was as though she were reading my mind.

"It's not that kind of stone, Becky," she said, taking my hand and sitting me down at the kitchen table. I felt myself plop into the chair and then she sat down opposite me. "It's called a tombstone, and it's made of granite. It marks a person's grave, honoring her memory. Papa decided to have the dedication today because it will soon be Rosh Hashanah and most people try to have it done before that date."

She looked at me and waited for the questions but I understood, more or less. What I couldn't understand was why they were going to all that trouble when Mama wasn't even in that grave and never had been. I could see that Sylvia expected me to ask some questions, and I had to oblige her. "What does the Rabbi do?"

"Well, he says a prayer for the dead and the relatives are there, the ones who are in town and the friends, but not the second wife, because that would look too . . . too . . . ." She turned her face away while I stared at her. Was Sylvia crying—calm, unexcitable Sylvia?

She rose suddenly. "All right now. If you haven't any other questions, run along. I have some work to do." She sounded exactly like a schoolteacher.

I had a very strong urge to tell her about Mama just to keep her there, to tell her everything, even that I knew Mama hated me. I bit my lip hard, fighting it. No one must ever know. No one, not even Papa. He would think, if my own mother hated me, there must be a good reason. He would believe that I must be very hateful.

I wandered up to my room and stood in the middle of it, undecided what to do. Should I write in the new scribbler? I looked at Mama's chair beside my dresser and the gnawing inside me got worse. I sat in Mama's chair facing the opposite wall, the same spot where she had stood when she had come to me that time, the only time when she'd still loved me. I stared at the corner near the ceiling. During that time before the funeral Mama had come back. Now they were putting a stone on her grave. . . . Would she come here again? I waited, as someone awaiting execution, with no hope of reprieve. Mama could get me anywhere. If I tried to hide, she could find me.

The chair felt suddenly hot. I jumped up and sat in my own place in front of the dresser. I leaned on my elbows and looked at my reflection in the mirror. If I stared at it hard enough, my eyes blurred so all I could see was a round blob without any features. I kept my eyes unfocused, my mind blank. It wasn't hard to do. In the mirror, my room was backwards and over my left shoulder where the ceiling met the wall, something . . . something . . . I blinked to clear my vision, and stared behind me. There was nothing. I must be crazy, I thought. The pain in my stomach grew stronger and my hands holding my head up were damp with perspiration.

I felt hot, then cold. My head hummed, as if a thousand bees had gotten loose in there, and my fingers and toes had gone to sleep. Was this what it felt like to die, Mama? Are you giving me a taste of it? But Mama wasn't here with me. I couldn't see her anywhere. I put my head down on the dresser top on my folded arms, the humming growing louder.

*Stay away from her,* Mama said. *Stay away from her.* How can I? She comes to me. I can't run away. *It's your fault. Stay away from her,* Mama said, *or you'll be sorry.* Suddenly the humming stopped. I lifted my head and stared around me. I couldn't hear the voice in my head. I rose to my feet and began to jump up and down, rubbing my hands together, feeling the pins and needles stabbing into my fingers and toes, the blood beginning to move again. What did she mean: or I'd be sorry? What would she do? A wave of cold air rushed over me, from head to foot. I ran out of the bedroom, down the stairs and into the room where Sylvia sat bent over the books. She glanced up.

"What's wrong, Becky? You're pale as a ghost!"

"Nothing's wrong!" I edged away from her. If I could stay away from her . . . if I only could, I would. Sylvia gave me a helpless look. She probably still thought I hated her. I told myself. She was probably thinking: I did my best to be friends, but she doesn't want to be friends, so what's the use? That's what I would think if I was her.

After one more worried glance in my direction, Sylvia sighed and went back to her work, writing figures down in the account scribblers. "Papa will be back in a little while, Becky," she said, "and he'll have some people with him. *If* anybody else came to the unveiling . . ."

"What's an unveiling?"

"That's when the stone is dedicated. Of course your Auntie Sadie and Uncle Morris are still out of town and so are the cousins." She frowned slightly, puckering her smooth forehead with thought. "Still, we should have tea prepared. Can you bring down the teacups for me from the top shelf? They probably need washing."

"Isn't Auntie Leah back yet?"

"Yes. As a matter of fact I phoned them the other day." She smiled, remembering. . . . "It was quite a shock to her, I'm afraid."

I dragged a chair into the kitchen and stood on it to reach the teacups and saucers, bringing them carefully down and carrying them to the sink. They were coated with a layer of dust. We washed and dried the dishes and the little silver spoons which were Sylvia's, and changed the tablecloth to a clean white one. She had baked a cake in the morning, and now she sliced it all around but kept the slices together so it still retained its shape.

Papa came in with Auntie Leah and Uncle Dave and Cousin Hinda. They didn't look very sad, I thought, so the unveiling wasn't the same as a funeral.

Auntie Leah hugged me. "Nu, Beckala, so how are you? Did you have a nice summer?"

I nodded.

"And Saul too? He's all right?"

"Sure." Why wouldn't he be all right? Nothing ever bothered him. He could play from the first thing in the morning till the middle of the night with all his millions of friends. Not like me.

We sat around the table and had tea and I watched Cousin Hinda drink hers and though how much she looked like a schoolteacher, even more than Sylvia when we'd first seen her. It was the way she wore her hair, parted in the middle and down over her ears and not very spiffy-looking at all. I would never, I vowed, wear my hair so I looked like an old maid. I studied her face critically. Too colorless, too wishy-washy. What Cousin Hinda needed was makeup and plenty of it.

She looked at me and smiled and I wondered if my thoughts showed on my face. *I hoped not.* If she wanted to look like an old maid, that was her business, not mine.

Sylvia refilled the glass sugar bowl and, passing it over my head, lightly touched my shoulder with her other hand as she placed it in the middle of the table. Could I be rude and shake her hand off right in front of everybody? *You'll be sorry . . . you'll be sorry . . .* The words ran around in my brain. . . . *Stay away from her or you'll be sorry. . . .* Why didn't Mama tell Sylvia to stay away from me?

Papa, in the chair opposite mine, stared at me. He had seen. He had seen and he was angry. I dropped my eyes to my tea; I wished I could explain. It was nothing against Sylvia, I would tell him. I can't help it. But he would only get angrier, because he said things like: Mama wants me to get married again! I knew that wasn't true but Papa believed it, so it was no use telling him anything. Besides, Mama would hear and she'd do something to me. . . . *You'll be sorry. . . .*

Papa shoved his chair back from the table and stood up. I didn't dare look at him. I knew he was glaring at me. He wheeled and walked out of the kitchen and through to the other room. I wanted somehow to explain, to get back in his good graces again. I heard him open the store door and ran to catch up with him but stopped when he didn't turn around. Papa's foot creaked on the top step that led downwards and as I stood, twisting my shoe, a vague feeling of uneasiness in the pit of my stomach, I knew something bad was going to happen. The room around me sat in a pale haze and time became elastic. It stretched and stretched between the moment I heard the first creak and when I should have heard the second one. But what I heard was a strange sort of cry or grunt and a thud and I was the first one to kneel beside Papa, who lay across the two steps, one leg twisted under him.

Sylvia pushed me aside with the others crowding around. I saw it all in my haze, the voices coming through thick cotton. I could only see Papa's prone body; the others were no more than shadows passing in front of me. I heard Sylvia's voice, anxious, and Uncle Dave's, crisp, talking into the phone. Mama had taken her revenge; this I knew as surely as I knew my own name.

Papa had used those steps eight billion times. He had never tripped on them before. I didn't see Mama push him, but I knew that she had. You'll be sorry, she had said. I thought she meant me, but this way was just as bad. A great coldness lay on me and Hinda's arm around my shoulder didn't warm me one bit.

Simply Simon came racing into the house, his face white. "There's an ambulance outside!" he cried, and then, looking at all of us, he ran to Papa. The ambulance men had lifted Papa onto the stretcher and Papa's face was contorted with pain. A shock of identical pain hit me. I knew what he was feeling in a mysterious fashion that frightened me even more. "What happened?" Simply Simon was shaking me as we watched the men in white coats carefully trundle Papa out the front door, Sylvia close behind them. "What happened?"

I shook my head. I would never tell the truth about it. In fact, I couldn't talk about it at all.

"Your father fell off the step and broke his leg," Hinda explained, as the ambulance drove away, Papa and Sylvia inside it. She made it sound so simple, like any other accident. "I guess he'll be in the hospital for a while but don't worry, he'll be all right. Anyway, we'll stay here and keep you company until Sylvia gets back so you won't be alone."

Standing on the veranda steps, staring at the street where the ambulance had stood, brought me sharply back to that other time, that other season, when Simply Simon and I had stood alone at the front window, watching the empty street where a taxi had stood. I felt peculiarly abandoned. I felt like a true orphan. I felt like the last person left alive in my family. It was only a matter of time. . . .


**5** In some strange way, I learned to live with my feeling of dread. It became part of me, part of daily living. There were even times when I forgot that life was a mere thread that could be snipped away by unseen scissors, when I could stop thinking about Mama waiting for the opportunity to strike me down.

While Papa was at the hospital Sylvia ran the business, and when he came home, his leg in a plaster cast, she continued to wait on the customers while Papa chafed and fretted on the chesterfield, his leg supported by a chair.

I became Papa's shadow, annoying him with my anxiety. I brought him cold drinks of water whether he wanted them or not, and newspapers or magazines to read, anything to allay my feelings of guilt. If it hadn't been for my making Mama angry, it would never have happened. To make it worse, I knew Papa had been angry with me too at that instant when it happened.

August. Long heat-filled days, lazy languid days that droned with buzzing flies near the ceiling, moist air wafting through the window screens, doing nothing to cool the inside. . . .

Papa, a very bad patient, hollered for Sylvia. She came in from the store. "What can I get you, Jake?"

"I told you, I want crutches. Did you talk to the doctor yet? I can't stand to sit anymore!"

"I'll phone him right now!"

Papa had the crutches the very next day, and helping him off the chair onto the crutches became a family project. Papa leaned heavily on them while Sylvia on one side and I on the other, and Simply Simon behind, all heaved together to get him started. He stood then, his encased foot raised an inch off the floor, all his weight on the other one, and leaned on the crutches. Now all he had to do was learn to walk.

"Be careful, Papa," I said as he clumped across the floor. Papa gave me a look.

"I'm careful. Thank you."

"Sit awhile now, Jake," Sylvia said after Papa had just barely got started. "Don't tire yourself out."

"Tire myself out? Who's tired? If I sit another minute, I'll get a blister! I have to get used to this. In two weeks, it's Rosh Hashanah and it's a long walk to Shul."

"Jake!" Sylvia's hand flew to her face. "You're not thinking of going to Shul this year?"

He stared at her in astonishment. "Naturally, I'm going to Shul. What do you mean?"

"But you can't! I'm sure God will forgive you if you don't go this year. You can't be serious. . . ."

Papa began to breathe heavily, reminding me of the Papa of olden times, when Mama tried to change his mind from doing something he wanted to do, or make him do something he didn't want to do. "I am serious," he said, emphasizing each word. "I am *very* serious. I will go to Shul, like I went to Shul every Yontiff of my life, even when those Russian bandits murdered my mother. With a little thing like this"—he indicated his foot —"I will still go to Shul. Only when I'm dead, I will stop going."

He made a slow, laborious right turn, and navigated the distance from the middle room to the kitchen in four minutes while Sylvia stood staring at him, a baffled expression on her face.

We became used to the clump-clump of Papa's crutches, and it didn't surprise me in the least when he soon began inching his way down the treacherous two steps into the store. Now Papa was back as the head of the family, running his business. Of course, he still made his bed on the chesterfield because going up a whole flight of stairs was another matter entirely. It was a lucky thing, I thought, that we had a bathroom on the main floor, or it would have been too bad.

I was sure that Papa could do anything he set out to do, and if he said he was going to walk to Shul . . . that was exactly what he would do. I didn't really want to think about Yontiff because it was so close and that meant that the First Day of School was even closer! I could see by the kitchen calendar that school would start the week after next.

As if to underline its imminence, Sylvia made a list of things we needed for school, including new shoes and a new dress for me to wear both to school and to Shul. I leaned against the back of her chair as she wrote, reminding her of things she might forget, and adding, hopefully, a new tunic, preferably one with deep pleats that stayed in even when you sat down.

Funny how the days seemed suddenly to have grown shorter, how they flew now that we were getting our school things. Sylvia shortened my tunic and it was already the day before school was to start. If I shut my eyes I could still pretend that it was the first day of holidays with the whole wonderful summer of idleness still ahead. Now . . .

I didn't really mind much. A new school term meant a new teacher and possibilities unlimited. And it meant seeing my friends again. I had never had friends other years and it was a marvellous feeling to look forward to seeing them. I had so much to tell them. Just wait till they heard my news!

Sylvia woke us early. Dressing up in the tunic which flared out in a very satisfying way, with a new white blouse and white socks with my new shoes, I felt stylish beyond belief. I felt sorry for Simply Simon because, even though he wore new pants and a green pullover, he felt like a sissy and it showed on his face. Girls enjoyed new clothes much more than boys. We tried to be very quiet when we came down the stairs but Papa was a light sleeper.

"Make sure you don't forget anything," he called from the front room. "Don't forget your pencils. . . ."

"They have everything, dear," Sylvia assured him.

We ate hurriedly and it was time to go. We went into the front room to kiss Papa good-bye. Sylvia stood waiting, smiling. My heart thumped loudly as I suddenly, and without warning myself that I was going to do it, kissed her cheek. It was cool and smooth and smelled faintly of butter. I saw her eyes widen and as I turned away, had a glimpse of her hand going up to touch her cheek.

How do you like that, Mama, I asked her in my mind. If you're going to do something to me anyway, I might as well be nice to Sylvia and make her happy, because *she is very nice to me.*

"Have a good day in school," Sylvia called through the screen door as we galloped down the veranda steps. Her voice sounded light as a feather, as though it were floating away on a bubble of happiness.

It was weird to see the sun shining as usual and flowers bowing in their untidy rows and the birds still hopping around. Yesterday it was summer. Today, because of school, fall had arrived.

We walked down College and stepped over cracks, and

pulled up a few marigolds that grew outside somebody's fence, because that made them public property. The marigolds stank but they were a pretty color so I forgave them. I would give them to my new teacher, whoever she would be. I knew only that I was to go to room 10, along with the others in my room who had passed. I hoped I would like the teacher, but I hoped even harder that she would like me.

Simply Simon swung his school bag in a wide arc around him. He always took it on the first day of school and then didn't even look at it all the rest of the year. The First Day. You always did everything exact, perfect on the First Day. After that you didn't bother because only the first impressions counted.

I thought about Betty and Marjorie and how excited they were going to be when they heard about everything that had happened the past two months. I remembered back to last year when I had stood in the background and listened to them tell each other about their holidays, while I had stood enviously by. This time, I had something to tell too!

I could just imagine their faces, their mouths open with envy and astonishment. Boy! would *they* be surprised. It was all so exciting. Suddenly, I made a little prayer to God. Please make my new teacher nice and have her smile a lot, not just on the first day like they all do, but *every* day. And please protect my little brother. Don't let him get Miss Harrison, because he's dumb enough to still like school, and if he gets *her* he won't like it long. That's all amen and thank you God.

Simply Simon suddenly stopped. "Hey! I found a dime!" It glinted in the sun as he held it up. Well, wasn't it just like that lucky fish? And here I worried over him. A lot of good it did me. We crossed the street and entered the zigzag lane. The gravel felt rough underfoot and crunched as we walked, and I renewed my acquaintance with the tall grass and wild flowers that bent towards me which I hadn't seen in two months. It delighted me to see the golden buttercups like confetti peeping between stones at the side of the lane. I clutched the marigolds still in my hand and skipped a little, and was past the gate of The Pest before I remembered to be wary.

"Oh, hi!" she squealed, running slightly to keep up with me, her crippled arm suspended in midair by the metal brace; because it was too late to avoid her, I walked fast on purpose. "Isn't it wonderful to go back to school? I missed it, didn't you?"

"No I didn't," I said without looking at her. "Only dumbbells miss school in the summer!"

She ran backwards in front of me, almost poking me in the eye with her brace. "It's dumbbells who don't like school!" She stuck her tongue out at me.

I laughed. Miss Goody Two Shoes had stuck her tongue out at me! I almost started to like her right then. At least she seemed more human and less Christian when she did that. "So why walk with a dumbbell then?" I asked her. "If I were you, I'd go to school through the front gate, instead of the back lane."

"I have a right to use my own back lane!"

I zipped up my mouth, fastened my ears shut, and pretended to myself that she had disappeared. I wasn't going to let her spoil my last few minutes of freedom, no sir! I ran past her, past Simply Simon, who was poking around in a garbage can, and right out of the lane.

Now I stood on the grassy boulevard facing Machray School, looking at the crowded school yard ahead of me. For a few seconds I was still me, alone and separate. There wasn't any point in rushing into the school yard.

"Hey, Becky!" A shrill voice ripped through my head. I turned in time to see Betty get out of her father's car. She wore a cute green dress with pleats all around and ankle socks to match. I felt suddenly slovenly in my new tunic, like somebody on relief.

"Hi," I called. "Did you have a nice summer?"

She came closer. "I sure did! We went to my uncle's cottage on the coast." We crossed the street together. "It's right on the ocean, and we went to a bay where the water feels like you're in a bath and it's so warm!"

"Really?" I cried, impatient to get a word in. "We went

to the beach and we stayed in a cottage, and the outhouse stank something awful!"

"Oh I know. We do that every year. My cousins have a boat. We went sailing a lot and had picnics on an island. Was it fun!"

"That's nice. And you know, the next-door cottage, there was this lady, her name was Mrs. Hanover, and she had the sweetest baby named Jennifer, but I called her Jenny-Wren and you know, she liked me better than her own mother?"

"Oh really? Anyway, while we were on the coast, that's Vancouver, you know, we went for a ride on a ferry? Not the kind with wings, I mean the kind that goes on the water. . . ."

"That's very interesting. Did I tell you my father fell and broke his leg?"

"Did he? That's awful. How did it happen?"

"It was on the step. I believe he was pushed."

"Who pushed him? Did you see who did it?" We were walking very slowly towards the usual corner of the building.

"No. There wasn't anybody around *to* see. But I bet he was pushed anyway."

"Gee that's too bad. I hope he'll be better soon. Hey there's Marjorie. Yoo-hoo Marjorie! Did you go anywhere this summer?

By now we were in the thick of a million of gabbling kids, everybody talking about their great vacations. An agony of words poured into the receptive air to be swallowed up into the overhanging trees. Nobody seemed to be listening to them.

"And then we went for fish and my daddy gave me his line to hold," I heard Debby say as she looked past everyone's heads. "And all of a sudden it started to jerk, and I got all excited and I screamed. . . ."

"We got the most gorgeous outfits in Minneapolis," Marjorie said, her eyes shining, as she looked at Betty's dress. "And three of them were for me. One is pink, with a frill along the bottom and short sleeves, and one is yellow. . . ."

"The salt in the water makes you float," Betty was saying. I didn't want to be left out of it.

"In the lake at the beach," I put in hopefully, "the water is so cold you freeze to death, at first, anyway...."

"So then daddy pulled the fish out of the water, and he said it was mine, and my mother cooked it and I ate all of it, even though I hate fish like poison. After all, I caught it!"

"The third dress is ... you know ... mauvey, sort of, and has these great big pink roses on it, and it's got buttons up the back and a wide skirt that really whirls around...."

"Well, while we were on the ferry, I saw the captain and he was so adorable in his uniform, and I went up to him and asked him how far we were from land, and he said ..."

"I'll bet I never eat another fish again as long as I live. If you only knew how much I hate fish!"

"All I need are new shoes to go with the dresses, but my mother said one pair, only!"

"See these snapshots of me and my uncle? They were taken on top of a mountain. If you look hard you can see almost all of Vancouver down there ... that sort of haze with little dots. ... See?"

I looked at the pictures because they were right in front of my face, but I couldn't see much of anything except a group of people I didn't know, and someone shorter who had to be Betty although you couldn't tell, everybody was squinting into the sun. I noticed that I still held the marigolds in my hand. They were wilted now and drooped, very dead. I opened my hand and let them fall to the ground. It was the worst possible thing to do, to give a teacher dead flowers as a present when you wanted to get on the good side of her.

Her name was Miss Comstock. She had iron gray hair with dark strands running through them and sharp blue eyes behind silver-rimmed glasses. She was new to our school, but old to teaching, and the first thing she said after we were all settled in our seats (I had found one in the middle somewhere) was: "I hate gum chewers, whisperers, people who don't do their homework, and latecomers. If you remember that, we will get along just fine. Be prepared to work, work, work!" Then she gave us a false teacher's smile.

An audible groan rose to the ceiling. Miss Comstock

pretended not to notice. I sat up very straight in my seat and listened to every word she said. This year, I was determined not to be the goat. This year I would be real smart, like Betty.

After a summer of doing nothing, it was hard to get back into a routine. By lunchtime, though, it felt as if we'd never been away. We already had homework, Miss Comstock having made up some arithmetic problems out of her head. She'd given out some of our textbooks and in the afternoon she would give out the rest, she said.

Simply Simon met me halfway home, still looking pretty happy. "Who's your teacher?" I asked.

"Miss Crawford."

It was no more than I expected. He was born lucky, that's all. I wondered what kind of year I'd have. Would it be like last year, or better? Of course, this year, I'd have Sylvia to help me. Anything she didn't know, Miss Comstock wouldn't know either.

What really cheered me was the fact that we'd soon have our Jewish holidays. Erev Rosh Hashanah was Saturday night, then all day Sunday and all day Monday. Papa still insisted that he'd go to Shul, crutches and all, and if I knew Papa, he would do it.

After four o'clock, I spread my homework out on the big desk at home. Sylvia appeared at my side as though I'd waved a magic wand. "May I see that?"

I moved to one side. She pulled another chair up beside mine. Now I had the advantage of personal tutoring and I didn't resent it in the least.

Later in my bedroom, I began to be afraid. I had flaunted friendship with Sylvia in Mama's face. When would she begin to take her revenge on me? I knew it would happen sooner or later. The question was, when? When I least expected it? I looked at her chair apprehensively, as if I thought she would suddenly appear sitting in her chair.

A breeze blew my curtains into the room so they flapped and then died down just as quickly. I walked over to the window and shut it, then pulled the blind down, closing out the night. For a minute I stood still, listening. I heard a faint tapping at my window. My heart thumped loudly, pounding inside my head. With only my eyes moving, I looked up towards the ceiling and the tapping stopped. I strained to listen, to hear even the sound of breathing, but I heard nothing over the beating of my heart.

I backed away from the window after tossing one quick glance over my shoulder to make sure I was alone in my room. I stood near the door, ready to bolt at the slightest sound. All remained silent. Trembling, I pulled off my tunic and with elaborate care, to put off the moment when I would have to get into bed, I hung it in the closet. I wondered if Mama could see me, if she watched my every move.

In my pajamas, with no excuse whatever for not plunging my room into darkness, I slid under the covers and reached for the cord. I covered my head. Now Mama couldn't see me, I told myself. I pulled the cord and heard the click and released the end of the cord, flattening myself right out in bed.

She was probably looking for me, feeling the empty air over my bed. With the Unseen Watchers in the Black Dark, she groped and groped, but somehow she kept missing me and as long as I didn't make any sound whatever, I would be safe from Mama.

I didn't hear the tapping again, because I kept my fingers in my ears under the blanket. I didn't hear it the next morning either. In fact, I managed to forget all about it until I opened my bedroom door at night to go to bed. Then I remembered, a chill flashing through me as I stood still, listening. There was only silence. Maybe I hadn't really heard anything, I thought. Maybe I had just imagined it.

I prepared for bed, trying not to think about it. Under the covers, convinced by now that I hadn't really heard Mama at the window, as my breathing began to lengthen out and I felt myself relax into the mattress, it came again, a knocking at the window, faint, irregular . . . taptaptap*taptaptap*taptaptap. . . . It was Mama. I was sure of it. I slept with my fingers in my ears again.

I wondered if it would do any good to pray for Mama. If I asked God to take her to Heaven then she couldn't be where she could hurt me. I decided that on Yontiff, when we went to Shul, I would pray for Mama and myself. I didn't want to die or have a broken leg. I was sure it would be terribly painful and I couldn't take pain. Even a splinter made me cry. I wasn't brave like Papa.

I wondered what Papa would say if I told him about the tapping. But I couldn't tell him or anybody; it would only make him angry with me again. He never let me say anything bad about Mama.

It was Yontiff; it was Saturday night and we were dressed in our best clothes to go to Shul. Sylvia locked the front door; then with Papa between us, we each hung onto him as he clumped stubbornly down the veranda steps. If he fell, we'd fall with him. We'd left early enough so we could walk slowly to the Shul together. The air was soft and balmy, like summer, with a few sleepy birds twittering in the still-green elms on the dusty boulevard. Simply Simon carried all the prayer books, and walked on ahead because he couldn't ever seem to slow down for anybody. It seemed unbelievable to me that only last year, Mama had been with us, in the world, going to Shul, and everything had been so wonderful, with the baby to look forward to. If I'd only known I might have appreciated more the ordinariness of our life then, and Mama had still loved me. . . .

Sylvia and I went up the rickety steps that seemed even more decrepit than before and found our seats in the balcony. She sat where it said Mrs. Devine. After all, Sylvia was Mrs. Devine. There weren't too many ladies there now. Most of them would come tomorrow morning. Only very religious people showed up for all the services. It was a funny way to run a religion but it was our way.

It seemed strange to see Sylvia sitting in Mama's place. I had wondered how I'd feel about it. Now I knew. It felt unreal. I could imagine that Mama still sat in her seat and right on top of her sat Sylvia. Staring at her, I imagined that I could see Mama invisibly underneath her. Mama didn't like it.

The interminable reading of the Torah began. I opened

my prayer book at random. It didn't matter where because I had other things to pray for. A few more ladies drifted in, some of them glancing toward us. I recognized one by her shape. She wore heavy suits and heavier furs and she looked for a moment as though she would lean over and wish Sylvia a Happy New Year because she had always wished that for Mama, but she changed her mind and sat down. I looked out of the corner of my eye to see if Sylvia minded but she didn't look as if she'd even noticed.

I watched the old ladies on the other side of the Shul, across the ancient chandelier that was missing some little bulbs, and wondered why they always cried when they prayed. They stood with their big prayer books opened, and went on and on, no matter where everybody else was up to; they had come to pray and that was what they did.

Finally, it was time to go. We wound our way down the steps with everybody else and now we were out on the street and Papa introduced Sylvia to some of his Shul pals, who shook her hand and wished her a Happy New Year. My stomach made hunger noises because I was so hungry and we wouldn't have supper until we had started the stove and warmed up what was precooked on Friday. On Shabbas we didn't use the stove because we weren't allowed to start a fire, but when the sun went down it was allowed. Shabbas was more important, Papa said, than any Yontiff, even Rosh Hashanah.

We walked slowly, keeping in step with Papa, who hobbled on his crutches like an expert. There were a few stars out, and the shadowy figures of other people on their way home from Shul veered off at their streets, and still we went on, towards Boyd. I could see from the light on the corner of our street that our house was watching for us, the windows dark. There wasn't even the whisper of a breeze.

# PART SIX

In October Sylvia became sick. Her face had a wan, hollow-eyed look, and it was Papa who woke us for school in the mornings, just as he used to. Sylvia stayed in the bedroom, not even coming out to say good-bye when we left for school. Papa, who could get around with the aid of two canes, slept upstairs again, and made sure we were awake before he went downstairs to prepare our breakfast. Once down, though, he stayed there, as it wasn't easy for him to handle the stairs yet.

Sylvia seemed better by lunchtime and managed very well, but just the same, I kept my distance in case it was contagious. Then, when we'd come home after four, I'd forget that she had been sick at all, she'd be so cheerful and gay. But of course, the next morning it would be back again.

I wondered if Mama had anything to do with Sylvia's sickness. It seemed probable to me, the way it came and went like that, as if Mama was having fun torturing Sylvia that way. But I couldn't voice my suspicions to Papa, not only because it would make him angry, but because I had enough to worry about without that.

I never knew, when I'd walk into my room, whether I was going to hear Mama tapping at my window that night or not. Sometimes, tensed to a deathlike stillness, I would stand inside my door for long minutes and listen, and hear nothing but my own heartbeats. Other times, especially when the wind howled wildly on the other side, she would try by beating on my window to shatter it. The coldness inside me froze to a hard fist in my stomach as I listened to the ferocity of her rage, and I knew if she ever got in, I wouldn't last two minutes against that fury.

Sometimes it stopped, sometimes it grew louder. The room vibrated with the blows being dealt to the fragile glass. I held my breath, expecting to hear the crash and tinkle which would signify the end of everything. I almost wished it would happen, and soon, so I wouldn't have to fear the inevitable anymore. I gritted my teeth and took out my scribbler, and sat at the dresser with it. This was my challenge to Mama. If she was going to do it, let her do it quickly. I didn't want to be afraid anymore.

I opened my scribbler, trying to ignore the sounds behind me, the taptaptap*taptaptapbang!* taptap. . . . I would write about . . . winter, I decided. Next week was the first of November, and even though we hadn't experienced our first snow of the season yet, it was only a matter of time. I loved the first snow, but I hated all the snows that followed it, the endless falling of snow that seemed sometimes to threaten us with suffocation, the silent white blanket that deadened the sound of footsteps and drew stark black silhouettes of skeletons of trees against leaden gray skies. Winter meant death.

Winter meant the wind, blowing from the north with fierce strength. This afternoon, I had felt its wild power, chilling, whirling dead leaves madly in front of my face, some of them landing at my feet, and one hitting my face with its whirling center. I wrote about the wind, and even as I wrote about it, I could hear it outside around the eaves, and Mama's tapping growing louder with it. This might be the night, I thought, when she would break the window and get in.

Facing myself in the mirror, my neck felt rigid as a metal pipe pushed through the top of my head and down. I wondered what it felt like to die, and how she would do it. Would she strangle me? I wanted to get up and run out of my room, but what good would that do? I would only have to come back again later on. I still had to sleep here. The tapping died away, then stopped. I drew a long breath and leaned over my scribbler again, and wrote at great length . . . about Mama, and what had made her change from the good, warm person who had always understood me and shielded me from Papa's anger many times to the vengeful spirit who waited relentlessly to kill me.

Suddenly, a feeling of terror took hold of me. I was positive Mama stood behind me, staring at the back of my head. I kept my eyes glued to the scribbler, afraid to look up and see my reflection in the mirror, and . . . something . . . behind me.

I wished someone would come upstairs, Simply Simon or Sylvia. I knew Papa wouldn't until quite late when it was time to go to sleep. By then it would be too late. I stared at the words I had written about Mama and wondered if she was reading them over my shoulder. If she was, I was sunk. My neck hurt from sitting so still. What if I looked up and saw . . . nothing? What if nobody stood behind me at all. I would look up and see.

I tried to raise my eyes but they wouldn't go up. What if something actually *was* there, a skull and crossbones for instance? Why didn't Simply Simon run upstairs right now, feet pounding on each step the way he always did, with a message for me? Why couldn't he come right into my room and look behind me and see nothing and say Hey, come on downstairs, Papa wants you. And I would say, Okay, wait for me, I'm coming. Then I'd get up and because he'd be there Mama wouldn't be able to touch me.

I could wait forever and that stupid Simply Simon wouldn't come upstairs. I would have to get up and walk out and go downstairs and pretend I didn't know she was in the room with me. If I gave myself away, by making a sound of any kind, like yelling or screaming, then she'd get me. She'd broken Papa's leg on only one step; imagine what falling down fourteen of them could do. I listened intently to the silence, then accidentally looked up and met my own frightened gaze in the mirror. I stared at myself. I must be nuts, I thought; I'm all alone here. There's nobody in this room but me. Quickly I left the room, leaving my light on. Going down the stairs, I held tightly to the bannisters, walking like a . . . lady.

It was amazing. Downstairs, Simply Simon listened to Charlie McCarthy on the radio, Papa sat reading the newspapers, and Sylvia, looking remarkably well, sat knitting something in white wool. I stared at them, so cozy together, so like a family. How could they just sit there and not have the faintest idea that I had needed them so badly? How could they be so insensitive?

"Is something the matter, Becky?" Sylvia counted stitches.

"No. Nothing's the matter."

Later, when we were going to bed, I went up behind Simply Simon, treading on his heels all the way. I was glad I'd left my light on. Still, I didn't want to go into the room by myself. "Come on." I pulled his sleeve. "I want to show you something."

I dragged him in by the elbow. He stared at me with suspicion and looked around. "Well? Where is it?"

My room looked exactly as I had left it, but it was the silence I was hoping for. Simply Simon became impatient. "What did you want to show me?"

"Oh. I can't find it. I thought it was in here. Oh well, forget it."

He gave me a disgruntled look walked out.

"Well, I can't help it if I can't find it!" I yelled at his back. For answer, he slammed his door.

While I was getting undressed, a sudden gust of wind crashed around the house. Mama began tapping loudly at the windowpane. She had been sleeping outside and the wind woke her up. She was cold, that was it. The wind caused all my problems, I knew now. But I wouldn't let her in, no I wouldn't!

I shivered into my pajamas and crept under the covers and pulled the blanket over my head. I wasn't going to turn out the light, not while Mama pounded on the window, and especially if she could get in. Sylvia could turn it out when she came upstairs if she wanted to, or Papa could, but I wouldn't. Even if it meant wasting lights . . . wasting electricity . . . I-would-not-turn-out-the-lights!

With my head stuffed under the blankets I could still hear the tapping, so I pulled my pillow under too, and shoved my head underneath it.

Sylvia shook me awake. I blinked in the hard glare of morning and stared up at her. She looked ghastly, but she buttoned herself into a loose-fitting dress. "Time to get up dear," she said, lifting my pillow and giving it a shake. "By the way, you left your light on last night. Did you know?"

I rubbed my eyes and pretended not to hear. In the light of day, last night seemed like a bad dream. There was no tapping, no sound at all except for the sound of Sylvia's slippers slap-slapping on the wood floor as she walked away. "Dress warmly," she called over her shoulder. "The wind we had last night brought the temperature away down. It may snow anytime."

I heard her open Simply Simon's door. I sat and listened for a moment, then slowly pulled on my stockings and bloomers. My skin crawled with goose pimples . . . the tapping had begun again, softly. Mama had waited until Sylvia had gone out. If I called her back, the tapping would stop and Sylvia would look at me as if I'd gone raving mad. I reached for my undershirt and then my blouse. Anyway, the tapping didn't sound as frightening during the day. I pulled my tunic on over my head. I decided to be extra careful on the stairs. I had a feeling that if it happened at all, it would be on the stairs.

Sylvia stuck her head back in the door. "Oh good," she said. "You're dressed. I'll see you downstairs." She withdrew her head.

The tapping *hadn't stopped.* It had gone right on but she hadn't heard it. She hadn't heard a thing! Nobody could hear it but me! Mama meant it to be that way!

Why did she pick on me and not the others, I wondered. Why only me? But of course, that wasn't true. What about Papa's leg? And Sylvia's sometimes sickness? It was my turn next.

All day I heard the tapping. I could hear it plain as anything in the classroom and I heard it as I walked home from school. I was haunted by the sound wherever I went. Carefully, I stepped over all the cracks in the sidewalk. I didn't take any chances. Then, while it was still light enough outside, I went into my room and turned my light on and closed my door so that Sylvia wouldn't see it and turn it off again.

I began to get used to the tapping, accepting it as part of my life. During the night, with my head under the blanket and my light burning brightly, I thought Mama sounded ferocious, as though she were getting very impatient. She banged on the window so it rattled, then slyly with just her fingertips against the glass. Taptaptap*taptaptap*taptap-taaaaa . . .

Snow fell for a week and swirled into drifts so it looked like sour cream piled in a bowl. The temperature dropped to zero and we had to admit that winter had finally arrived. Winds howled and blew outside my window, and the tapping never stopped. Whether I was in my bedroom or at school, I heard it. I couldn't tell anymore whether the sound I heard was real or imaginary and it didn't matter. Now I needed the sound to feel safe. If I didn't hear anything for a minute, I became tense and frightened as if the blow would fall any-time. I tiptoed around the house hoping Mama wouldn't hear me, drew up elaborate schemes to keep from being caught off guard. I stayed near Simply Simon whenever possible so that I wouldn't be alone. It was the middle of November and I thought it would be this way forever. Then Papa said:

"Becky, what's this I hear? Every night you forget to turn your lights off? Don't you know electricity costs money?"

I felt as though a giant hole had opened up under my feet. I could feel myself slipping down, down. I shivered, holding on to the back of a chair. Papa's eyes didn't leave my face, accusing, staring. I stared back. "Why don't you answer?"

What could I say? I looked at the floor, seeing the worn-out spots on the linoleum. We still hadn't got a new carpet for the floors, I told myself. My heart thudded hopelessly.

"Well?" Papa prodded.

I licked my lips. They felt dry and corrugated, like old cardboard. There was a rustling behind me, and I sensed that Sylvia drew nearer, the knitting stilled. I shivered again, a hollow cave opening up inside my head. My brain flew out through the hole. I couldn't think anymore.

"I'm waiting to hear something. . . ." Papa's voice held an ominous threat.

I shrugged then and looked at him, my mind blank. Simply Simon, who had been listening to the radio, clicked it off and shuffled towards us. I heard his steps like echoes in my head. I was in the center of a whirlpool and all around me eyes stared at me, Papa's, Sylvia's, Simply Simon's, and away out above the roof, Mama's. I could hear laughter, wild shrieking laughter in the howling wind.

"What's the matter with you?" Papa exploded. "Can't you say *something*?"

Sylvia's hand came out. I saw it appear in my range of vision. I looked at it, saw the smooth skin, the pink fingernails cut even with the fingertips, the wide knuckles, the plain gold ring on her third finger where Papa had placed it in June at Auntie Sadie's.

"Wait," she said. "Let's start over again, and this time, let's not lose our tempers." I knew she was talking to Papa and I felt vaguely grateful.

"I'm not losing my temper," Papa said crossly. "Why doesn't she answer when I ask a question?"

"Maybe she'd rather not speak in front of Saul?"

"Boy!" Simply Simon exploded. "Every time something interesting is going on, I have to leave! Well, *okay* then!" He stomped out, slamming the door. We could hear him grumbling all the way up the stairs to his room, then his door banged and there was silence. I knew the time had come, but I didn't know what to tell them.

Sylvia leaned towards me. Now I saw all of her, including something I'd been too miserable to notice before. Sylvia was getting fat! But I didn't really have time to digest this. Her hand rested lightly on my shoulder. I bit my lip, feeling something egg-sized come into my throat, trying to choke me. I swallowed it down again. "Becky," she said, "Are you afraid of the dark? Is that why you've been leaving your light on? If that's the reason, don't be ashamed to say so. It's quite a normal thing for a child to be afraid of the dark."

"Well," Papa said. "Is it true? Are you afraid of the

dark, a big girl like you?"

"No, Jake!" Sylvia sounded angry. "If she's afraid we have to show her there's no reason to be. I don't want her to be ashamed of it."

The egg slid up into my throat again. I blinked at the table, then swallowed harder. The egg moved up and down like the elevator at Eaton's Store.

"Now," said Sylvia, firmly in control, "do you want to tell us about it?"

I opened my mouth, sure no sound would come out. I made a croaking sound, then cleared my throat. Papa and Sylvia leaned closer, waiting. "You'll think I'm crazy."

"How do you know? You might be surprised to find out how much Papa and I understand. . . ."

I gave her a long look, then looked at Papa. He frowned. I fixed my eyes on Sylvia's face. At least there was sympathy there.

"You'll get mad when I tell you."

"No I won't. And that's a promise."

"Papa will."

"He won't."

Papa began breathing hard. "Tell us, Becky, or you'll see how mad I can get!"

I had no choice. "It's . . . about . . . Mama!"

"*Again* about Mama? Papa's voice sharpened. "What about Mama this time?"

I felt my face stiffen as though it had been pushed through the wringer of a washing machine. Sylvia's hand squeezed my shoulder. "Go on, dear. What about Mama?" Her voice smoothed out my apprehension.

"She wants to kill me!"

I heard Papa's breath go in with a wheeze, but Sylvia cut him off. "Why would you think such a terrible thing?"

"Because she hates me, that's why."

"That's not true," Sylvia said. "Your mother loved you. She loved you very very much. Did you say . . . hates? In the present tense? You know your mother is dead, don't you? You do know that?"

"Yes, but she comes back. She comes into my room."
Papa and Sylvia exchanged glances.

"It's true," I insisted. "She used to come into my room
and talk to me when I was sleeping, and she told me to stay
away from Sylvia."

"Why would she say that?"

"Because she doesn't want you to take her place. And
she was mad at Papa for getting married again. She said I
would be sorry, and then she pushed him so he fell and broke
his leg!" My words spilled over each other, so I could get
them all out before Papa could interrupt with his grown-up
logic.

Papa said: "Nobody pushed me. Nobody! I fell, because
I wasn't looking where I was going. I didn't watch my step
that one time and that's why I fell. Plain and simple."

I shook my head. I had known he wouldn't believe me.

"Didn't I tell you Mama wanted me to get married
again? I told you, didn't I? She made me give her my
promise." Papa looked like he was getting sick of the whole
subject.

"But she came after that and told me to stay away from
Sylvia."

"How did she look?" Papa's voice was skeptical.

"She had a white thing on . . . and wings. And she came
into the corner of my room once, right at first."

"Becky," Papa said. "she didn't come back. If she could
she would come to me, not to you. But she couldn't. She can't
talk or be mad at anybody. When you're dead, that's it.
Whatever you think you saw, it wasn't Mama."

"It looked just like Mama."

"Mama never did a bad thing to a person in her life.
Now when she's dead, you think she would come and push
me so I would break my leg. Does this make sense?"

"I don't know! I don't know! I only know I saw her. I
did! I did!"

Sylvia leaned her face into mine.

"But why, Becky? Why do you think Mama wants to
kill you? This business of leaving the lights on all night

started a couple of weeks ago, and Papa fell and broke his leg in August."

"Well, you see," I turned to Sylvia, anxious to make everything clear now that I'd started. "It's because I was so mad at her for pushing Papa, and to get even I did what she told me not to do; I let myself get close to you. I wanted to anyway, and every time I tried she made my stomach hurt."

Papa and Sylvia looked at each other again, and from their expressions, I imagined they were feeling sick inside. "Why didn't you say something sooner?"

"I wasn't going to tell you, ever! Because I knew you wouldn't believe me."

Sylvia sighed and sank into her chair. "So that's the whole story?"

"No. That's when the tapping started. I think, when I didn't want Mama to come into my room anyme."

"What tapping?"

"The tapping at my window. Every time I go into my room, Mama taps on the window, that I should let her in. Sometimes she taps very hard and sometimes very soft. If I let her in, she'll kill me, so I don't go near the window."

"Whatever you think you hear, Becky," Sylvia said with steel in her voice, "it's not your mother. To prove it, we'll go up to your room right now and listen for the tapping."

"It won't work! Do you think Mama would try to come in with everyone there? I'll bet a million dollars there won't be any tapping."

"Let's go and see," Sylvia said with determination. Even Papa went up the stairs, with Sylvia coming up behind him, holding him. I figured with all the noise we were making, Mama would know we were on the way up and wouldn't make a sound. The experiment was doomed, and Papa was going up for nothing.

At the top of the stairs, in the dark, Sylvia took firm hold of my hand while Papa went to my room. Nobody spoke as Papa creaked my door open. I was prepared for absolute silence. My heart lurched with shock. Clearly, I could hear the taptap-tapping. Did they hear it too?

We stood in the doorway of my room as Papa limped over to the window. I held my breath and bit my lips to keep from screaming. I wanted to yell, *Be careful*, Papa. He raised the window blind. The tapping continued, getting louder, getting softer. Sylvia's hand squeezed mine.

"What is it, Jake?" she whispered.

Papa looking out of the window at an angle, said, "It's a wire, from the telephone. It's not nailed down good to the house, so it leans on the glass. When the wind blows, the wire hits the pane. Do you want to see, Becky?"

I couldn't believe it. Sylvia pushed me ahead of her towards Papa. He moved aside and placed me in front of him, pointing with his finger. I could see the wire. It was the one the telephone men had put in this summer. As I watched, it bumped against the window, and each bump went tap, tap, tap, tap. A strong gust suddenly blew the wire so it went *taptaptap*, tap, tap, tap. I stood and stared at it, my mouth open. I had been terrified half out of my mind, and all it was, was this measly telephone wire! I didn't know what I wanted to do more . . . laugh, or cry! I did both, while Papa held me, his hand awkwardly patting the top of my head.

"I could *feel* Mama in the room. I could *feel* her eyes on me, staring!" I mumbled into Papa's vest.

"Your imagination, Becky," Sylvia said. "You have a very active one."

"But I *saw* her, I *saw* her! Right in that corner!" I looked squarely at the forbidden corner. There was nothing there but some cobwebby dust, which Sylvia flicked away with her hand. Mama didn't appear. I felt . . . silly . . . stupid. . . . I felt like the dumbest idiot alive. "But I did see her," I said quietly.

Papa looked at me, "I think," he said, "you and me are going somewhere tomorrow, right after school." He gave Sylvia a meaningful glance over my head. I looked quickly and saw her nod.

"Where?" I became very interested, looking up at him.

"Tomorrow," Papa said, "You'll see. . . ."

Sylvia stared out of the window into the dark night.

"What can we do about that wire?"

"I'll call the phone company. I'll tell them they should fix it, so it doesn't touch the window."

The tapping continued, but now that I knew what it was, it didn't sound sinister anymore. It was just a wire tapping against the pane . . . not threatening or menacing. "Never mind, Papa," I said. "It isn't scary now. You don't have to bother."

"I think I'll putty around the window too," he said. "Some of the noise is the rattling from the window, shaking because it's loose. That means the wind is getting in. Tell Saul to run downstairs and bring me the putty and putty knife, while I'm here already."

"Okay, Papa!" Simply Simon said from behind us. I hadn't even noticed him there. I wondered how much he had heard. Not very much, I hoped.

It seemed impossible to me now that I could have been so afraid only last night . . . only this afternoon. Why hadn't I looked out of the window the very first time? I sat on the edge of my bed, Simply Simon beside me, as we watched Papa soften the putty and work it into the window's edge. There was a scraping sound behind us. Sylvia had pulled Mama's chair away from the wall, and very carefully, sat on it.

"This chair," she told me quietly, "can come downstairs now, can't it?" Of course she knew which chair it was. I nodded. In my mind, Mama began to lie down.

In the morning, I stood beside the window and touched the puttied edges. I could see the wire and I could watch it move and hear the sound it made. But I didn't laugh at myself. I was too worried about where Papa was taking me today. During the night, when I couldn't fall asleep right away with thinking about everything, I had wondered if he was taking me to have my head examined. I dressed quickly and ran downstairs where Simply Simon sat eating his breakfast.

Sylvia looked up from her place at the stove and smiled at me. "How are you this morning, dear?"

"Fine." I sat in my chair, noticing that Mama's chair

had been placed beside the stove near the back door. So Sylvia couldn't quite bring herself to use it, I thought.

The day passed slowly, worry nibbling at the back of my mind about where Papa was taking me after school. One thing I noticed though. Where before Mama had whispered and threatened me while I sat in school, now there was only flat silence, and I couldn't see her face with its angry eyes. I both dreaded and waited expectantly for the time when Papa would take me to have my head examined. At least then I'd find out once and for all if I was crazy or not.

A taxi drew up to the curb as I ran up the veranda steps to the house. Papa wore his heavy winter coat. "Put down your books and come," he said.

My heart drummed against my ribs. Papa was in a great hurry to find out, I thought, handing Sylvia my books. She smiled at me. "Don't look so worried," she said. "It may not be as bad as you think."

She handed Papa his cane: he could manage on one pretty well now. I followed Papa out of the house and tried to help him down the steps. Papa very impatiently waved me away. He was an independent man. We climbed into the backseat of the taxi, Papa leaning forward and saying something in the driver's ear. I wondered where we were going that we needed a taxi. I'd never been in one before, but from what I knew of them, they usually meant bad news.

It was a long ride. I leaned forward against the upholstered seat that smelled of old leather, stale tobacco and perspiration, and watched the side streets slip past. Then we were at the city limits where the rows of houses thinned out to the odd farmhouse and barn. The driver turned north. Now we were out in the country. But where?

Snow lay in smooth layers over everything, topping barns, cabins, run-down shanties. When the taxi finally stopped, we weren't at any doctor's place. We were in front of tall metal gates with Hebrew letters along the top. It was the cemetery.

Papa told the driver to wait, and we got out. The wind caught us squarely, taking my breath away. We trudged silently over a barely discernible path, Papa leading the way. His cane made small holes in the snow. I hunched deeper into my coat, my hands shoved into my pockets. I knew now where Papa was taking me.

We walked past rows of gravestones that stuck out of the snow. Some of them leaned a little and others looked as though they had been there since the world began. It wasn't as spooky as I had expected, the way cemeteries looked in horror movies at the Palace Theatre. It was just . . . a cemetery, and cold. Suddenly Papa stopped, so I stopped too. He looked down at a mound of snow in front of a new-looking, gleaming white gravestone. "Here is where Mama is buried," Papa said.

I looked down at the hill of snow; then I looked at the gravestone. There were Hebrew words carved into it, with Mama's name, the date she was born and the date she died. And in Hebrew it said Rest in Peace.

Mama was here underneath the snow and the earth. She had been here since the first minute. She was never in my head or my heart or my stomach. She wasn't in my bedroom or at the beach or anyplace. Just here. She had been here all along, I thought, under the snow. With the toe of my overshoe I dug into the snow.

Hello Mama, can you see me? I can't see you but I know you're there. I made a big mistake but I won't ever make it again. I know you always loved me. And I don't think you can feel anything anymore. I dreamed you. That's what I did. Rest in peace, Mama.

With the toe of my overshoe, I smothered the hole again, and left the imprint of the bottom of my overshoe, a criss-crossed grill. In my mind, Mama lay all the way down now and slid under the ground. I saw the grave close gently. I looked up at Papa. He stood, his head bent. Suddenly, I pressed my face against the wool of his coat, the tears I hadn't been able to shed for a long time bursting out in painful gusts. I clung to Papa's coat sleeve and felt his other hand come up and touch my head. Then we both turned and walked back along our footprints to the gates, where the taxi waited. I knew we couldn't afford anything as luxurious as a taxi, but Papa had made the sacrifice.

After supper, when the dishes were done and put away, Sylvia sat us all down, and with Papa right there looking happy, she told us the big news. There was going to be, God willing . . . a baby in the spring.

# epilogue

Sylvia leaned over, lighting the candles on my birthday cake. I waited, taking deep breaths to prime myself for the blowing-out ceremony. I wondered what I should wish for, because at the moment there didn't seem to be anything that I wanted. Now that I was eleven I felt I had outgrown any childish desires, but at the same time I wasn't altogether grown-up either. As I watched the flames dance on the tiny candles, I had no worry over who I was; I was the honored guest at the table.

"Now make a wish and blow them out." Sylvia stepped away, smiling.

I thought hard, watching the tiny flames bob and leap while the wax in the candles began to make small inroads into the icing. Sylvia stood beside me.

"Hurry up and blow them out!" Simply Simon cried impatiently. "The candles are starting to drip!"

I wish . . . I wish that all dreams could come true. I wish for everybody to be happy, that we could always be just the way we are now . . . happy with each other. I wish for love and to be famous and for the glory of being a writer.

I blew real hard; the flames went out and Papa and Simply Simon applauded and Sylvia began to sing: "Happy birthday to you. . . . " And I thought it was probably one of the best birthdays I'd ever had.

Sylvia said, "And now, the presents!" She handed me a big package which I'd been eyeing since the moment I'd first seen it. It was always so exciting to open presents, and wonder what was inside them while you were doing it, especially on your birthday.

There were two dresses in the box, dresses I needed because I'd shot up in the last few months and nothing fitted me very well. They weren't terribly fancy ones, but I didn't care about that. They were new, they looked nice. . . . I kissed

Sylvia, then Papa.

"Clothes!" Simply Simon jeered. "What kind of a present is that? I think you got gypped!"

Sylvia smiled and held something behind her back. "Maybe he's right," she said. "So here's something extra, from me to you!" She held out a smaller but solid-looking package.

"Gee, two presents!" I hadn't expected anything else. I opened the brown-paper wrapping quickly, wondering what it could be. It was a book . . . a leather-covered book, but instead of a title, on the bottom of the cover, my name had been stamped in gold.

I opened it to the first page. It was blank . . . beautiful white blank paper. I riffled through it, my excitement mounting. This book had nothing in it but blank pages, hundreds of blank pages for me to write on! It was a journal, a diary, sort of! I looked at Sylvia, who watched me expectantly. "Do you like it? See, it's bound so the pages won't drop out. It's like a real book, isn't it?"

I couldn't believe it. I turned it over and over in my hands, loving the heavy feel of it, and my own name in gold, as if I was an author already. How could she have known the one thing I would love over everything else?

I hugged her. I hugged her as hard as I could without smothering the solid mound of flesh between us. She hugged me back looking so happy that I felt I didn't really deserve to be so lucky.

We cut the cake then and Papa had to go and look after a customer and Simply Simon went up to his room to do his homework. I stayed downstairs with Sylvia, still holding on to my book. I wouldn't let it out of my hands. I sat down opposite her and licked my lips. There was something I'd been meaning to say to her for a while now, and this looked like a good time to say it.

"Sylvia," I said. "Now that you're going to have a baby and all, I don't think we can call you by your first name anymore."

She looked surprised. "Why not, dear?"

"Well, because, it might get the baby all mixed up when she's older. She might start calling you Sylvia too, see?"

"That hadn't occurred to me," she said thoughtfully. "You may be right. What do you suggest?"

"I don't know. I thought maybe you'd have some ideas."

"No. Not even one. I'll have to leave that up to you."

"Well I can never call you Mama. You know that. It wouldn't sound right."

"No, I guess not," she said, her voice sounding sad.

"And 'Mother' sounds so . . . so phoney to me."

"Yes . . . to me too. A bit too highfallutin."

She waited expectantly. She knew, I could tell, that I had made up my mind what to call her before I'd ever mentioned it to her. She blinked her eyes, her hands folded over her stomach.

I took a breath, "Well, I thought maybe you wouldn't mind. . . . Betty Greenberg calls her mother . . . 'Mummy' . . . and I thought maybe . . . we could call you . . . Mummy too. Would that be all right?"

"Why don't you try it and see?"

"Okay." I waited, the word on my lips, then I said it carefully.

"Okay, Mummy." I looked at her then and we both smiled at the same time. "It sounds okay, doesn't it?"

"It sounds just fine."

She held her arms out to me. I went around the table towards her. I felt kind of funny about it because I was now eleven years old, sitting on her lap as if I was a baby.

"I might hurt her," I said, trying not to lean too hard on her stomach.

"Oh don't worry about her . . . or him . . . she's well protected in there, you know." She squeezed me harder. "Anyway, she's a lucky girl or boy to have a big sister like you, so she'd better just start to get used to it. We don't want him . . . or her . . . spoiled. She'll have to share my lap with both of you."

"You don't have to say 'her or him,' you know, Mummy," I told her confidently. "She's going to be a girl."

Mummy laughed. "We'll see."

I had a strange sort of feeling that if Mama could see us now, which of course she couldn't, she'd be very pleased at how everything had turned out. The book pressed into my side, with Mummy hugging me, and that reminded me ...

"You know what I'm going to do?" I leaped up. "I'm going to take my scribblers and tear them up and put them in the stove to burn. Then I'm going to start all over again, in my ... book."

"Shouldn't you read them over first? There may be good material there and it would be a shame to waste all that effort."

"No. There's nothing good in there. Nothing at all. I'm going to get rid of them once and for all, and start fresh, with a lot of happy feelings."

I detached myself from her clinging hand. "You wait here," I said. "I'll be right back."

We had a small ceremony when I returned with an armful of scribblers. I tore each one in half, then in quarters, and tossed each part into the fire. Mummy stood beside me and watched.

"Maybe we should say a few words," she suggested.

"Okay. How about: Burn and make big and beautiful flames, O books, and help me to make my next books better ones, that will last forever, so I may be a writer someday. Amen, how's that?"

Mummy smiled. "Good enough. Now I'll say some: May you work hard and keep to your course and not be discouraged if fame doesn't come quickly. May you write and rewrite if necessary, and love whatever you do. And may your dedication be rewarded."

I put the lid back on the stove. "Amen," I said. "Now I think I'll start on my book." I sat at the kitchen table and opened to the first page. With pencil in hand, I looked up at her. "How should I start it?"

"Why don't you start by telling who you are?"

I wrote: "I am Rebecca Devine. I am a writer. I will always be a writer. I am Me, Myself and I."

# GLOSSARY OF YIDDISH WORDS

*Blintzes*—crepes rolled around filling such as cottage cheese
*Bobbe*—grandmother
*Bobbe-Myseh*—old wives' tale
*Boruch Atoh*—first words in Hebrew blessing: Blessed art Thou
*Chanukah*—the Festival of Lights, a secular Jewish holiday lasting 8 days
*Cheder*—Hebrew School
*Chozzerai*—nonkosher food products
*Daven*—pray in Hebrew
*Faigele*—literally, little bird; used as a term of endearment for girls
*Goy (plural: Goyim)*—non-Jew
*Haggadah*—book used during Pesach Seder which tells about exodus from Egypt
*Kinderlach*—children
*Kroit borscht*—cabbage soup
*Landsman*—compatriot, fellow countryman
*L'chayim!*—Cheers! (used as a toast)
*Mazel tov!*—Congratulations!
*Mensh*—a decent human being; respectable
*Meshuggener hindt*—mad dog
*Metsieh*—something found; a big bargain
*Pesach*—Passover; Erev Pesach: Passover Eve
*Rosh Hashanah*—Jewish New Year, celebrated in late summer or early fall
*Seder*—ceremonial meal eaten at Pesach
*Shabbas*—the Sabbath, which lasts from sundown Friday to sundown Saturday; Jews may do no work on Shabbas.

*Shah*—hush, be quiet, shut up

*Shaygets*—non-Jewish boy

*Shiva*—traditional mourning period

*Shiddach*—a match, as in pairing a man and woman with matrimony the object

*Shochet*—one who is authorized to slaughter animals according to ritual requirements

*Shul (Sheel)*—Synagogue

*Shvartz yor (plural: yoren)*—literally, a curse (black year); homely or ugly

*Toig oyf kapores*—good for nothing; bad, as in business at a standstill

*Torah*—the five books of Moses

*Traife meat*—meat that is not kosher

*Tsedrayteh*—crazy one, crackpot (tsedrayt: crazy)

*Yarmelke*—skullcap

*Yom Kippur*—the Day of Atonement, when Jews fast and pray

*Yontiff*—any Jewish holy day